RANDOM HOUSE

LARGE PRINT

Dear Friends,

I'm so delighted to share with you my new novel, **Last One Home.** Like that of the sisters in this book, one of my fondest memories from childhood is playing hide-and-seek in the park with my neighborhood friends. And, like Cassie, our main character, I often would squeeze through the thick branches of a huge bush so as not to be seen. We always played until dusk, waiting for the porch light to be turned on, our parents' signal that it was time to come in. Then we'd all race for home.

In the novel, my character Cassie has, as an adult, become estranged from her family. When the book opens, she hasn't seen them in thirteen years. The idea of "coming home" seems almost impossible to her, but it is what she longs for most, a feeling I think we all can understand. While I didn't have a sister growing up, I had lots of cousins who I was very close to, and I can't imagine losing touch with any of them.

Now please turn the page and meet one of the strongest heroines I feel I've ever written. Cassie is eager to tell her story, and I hope you are just as eager to read it.

Warmest regards,

Debbie Macomber

P.S. Hearing from my readers is one of the many pleasures I have as an author. You can reach me through my website at DebbieMacomber.com or on Facebook, or if you would rather write a letter, my mailing address is P.O. Box 1458, Port Orchard, WA 98366.

Last One Home

DEBBIE MACOMBER

Last One Home

A Novel

RANDOM HOUSE
LARGE PRINT

Copyright © 2015 by Debbie Macomber

All rights reserved.
Published in the United States of America by Random House Large Print in association with Ballantine Books, New York. Distributed by Random House LLC, New York, a Penguin Random House Company.

Cover design: Belina Huey
Cover illustration: Stephen Youll

The Library of Congress has established a Cataloging-in-Publication record for this title.

ISBN: 978-0-8041-9469-3

www.randomhouse.com/largeprint

FIRST LARGE PRINT EDITION

Printed in the United States of America

10 9 8 7 6 5 4 3 2 1

This Large Print edition published in accord with the standards of the N.A.V.H.

To Roberta Stalberg,
dear friend, fellow author and knitter,
traveling companion,
and
plotting partner

Last One Home

Prologue

Summer had always been ten-year-old Cassie's favorite time of year. Larson Park, just down the street from her house, was the neighborhood play yard where her sisters and kids from the block gathered in the cool of the evening. The most popular after-dinner game was hide-and-seek, and the huge chestnut tree in the center of the park was their home base.

"Olly olly oxen free," twelve-year-old Karen called out. Cassie's older sister was it, and she was good.

Cassie struggled to hide her giggles. She'd gotten good at hiding—no one knew of her secret place inside a huge bush that grew low to the ground. The day had been blistering hot, but a cool breeze set the leaves to whispering. When she closed her eyes, Cassie could hear the trees singing to one another.

Cassie was just small enough to squeeze in between the thick branches of the bush and hunker down out of sight. She held perfectly still as crickets chirped in the background. The scent of the freshly mowed lawn nearly caused her to sneeze, which would have ruined everything. The best part about her hiding spot was that she was able to peer out between the greenery and watch when Karen left the chestnut tree.

Fun and games with her two sisters and friends was a perfect ending to what was probably the best day of Cassie's entire life. Earlier that afternoon a big truck had parked outside their house with a delivery. It was the piano Cassie had dreamed about ever since she started taking lessons two years earlier. Recently Mrs. Schneider, her teacher, had encouraged her parents to invest in a piano.

According to the teacher, Cassie had musical talent. She loved to sit at the piano, fascinated by the sound each key made and what happened in her head when she heard a song on the radio. Mrs. Schneider claimed Cassie had been born with a musical ear. Cassie wasn't quite sure what that meant and thought it might be her ability to hear a song and then find the keys to play it all on her own without looking at sheet music.

Unfortunately, the only place she'd had to practice was at the old upright in the school gymnasium. The piano was available after school and at no other time. Mrs. Schneider was certain Cassie would excel if she had access to a piano of her own. But pianos were expensive and her mother had sadly explained that the family couldn't afford to take on that big of an expense.

Her dad, however, had overruled her mother. He insisted that they would find a way to pay for a piano, and he had. He'd found a rent-to-own program and vowed to squeeze the twenty-five dollars a month out of their already tight budget.

When the delivery men rolled the piano into the house, Cassie could barely contain her joy. She'd sat and played until it was dinnertime and her mother made her quit because it was her turn to set the table.

It was hard to tear herself away from the piano for their nightly games, but the house was hot and the cool night air beckoned her. Cassie's parents sat in the center of the gazebo her father had built, drinking coffee and keeping an eye on the park.

Their nightly game of hide-and-seek involved nearly the entire neighborhood. They could play until it was dark and the porch light went on at the house. That was their signal it was time to come home and get ready for bed.

Cassie squirmed, certain she was about to sneeze. A loud clap of thunder shook the sky. Heat lightning wasn't uncommon this time of year.

"Olly olly oxen free," Karen cried out again.

Cassie saw several of her neighborhood friends dash for the tree. Seeing that the coast was clear, Cassie left her secret spot and was on her feet and running. Right away Karen spied her and was after her, chasing her with a determination that nearly caused Cassie to stumble. If she made it to the chestnut tree before Karen could tag her, she'd be safe.

Zigzagging across the lawn, Cassie twisted and turned in an effort to avoid her sister's outstretched arm. By the time she was close to the tree she was breathless. From the corner of her eye, Cassie saw her youngest sister, Nichole, emerge from her own hiding place behind a bench and run for the tree as well. She tried to hurry and reach it first.

Cassie nearly made it, but Karen was too quick for her. Just before she lunged forward to touch the tree, Karen slapped her shoulder. Cassie had been caught.

The three sisters sprawled onto the grass, gazing up at the darkening sky. Holding on to their stomachs, they panted and laughed. Up and down the streets porch lights were coming on one by one. Soon their neighborhood friends headed off into the dusk until only Karen, Nichole, and Cassie were left under the big chestnut tree.

Cassie's heart swelled with happiness in the glow of her one perfect day. It spilled out into a huge grin as she stretched out her arms to either side of her and touched her sisters, wanting to share this joy with them.

Their father stood in the gazebo and called, and all three girls leaped up. Karen shouted, "Last one home is it." Both Karen and Nichole got a head start, but Cassie was right behind.

Chapter 1

The impossibly thin woman sitting next to Cassie Carter in the King County Courthouse in Seattle trembled like an oak leaf in a storm. When the judge entered the courtroom and they were asked to rise, Maureen could barely manage to get to her feet. Cassie wrapped her arm around the other woman's waist and helped her to stand upright. Maureen was skin and bone, so thin Cassie could feel her ribs. She'd been that thin once herself. Like Maureen, she had been beaten down, battered, and emotionally broken.

"You're doing great," Cassie whispered. She understood all too well what courage it took for Maureen to testify against her husband. Cassie had sat in a similar courtroom in Florida, only she'd sat alone. Duke, her husband, had glared at her as she'd slowly walked toward the witness stand, his dark eyes filled with hatred. Eyes that said he would kill her if he got the chance.

He nearly had.

They'd been married only a few months when Duke hit her the first time. He'd had a few beers with friends and come home and found Cassie didn't yet have dinner ready. To show her how displeased he was, he'd slapped her. Cassie had been stunned. Her father had never laid a hand on her mother or her, nor her two sisters. Horrified, she'd pressed her hand to her cheek, hardly knowing what to think.

That was the first of many such slaps. Afterward he was sorry. He felt horrible that he could do anything to hurt the woman he loved beyond life itself. He'd cover his face and weep, begging her forgiveness. The irony of it was that she, the one who'd been hurt, would rationalize his anger and comfort **him.** Shocking, really, when she thought about it. Duke hit her and **she** was the one who apologized.

As the years progressed, the slaps turned to slugs and the slugs into beatings. During the last beating she'd seen that very look in his eyes, the same one he gave her the day she stood in a Florida courtroom.

The look that said her days were numbered. She would pay for what she'd done.

That final time, as Duke's fists pounded down on her, Cassie had been terrified by the cold hate in her husband's eyes. Duke would not stop until he killed her. It was as clear as the writing on a highway billboard. In that breathless moment, Cassie knew beyond a doubt that she was about to die. She lost consciousness briefly, and when she came to again she heard him rifling through the kitchen drawers. She knew he was searching for a knife.

Carried by adrenaline, numb with fear, she managed to escape into her daughter's bedroom and blocked the door by tilting a chair beneath the knob. She grabbed seven-year-old Amiee and fled out the window.

She didn't take her purse or her identification or any money. And she had no friends, no resources. Just her daughter and the clothes on her back.

Cassie hadn't needed anything else. The one precious thing that had come out of her marriage had been her daughter. Fleeing to a women's shelter, Cassie was given housing and assistance. Duke was arrested and sentenced to a six-month jail term.

Cassie had taken those months to put her life together. And to try to make her way back to the good life she'd left behind. The hardest part hadn't even been leaving Duke after all—it was that she didn't have her family's support. She was on her own, without her parents, without her sisters. She had to do it alone, and so she had.

"What if the judge doesn't believe me?" Maureen whispered, her voice trembling to the point that her words were barely discernible.

"He has the police report," Cassie assured her.

"I . . . I don't know that I can do this." Maureen started to shake again, even worse than before. "Lonny doesn't mean to hurt me . . . he can't help himself. He has a temper, you see, and it gets away from him. He doesn't know what he's doing. He can't help himself."

"Maureen, we've been through this. It isn't your fault that your husband hits you. You've done nothing wrong." Cassie recognized the thought process: If only she'd been a better wife, a better housekeeper, a better mother, then Duke wouldn't be upset. It was her failings that brought on the abuse. Only later, with counseling and patience, did she accept that the blame wasn't hers. She had done nothing to deserve the beatings Duke gave her.

"But . . ."

"I was married to a man who beat me," Cassie reminded her. "I thought it was my fault, too. If only I hadn't put mustard instead of mayo on his ham sandwich he wouldn't have hit me. I should have remembered. How could I have been so stupid? Maureen, think about it. Would you pound your fist into your daughter's face for something like that?"

"No, never . . . I'd never hit one of my children."

"I didn't deserve it, either, and neither did you."

Maureen stared up at her with wide, blank eyes. At one time Cassie's eyes had had that same hollowed, hopeless look.

"I'll be right here," she promised the other woman. "I'm not going to leave you. Once we're finished I'll take you back to the shelter."

Maureen gripped her hands together in a hold so tight her fingers went white. "I can do this."

"Yes, you can," Cassie assured her and gave her thin body a gentle squeeze. "Think of your children."

Maureen briefly closed her eyes and nodded.

"Lonny is going to jail, if there is any justice," Cassie assured her.

"But what will I do then?"

"The shelter will help you get a job and find housing." Cassie had already been through this with Maureen a number of times, but the fragile soul needed to hear it again.

"The paperwork . . ."

"I'll help you fill out the forms, Maureen."

Cassie understood the other woman's fears. As easy as it might sound to others, little things like obtaining a driver's license or completing a job application seemed overwhelming. Duke had refused to allow Cassie to drive. It became a control issue with him. If she had access to a car she might leave him. When they'd married she'd had a license, but it had long since expired and was from a different state. Moving her away from family and friends had been one of the first things he'd done, taking her from Spokane all the way to Florida, where there were supposed to be good jobs. The job had never materialized, but he'd succeeded in getting her far from family, friends, and all that was familiar.

To anyone who hadn't been the victim of domestic violence, the hesitation to testify, to put the aggressor behind bars, was incomprehensible. Only those who'd walked through this madness understood what courage it took, what fortitude and pure nerve were required to stand up in court and admit what they had endured.

When Maureen was called to the witness stand, Cassie held her breath. She slid to the very edge of the hard wooden seat as the young mother reluctantly stood.

"Don't look at Lonny," Cassie advised, giving the other woman's hand a gentle squeeze as she scooted past. "If you need to, focus on me instead."

Maureen was deathly pale and her nod was barely noticeable. Her walk from the back of the courtroom all the way to the witness stand seemed to take thirty minutes. Thankfully, she followed Cassie's advice and kept her gaze lowered, refusing to look in the vicinity of her husband.

Twice the judge had to ask Maureen to speak up in order for her to be heard.

Cassie wanted to cheer when Maureen squared her shoulders as resolve came to her. She looked directly at the judge and said clearly, "Please don't let him hurt me again." With that, she stood and started to leave the witness stand.

Lonny roared to his feet and started toward her. Maureen screamed and two deputies rushed forward, restraining Maureen's husband while he blurted out profanities and threats.

The judge's gavel pounded like shotgun blasts through the courtroom, the sounds sharp and discordant. "Order," he demanded. "Order in the court."

Maureen fled to where Cassie waited. Cassie immediately wrapped her arms around the other woman and led her out of the courtroom. She'd testified and nothing more was required of her. Cassie was certain Lonny's outburst hadn't done him any favors in the judge's eyes. The prosecuting attorney would touch base with Cassie later in the day after he'd spoken to Maureen. The case was rock-solid and there was no reason to believe Lonny would escape jail time.

Part of Cassie's work as a victim advocate was to provide transportation for Maureen to the courthouse and back to the women's shelter where Maureen and her two children were currently housed. She helped the shaking Maureen across the parking lot.

At this point all Cassie's work was on a volunteer basis. She'd taken the formal training, and one day, God willing, she'd have the chance to go to college for a degree in social work with a minor in criminal law. That, for now, was a pipe dream.

Maureen didn't speak until they were in Cassie's car. Once her seat belt was in place, she released a stuttering sigh as if only now was she able to breathe.

"You did it," Cassie said, praising her.

"Yes. The worst is over."

Cassie didn't have the heart to tell her that this was only the beginning. When someone had been beaten down for years, making even the simplest decision seemed paralyzing. Maureen and her children would need counseling and hand-holding. Fortunately, Maureen was already in a support group. In an effort to lend encouragement and guidance, Cassie had sat with her for a couple sessions. Maureen had listened without speaking, although she'd nodded a couple times. Lacey Wilson, who facilitated the group, did an excellent job of steering the conversation. The women who attended were at different stages of the healing process.

They drove to the shelter, and Cassie walked Maureen inside. She glanced at her watch and saw that she was already late for work. Maureen seemed reluctant to let her go. "Will I see you this evening?" she asked, following Cassie back to the door.

Cassie knew Maureen needed her, but she would be doing the other woman a disservice if she allowed her to become too dependent. Maureen blocked the entrance to the shelter, her look imploring Cassie to stay with her.

"I'll be back later," Cassie assured her.

"You promise?"

How needy she sounded, uncertain and afraid, looking at Cassie with wide eyes, full of fear, fear of the unknown, fear of the future. Cassie knew about that, too. Leaving Duke had required grit and raw courage, but everything afterward had as well.

"You promise," Maureen repeated.

"I promise, but for now I need to get to work." Cassie had a job, one that supported her and Amiee. She worked as a hairstylist at a local salon in a quaint community in the south end of Seattle known as Kent. The shelter had supported her while she got the training she needed, and in exchange she'd worked at the shelter, cleaning and cooking. It'd taken her five years following her divorce to crawl out of the black hole that had become her life while married to Duke. Thankfully, she hadn't seen or heard from Duke since that fateful day when she'd testified against him in a Florida courtroom.

By the time Cassie arrived at work, every chair at Goldie Locks was filled, with the exception of Cassie's. Working as an independent contractor, Cassie paid Teresa Sanchez, the shop owner, a rental fee for the hair station. This meant she was responsible for paying for her own products, setting her own schedule, building up a clientele, and, probably the most difficult, setting aside money each quarter to pay the state business tax and her federal income tax.

"Mrs. Belcher is here for her haircut," Rosie, the receptionist, mentioned as Cassie reached for her protective top. She zipped it into place and grabbed a banana off the fruit bowl in the middle of the table. That would have to do for lunch. The hearing had taken more time than she'd expected.

"A letter came for you," Rosie said, as Cassie peeled away the banana's skin.

"Here? Really?"

"The envelope is handwritten and has a postmark from Spokane. You know anyone in Spokane?"

Cassie went still. The only person who would write to her from the Columbia Basin was her older sister, Karen. When Cassie first moved to Kent she'd stayed briefly in the same shelter where Maureen and her children were currently housed. Right away she'd reached out to her older sister in Spokane but explained this was only a temporary address. If Karen wanted or needed to get in touch for now, the best address would be the hair salon where she was employed. Until now Karen hadn't contacted her.

Despite efforts to reconnect with her family,

Cassie had a tenuous relationship with her two sisters. After a bitter argument with her parents and older sister, Cassie had run away to marry Duke. They had never forgiven her for leaving the way she did and for not contacting them afterward. Little did they know . . .

"It's in back. Do you want me to get it for you?" Rosie asked.

"Not now." It amazed her how unsettled she felt. The bite of banana seemed to stick in her throat and it took considerable effort to swallow.

Cassie couldn't imagine what her sister would have to say to her. Then again, she could. Karen had done everything right. Following graduation, she'd gone on to college, married, and had two perfect children. She'd stayed in Spokane and helped their parents. Their father had died unexpectedly of a brain aneurysm only a few weeks after Cassie had broken free of Duke. She had been penniless and living in the shelter, and there was no possibility of Cassie returning home for the funeral. Her mother and sisters were in shock themselves. Cassie was too proud to explain her circumstances. All her family knew was that she'd left Duke and was living in Florida. When her father died no one had offered to pay her way home, and so she'd remained in Florida and wept alone over the father she loved and hadn't seen or talked to in nearly eight years.

Cassie had always been especially close to her father. Of the three girls, she'd been his favorite. He'd been proud of Cassie's accomplishments, her high grades, the four-year scholarship she'd garnered upon graduation. Then she'd thrown it all away for Duke. Her father had never gotten over her turning her back on that scholarship and marrying Duke. Her sisters, either.

"Cassie?" Rosie said, breaking into her thoughts. "Mrs. Belcher is waiting."

"Yes . . . I'm sorry."

"You looked a million miles away."

"I was," she said, forcing a smile. She left the break room, leaving the banana behind, and collected Mrs. Belcher, who sat in the waiting area, reading the current issue of **People** magazine.

"I don't know any of these people anymore," she said, when she looked up at Cassie. "Who are these stars, anyway?" She shook her head and set the magazine aside.

Cassie led her customer to her station and slipped a plastic cape over the older woman's shoulders, securing it with snaps at the back of Mrs. Belcher's neck. "I hope I didn't keep you waiting long," Cassie apologized.

"Not at all," Mrs. Belcher assured her. "I'm just grateful to get an appointment. You're always so busy, and Cassie, my dear, just look at how long my hair is. I'm desperate. I can't do a thing with it.

My husband told me this morning that I resemble a shaggy dog, and he's right."

Cassie met the other woman's eyes in the mirror and smiled. "I'll take care of that in short order. Now let me take you to the shampoo station."

It wasn't until five o'clock that Cassie had the chance to retrieve her sister's letter. She stared at the envelope several moments before she had the courage to tear it open.

Inside was a single sheet of paper. Rosie watched as Cassie read the letter. It didn't take her long.

"Well?" Rosie asked. The receptionist was the salon owner's cousin and not the least bit shy about asking awkward questions.

"This is the first time Karen has reached out to me since my divorce," Cassie said, unable to tear her gaze from the letter.

"Do you think your sister wants to mend fences?" Rosie asked, lowering her eyes toward the printed page as if hoping to read a few lines herself.

"I don't know." Cassie wasn't getting her hopes up.

Rosie's dark, expressive eyes widened. "Are you mad at her?"

"I was never angry with her," Cassie explained. Once Cassie had left the women's shelter, her first thought had been to go home. She'd contacted her family, needing financial help. Grief-stricken, dealing with the aftermath of her husband's sudden death, Sandra Judson, Cassie's mother, had asked Karen and Nichole to answer Cassie's plea.

According to Karen, who spoke for both her and Nichole, neither sister was financially able to help. Karen's husband had gone through a period of unemployment and they were barely making it. And Nichole had recently married and wasn't in a position to be lending anyone money. The bottom line was that Cassie had made her own bed and it was up to her to climb out of it.

As for their mother, she was completely overwhelmed dealing with the insurance company and attorneys. The death of their father had been unexpected, and she, too, was under a financial strain.

When Cassie had defied her family and married Duke, her father had predicted that one day she'd come crawling home. At the time, he'd been angry and upset. But Cassie figured he was right—she'd gotten into this mess all by herself. So she'd better be able to get herself out of it, too. With no help from her family, Cassie had struggled for years, working odd jobs, living on food stamps and in government housing, and eventually getting her certificate in cosmetology. Only then, after working a year in Florida, did Cassie have the means to return to the West Coast. For safety reasons, Cassie chose to move to the Seattle area. If Duke were ever to look for her, it would be in Spokane, not South Seattle.

Despite her brave front, Cassie had been hurt and angry to have been abandoned by her family. In the years she'd lived with Duke she'd held on to the hope that if she found the courage to leave she could rely on them. That had been an empty dream. She'd been foolish, and it seemed that in her family's eyes, what she'd done was unforgivable. Cassie had been living in Washington state for two years and this was the first time that either of her two sisters had reached out to her.

It felt as if the letter was hot enough to burn her fingers. Cassie had been waiting a long time for this moment. She'd been eighteen and pregnant when she'd run away with Duke. Now, at thirty-one, Cassie was wise beyond her years.

Chapter 2

Cassie's tiny two-bedroom apartment was walking distance from the school where Amiee attended seventh-grade classes. It was hard to believe her twelve-year-old daughter was in junior high.

By the time she finished with the last hair appointment of the day, Cassie was tired. She'd been up since four that morning and the day had run her ragged both physically and emotionally.

"I cooked dinner," Amiee announced proudly, when Cassie walked in the door.

"Great. What are we having? Cordon bleu? Steak Diane? Don't tell me you made my all-time favorite . . . lasagna."

"Mom," Amiee groaned. "I don't know how to cook any of that stuff. I made tuna casserole, only I tried to do it on the stovetop 'cause the oven doesn't work."

Cassie had complained to the landlord, not that it'd done her any good. The stove was on the fritz, the faucet leaked in the bathroom, and there was only intermittent hot water that went from hot to freezing cold without warning, most often when Cassie's head was covered with shampoo.

"I saw a recipe on YouTube and it looked pretty easy," Amiee explained as she stirred the pot. She beamed with pride at being able to cook dinner, and Cassie was pleased that Amiee took the initiative.

Cassie flopped down on the sofa and removed her shoes before she rubbed feeling back into her toes. Next paycheck she'd get new shoes. Her current ones hurt her feet.

"How did the court case go with Maureen?" Amiee asked, as she continued to stir the pot.

"Really well." Cassie had gotten the phone call shortly before she left the salon. Lonny had been sentenced to a one-year prison term with a $5,000 fine. He wouldn't be bothering Maureen for a long time. "Maureen and her children are safe."

Amiee studied her mother. "That's good! Right?"

"Very good." Cassie set her feet on the coffee table and leaned her head back to momentarily close her eyes. She didn't dare let herself drift to sleep, although it was a tempting thought. After dinner she'd visit Maureen and then help Amiee with her homework. "How was school today?"

"Okay, I guess."

"Anything important happen?"

Amiee shrugged. "Not really. Claudia posted an ugly picture of Bailey on Facebook and then Bailey got mad and they wanted me to take sides. But I didn't and then Bailey put a snarky comment about Claudia on Twitter that went all over school and then Mr. Sampson got involved and called both mothers to the school." She paused and released a drawn-out sigh. "Do you want to hear more?"

"Not really."

"I don't blame you. The whole thing was cool."

"Cool?"

"Bogus. Cool can mean a lot of things now, Mom, more than just . . . cool."

"Right. It's hard to keep up with it all," Cassie said, doing her best not to smile, as her daughter was completely serious.

"I like Claudia, but Bailey is my BAE."

"Your what?"

"My BAE. My best friend. **B**efore **A**nyone **E**lse. Get it?"

"Oh." It was getting more difficult to keep up with her daughter.

Amiee brought down two mismatched plates from the cupboard and set them on the table and then carried over the pot with tuna casserole and placed it in the middle. "You ready to eat?"

"Ready and able." Cassie's half-a-banana lunch had long since left her starving. She moved from the couch to the table and noticed that the tuna casserole resembled a thick soup more than a casserole. From the time she was young, Cassie hadn't been fond of canned tuna fish, but she didn't have the heart to mention it to Amiee, who couldn't get enough of it. Her daughter's all-time favorite food, however, was KFC. Cassie swore her daughter would eat an entire bucket of chicken by herself if given the opportunity.

They sat across from each other, and after a brief prayer, Cassie dished up her plate. "This looks good."

"Mom, you don't need to say that. The sauce is runny and I overcooked the noodles. It looks awful, but at least I tried."

"Honey, I came home to a cooked dinner; I'm not going to complain. Besides, while it might not look like much, it tastes great." A slight exaggeration, but one that was warranted.

Amiee tried to hide how pleased she was. "So," she said, looking across the table at her mother, "how was work?"

"Good."

"Sorry, Mom, you can't answer with one word— remember the rule. It's got to be more than **good** or **okay.** We need to communicate. Isn't that the word you used?"

"Right."

Amiee wagged her index finger like a pendulum. "No one-word answers, Mom."

"Okay, give me a minute to think. I was late for my appointment to cut Mrs. Belcher's hair, but she didn't mind. Oh, and I got a letter from my sister." Was it a mistake to mention it, especially in light of the unfriendly tone?

Right away Amiee's eyes brightened. "Which one?"

"Karen."

"The one who lives in Spokane?"

Cassie nodded. Her daughter had a fascination with the aunts, uncles, and cousins she'd never met. Karen lived not far from the very home where they'd all been raised, and Nichole lived in Portland, Oregon.

"What did she say?" Amiee asked excitedly.

Cassie was sorry she'd mentioned the letter now. Her daughter wouldn't understand the family dynamics with Cassie and her two sisters. Furthermore, it would be much too difficult to explain. "Not much," she murmured, hoping to avoid details.

"Is she coming to visit, because she can sleep in my room and I can meet my cousins and they can sleep on the couch and I'll sleep on the floor in a sleeping bag and we can watch movies and pop popcorn and stay up all night and talk and get to know each other. Cousins do that, you know. Bailey has a cousin who lives in Gig Harbor and she spends a lot of weekends with her. They're BFFs.

Wouldn't it be cool to have a cousin who's your BFF?" All this came out in one giant breath.

"Your BAE?" Cassie teased.

"That would be so cool," Amiee said, sighing.

How Cassie wished life were that simple. Unwilling to disillusion her daughter, she made up an excuse why it was impossible for the families to get together. "Unfortunately," Cassie said, "my sister Karen has an important job with a title company and she can't take time off work, so she probably won't be visiting Seattle anytime soon."

"Oh." Amiee's shoulders sagged with disappointment. "What did her letter say?"

It could be a mistake to mention this, but Cassie did anyway. "She basically said she had something for me, but she didn't say what and she said I should call her since she lost my phone number."

"Did you?"

"Not yet."

"Mom," Amiee cried in a high-pitched half-moan. "What are you waiting for? Call your sister!"

"I will." Cassie needed to think about this before she placed the call. It was those difficult family dynamics again. It didn't help that Karen had made it perfectly clear that as far as she was concerned, Cassie had burned her bridges with the family.

"Call her, Mom." Amiee insisted. "Why would you even hesitate? This is your sister. Do it."

"But Karen's probably just getting home from

work and busy with dinner. Her daughter is only ten and is likely not as helpful in the kitchen as you," she said, grinning.

"Can we visit her?" Amiee asked next.

This was a tricky question, too, and Cassie had to be careful how she answered. "Not for a while, I'm afraid. Our car, old and run-down as it is, would never make it to Spokane."

Amiee was instantly unsettled. "I hate that car," she cried. "It's so old it should be in a museum. We could probably sell it for lots of money as an antique."

"It gets me to and from work, so I'm not complaining." Although, with more than 250,000 miles on it, how much longer her Honda would last was a major concern. Cassie was convinced heavenly intervention was the only reason the car continued to run.

"Call your sister, Mom. Please." Amiee folded her hands as if she was in church and praying. "It's not right that I've never even met my cousins."

"Okay, okay." Deep down, Cassie wanted to speak to her sister, but she was afraid. Until now, Karen had made it clear she'd prefer it if Cassie kept her distance. The letter she'd received hadn't been written out of love. She wasn't entirely sure what had prompted her sister to write it, but Cassie had the feeling she'd find out soon enough.

Even now, all these years later, Cassie remembered fighting with Karen. They had the same argument often. Her mother had told Karen to cook dinner so that Cassie could practice the piano. Then later, after Nichole had set and cleared the table, their father had asked Karen to wash dishes while Cassie played for him. He claimed listening to Cassie play helped him to relax.

That night Karen and Cassie had gotten into a huge fight.

"You're spoiled rotten." Karen had hurled the words at her like a World Series pitch right through the strike zone.

"I'm not," Cassie had insisted.

"Are too. And don't think I'll help you study for that math test, either. If you're so smart you'll figure it out yourself. Or else run to Daddy for help. You're his favorite, anyway."

"I'm not, either," Cassie insisted, but deep down she knew it was true. Their father had even promised her the cameo, which was a family heirloom, handed down from their grandmother to their father.

"You think you're so special because you can play the piano."

"You think you're better than anyone else because you got your driver's permit," Cassie flashed back.

And so it had gone on, until it became a shouting match. Eventually their father had stepped in and separated them. Even then, as teenagers, their relationship was strained. From those dreamy summer evenings as children playing in the park it had all seemed to go downhill. It hadn't gotten any better in the intervening years, either. But that angry exchange of words didn't compare to the final one just before Cassie ran away from home.

"Mom?" Amiee's voice broke into Cassie's musings. "You okay?"

"Of course," Cassie said, returning to her dinner, taking another bite and chewing it with gusto.

Perhaps if their mother had lived, the relationships among Cassie and her sisters might have smoothed themselves out. Sadly, shortly after their father died, her mother was diagnosed with lung cancer. She'd smoked for as long as Cassie could remember, knowing the health risks and ignoring them. While Cassie was in cosmetology school in Florida, Karen had contacted her to let her know their mother was seriously ill. For a while Karen sent tersely written updates on their mother's treatments and condition. Cassie mailed encouraging notes and received two or three short letters from her mother. The chemotherapy and radiation treatments had completely drained Sandra of strength.

Cassie wanted to call their mother, but Karen had let it be known that hearing from her at this point would be more upsetting than comforting. Cassie wasn't sure what she could say, anyway. Duke was in jail. He'd tried to kill her and she'd barely escaped with her life. It wasn't the conversation her mother needed to hear.

And then time had run out. Her mom had died and she'd been unable to afford to come to the funeral. She'd been living hand to mouth then—and still was, mostly.

Amiee scooted her chair back and handed Cassie the phone. "Call your sister."

Cassie reluctantly reached for the phone, dragged out the letter, and typed in the number listed at the bottom of the page.

A young girl answered on the third ring. "Hello."

"Is this Lily?" Cassie asked, forcing a cheerful note into her voice. She knew very little about her sister's life, but she did know Karen and Garth had two children, and that Lily was the oldest and their son, a couple of years younger, was named after his father and called Buddy.

"Yes." The ten-year-old sounded skeptical.

"This is your aunt. My name is Cassie."

"I don't have an Aunt Cassie."

Hearing that didn't come as any big surprise. Apparently, Karen hadn't bothered to mention she had **two** sisters.

"Lily, who's on the phone?" Cassie heard someone call in the background. It sounded like her sister.

"Someone who says she's related to us."

Not more than a few seconds later Cassie's oldest sister took the phone away from her daughter. "Cassie?"

"Hi." She kept her voice even, not wanting Amiee to know how difficult this conversation was sure to be. Amiee stood next to her, listening anxiously. "I got your letter," Cassie continued.

"You phoned." Karen sounded like she was talking to one of her clients, brisk and businesslike.

"Yes . . . you asked me to and wrote down your number."

"Tell her you have a cell now," Amiee instructed. "Give her your number so she can call anytime she wants."

Cassie waved her off.

"How are you?" Karen asked with stiff politeness.

"Good. Amiee and I are doing well." Her answer was equally stiff.

"The divorce is final?"

Cassie exhaled in order to keep her cool. "Yes, it was final over four and a half years ago now." She didn't want to have to cover ground that she'd already traveled. "Your letter suggested you had something for me."

"I do. It's been almost eighteen months now since Mom died."

A lump filled Cassie's throat. Both of her parents had died before they'd ever met their oldest grandchild.

"The house finally sold," Karen went on to say.

"I'm sorry I wasn't able to be more of a help." Cassie did feel bad that the burden of looking after their parents and the estate had fallen heavily upon her two sisters.

"I didn't have any choice, did I? When Dad died so unexpectedly, he hadn't done anything about setting up estate planning. I did what I could to help Mom, but she was in no kind of emotional shape to make important decisions, and then she went so quickly. I don't mind telling you the last few years have been rough."

They'd been rough for Cassie and Amiee, too.

"Anyway, the reason I wrote is to let you know that I've placed some pieces of Mom and Dad's furniture in storage. Nichole and I decided you can take what you want. We both took everything we wanted—what you don't take will go to charity."

Cassie was speechless. Unexpected tears welled in her eyes. "You're willing to let me have some of their things?" She choked out the question, hardly able to believe Karen would offer her any part of what had once belonged to their parents.

"Yes. There isn't anything left that interests us."

"Mom's dining room set?" Some of Cassie's fondest memories were sitting around that table for holidays when her mother brought out the good china and the family used real linen napkins.

"Yes, it's there. It's pretty worn, and a couple chairs are broken."

Cassie didn't dare ask about the piano. That would be long gone, possibly sold after she left with Duke.

"Thank you." Cassie struggled to hide the fact she was choking back tears.

When she spoke again her sister's voice softened slightly. "Nichole and I have husbands and homes."

Cassie recognized the dig. Her sisters were far better off than she was, and she was a charity case. But she didn't care what they thought of her. The tears blurred her eyes. Amiee hurried into the bathroom and returned with a wad of toilet tissue. "I don't know what to say," Cassie said, her voice breaking up. "I'm overwhelmed and so very grateful."

"Yes, well . . ." It appeared Karen hardly knew what to say herself.

Cassie grabbed the tissue from her daughter and dabbed at her eyes.

"Now," Karen said, her tone stiff once more, "when can you come collect the furniture?"

Cassie's shoulders sagged. "I . . . I don't know." She had no way of getting to Spokane—not with her Honda—and she didn't know anyone who owned a truck.

"I've paid for two months' rent in advance, but I really can't continue paying these fees indefinitely, Cassie."

"Of course not. I'll find a way to come pick

it up." She'd move heaven and earth to make it happen.

"Good. Let me know when you're available, but make sure you give me plenty of advance warning. Buddy's on a softball team this spring and Lily is taking clarinet and dance classes. Frankly, I don't have a lot of weekends free."

"I'll give you as much advance notice as I can." Her heart raced with excitement. "Thank you."

"Yes . . . sorry to cut this short, but I need to get dinner on the table."

"I'll be in touch," Cassie promised, and disconnected.

Amiee looked up at her expectantly.

Cassie hugged her daughter close. "We have furniture, Amiee, my parents' furniture." Grabbing hold of her daughter's hands, she did a little jig right there in their tiny kitchen.

This was the best news Cassie had gotten since she'd heard Duke Carter pronounced guilty.

Chapter 3

Karen Goodwin wasn't sure what to think about the conversation with her sister. She hadn't had an email address or a home address and had taken a chance mailing it to Cassie's place of employment, the last address she had.

It'd been awkward, each of them feeling their way, she supposed. Frankly, Karen preferred that they keep their distance. Cassie was troubled and needy, and both Karen and Nichole had their own lives and families to worry about. They didn't want to take on Cassie's problems, too. Still, she was blood, and she deserved some family mementos. It was up to Cassie to collect them within sixty days. It would be unreasonable and unfair for Karen to continue to pay storage fees until it was **convenient** for Cassie to come to Spokane.

Busy as she was, Karen had enough on her mind, including dinner that evening.

"Lily," she called over her shoulder from the kitchen, as she hurried to finish their dinner preparation. "Do you have any homework?"

"A little."

"Then do it."

Lily sighed expressively. "I thought you wanted me to set the table."

"I do. Then start your homework."

Lily approached the silverware drawer. "How come I have to do it now? Why can't I wait to do my homework until after dinner?"

"Because I have a PTA meeting tonight and if you need help I won't be here."

"Dad can help me," Lily argued.

"I'd rather you finish it now." Garth was way too lax with their children. From the beginning, Karen had been forced into the role of the disciplinarian. Her husband worked as a consultant for an engineering firm and at the end of a workday he was emotionally and mentally exhausted. Asking him to do anything beyond changing channels on the television was a strain on his mental capacity.

Lily obediently laid out the silverware at the table. Karen inspected it to be sure her daughter had placed each utensil in the proper position. Little things like that were important to her. In far too many families, etiquette and manners had gone by the wayside. Not in her home, though. Karen made sure her children sat up straight at the dinner table and never talked with food in their mouths. Nothing, absolutely nothing, irritated her more than bad manners.

Lily reluctantly sat down at the kitchen counter with her homework. Karen finished stirring the sour cream into the stroganoff, one of Garth's favorite dinners. She glanced at Lily and noticed her daughter was involved in writing out her spelling words for the week. Lily had her cell phone by her side and looked up each word on the dictionary app Karen had installed for her. She wondered if other parents had thought to do this. It certainly made Lily's assignment easier. Lily's last report card had earned her a cell phone. Buddy wasn't responsible enough for his own phone just yet. Their youngest often misplaced his belongings.

The door off the garage opened and Garth walked in. As he did every night, he placed his keys on the peg just inside the kitchen door, kissed Karen's cheek on his way into the family room, and immediately picked up the remote and turned on the evening news.

"Where's Buddy?" Karen asked, looking up from the stove.

"You mean he isn't home?" Garth asked, surprise showing on his face, his eyebrows raised.

"No, he's at baseball practice," Karen reminded

him, and then grinned, remembering the date. "Is this an April Fools' joke?"

"Is today the first?"

"Garth, be serious. Where's Buddy?"

Her husband rubbed his hand across his forehead. "Was I supposed to pick him up?"

He was serious, and this was no joke. "Yes, sweetheart. I reminded you this morning, don't you remember?"

"Apparently not," he muttered, and did a quick reversal, grabbing his car keys on the way into the garage.

Karen followed him and stood in the doorway as he climbed into the SUV. "How could you forget your son?" she demanded.

He ignored the question. "I'll be back in twenty minutes."

Her husband's forgetfulness played havoc on Karen's schedule. As much as possible she felt it was important for all of them to eat dinner together. It bothered her that too many important rituals in family life had disintegrated over the years. With busy schedules—sports, music, Scouts, church functions—it would be far too easy to do as several of her friends did and simply leave dinner on the stove. She knew for a lot of families, dinner was eaten in fits and starts, dished up whenever individual family members were available. By not sharing the everyday details of life, something important was lost. Karen didn't want to see that happen with her children and Garth. It had been ingrained in her from her own childhood—her parents had insisted they eat together as a family every night.

Putting the stroganoff on simmer, Karen collected her notes for the PTA meeting. As the secretary, she needed to have the minutes from the previous meeting prepared and printed. Thankfully, she'd seen to that the night before and the necessary paperwork was neatly tucked in her briefcase.

The noodles were already boiled and rather than let them get soggy, she drained off the liquid and combined them with the creamy mixture. The salad was in a bowl in the refrigerator and the frozen peas were in the microwave, already zapped.

Because Garth had forgotten to pick up Buddy, Karen wouldn't be able to join the family for dinner. It exasperated her that her husband could be so irresponsible as to forget their son. She hated the thought of Buddy waiting at the baseball field because his father had forgotten to come for him.

"Mom." Lily looked up from where she sat at the kitchen counter. "I didn't know we had another aunt."

Karen should have realized there would be questions. "Her name is Cassie."

"How come you never talked about her before now?" Lily asked, chewing on the end of her pen.

Karen removed the pen from her daughter's mouth. It was a disgusting habit, and Lily knew she didn't like it. "Well, because . . ." She tried to think of how best to explain this situation. "Cassie ran away from home when she was eighteen."

Even now, after all these years, Karen remembered the shock of waking that morning and finding their sister gone. Cassie had left a note on her pillow saying she was marrying Duke, a man her parents were dead set against. She'd gone against their wishes, brought untold grief into their family, and made the biggest mistake of her life. Their family was never the same afterward. Worse, there'd been no contact from Cassie for years.

"Where did she go?" Lily asked, cutting into her thoughts.

"To Florida." The less said, the better. Karen's hand was poised with the spoon above the stroganoff, which she immediately resumed stirring.

"Weren't Grandma and Grandpa upset? Didn't they go after her?"

Not wanting to get into the particulars and looking to distract her daughter, Karen asked, "Are you finished with your homework?"

"Yes! Tell me more about your sister. Is she younger than Aunt Nichole?"

"No, she's the middle sister."

"You never talked about her."

"There was a reason for that, Lily. Cassie made

a mess of her life. She didn't set a good example, and I wanted to protect you and Buddy. We didn't hear from her for a very long time."

Lily took a minute to digest this and was about to ask more questions when the door off the kitchen opened and Buddy raced in. "Dad left me at the field." His young face was streaked with tears and was red and angry. "I was the only one left and Coach had to stay with me and he was upset and—"

"Buddy, I'm sorry," Garth said, and tried to hug his son, but Buddy was having none of it. He jerked free of his father's hold and then rubbed his hands down his face to wipe away any evidence of emotion.

"Wash your hands," Karen called out. "Dinner is on the table." It wasn't, but it would be in short order. She dished up the stroganoff, the freshly cooked peas, and the salad and placed them in the center of the table, while Lily poured the milk. Then, grabbing her purse and briefcase, Karen headed out the door.

"Make sure Buddy does his homework," she reminded Garth.

"Will do."

"And that the dishes get put in the dishwasher and the stove and countertops get wiped down."

"Okay, okay. What time will you be home?"

Karen glanced at her wrist. "I shouldn't be any later than ten."

"I'll wait up for you," Garth said, and kissed her before sitting down at the table with their two children.

As it turned out, Karen was home at 9:45 p.m. As she expected, Garth was planted in front of the television. At first glance the kitchen was reasonably clean, and other than the TV, the house was relatively quiet, which meant both kids were in bed for the night.

Garth turned around when he heard the door open. "How was the meeting?"

"Okay, I guess. We decided against the carnival for the last day of school, thank God. We appointed a committee to come up with an idea for another fund-raiser. We agreed the carnival is simply too much work."

"Good." Garth sounded distracted.

"Everything go okay tonight?"

"Sure," Garth said.

"You okay?" she asked, setting her purse aside and moving into the family room.

"Of course. Why wouldn't I be?" he asked, studying her. He held out his arm in silent invitation for her to join him on the sofa.

Karen nestled down next to her husband and he wrapped his arm around her shoulders as she leaned against his torso. "Did you have a good day?" he asked, and kissed the top of her head.

"A busy one."

"Every day is busy," he commented, and it was the truth.

Karen released a long, slow sigh. "Cassie got my letter and called. Lily answered the phone and asked about her."

Garth's lips lingered on the top of her head. "What did you say?"

Her daughter's questions had nagged in the back of Karen's mind all evening. "I wasn't sure what to say. I should have thought this out more carefully before I wrote to my sister. It only makes sense that the kids would have questions." Karen remained uneasy about the situation with Cassie. "Nichole and I did the right thing, didn't we?" she asked, twisting her head so she could look up at her husband.

Garth nodded, his look thoughtful. "You are generous to offer her the furniture."

"But that and everything else is all stuff neither Nichole nor I wanted." Most of it was old and outdated and not worth much. What amazed Karen was how emotional and grateful Cassie had sounded. She wasn't entirely sure, but it seemed she'd heard tears in Cassie's voice.

"Are you feeling guilty about splitting the money from the sale of the house with Nichole?"

Karen sighed again, unsettled and unsure. "I don't know what I'm feeling anymore. Cassie was Dad's favorite, you know. It about killed him when she ran off with Duke. She didn't tell Mom or Dad until after she was married that she was pregnant with Amiee."

"Pregnant?"

Karen could see her husband was adding the years up in his head. She answered his question before he could ask. "Mom mailed her gifts and was all excited about her first grandchild. She hoped to make peace after the way she left, but we never heard anything back." For the first time, it occurred to Karen to wonder if her sister had even received the baby gifts.

"What happened with Duke?"

Karen didn't know. "They're divorced. About five years ago, shortly after Dad died, Cassie phoned Mom, looking for help."

"Help?"

"Money. She'd left Duke and wanted to get back to the West Coast. Mom was still dealing with the aftermath of Dad, and she asked Nichole and me to help Cassie."

Garth frowned. "You never mentioned this before."

She probably should have talked to Garth—he might have had an idea on how to handle Cassie, but Karen had been angry and disinclined to help her. In addition, she was overwhelmed dealing with the aftermath of their father's sudden death. Those days remained a blur in her mind.

"At the time nothing had been settled with Dad's

estate and Mom was in a financial crush herself, with the bills piling up. Paying for Dad's funeral was far more expensive than any of us realized it would be. It fell to Nichole and me to come up with the cash to help Cassie and we simply weren't in a position to do it. We also felt that she was too irresponsible. To just send her cash after the mess she'd already made would be like throwing it away. Of course, there was the money from the sale of our parents' house, but that had been set aside as retirement income, and had come well after Cassie's call, anyway. In retrospect, I wish we had been able to help her more, but it was such bad timing."

"What about Nichole? She couldn't do anything to help Cassie, either?"

"You're kidding, right?" Her youngest sister had never been especially good with money and left those matters to her husband, Jake. "Right," Garth responded with a half-laugh.

To Karen's way of thinking, Cassie was simply suffering the consequences of making a bad decision. She didn't mean to be unkind or unforgiving, but how did anyone learn responsibility if their family kept bailing them out? It was like with kids—you had to let them learn from their mistakes or they'd just keep repeating them.

"That's all water under the bridge now," her husband reminded her.

"You're right, of course." Still, Karen remained

unsure how best to explain to their children that they had a second aunt that they knew nothing about until now. "What should I tell Lily and Buddy?" she asked, seeking her husband's advice. "They're sure to ask, and I feel we should be prepared to explain why she hasn't been a part of our lives all these years."

"Tell them . . ." Garth hesitated, and then shrugged.

"See, it isn't as easy as it sounds."

"What did you say to Lily earlier?"

Again Karen wished she'd handled her daughter's question with a bit more finesse. "I explained that I hadn't mentioned Cassie because she wasn't a good example. Lily would have drilled me with more questions if you and Buddy hadn't arrived when you did."

"Knowing Lily, she won't let up until she has answers, so you'd best think of what you want to tell her now."

Karen scooted closer to her husband, enjoying the feel of his arm around her. It was far too tempting to close her eyes and lean against Garth. Thinking about Cassie and the mistakes her sister had made drained Karen. Of the three sisters, Cassie had shown the most promise and she'd screwed up her entire life over a man.

"She accused Dad of being jealous of Duke," Karen murmured.

"Was he?"

Garth's question surprised her. At the time the accusation had seemed ludicrous, but in retrospect Karen realized that Cassie had probably been right. As her father's favorite, he'd carefully scrutinized the boys Cassie dated more than he ever had any of the boys who showed interest in Karen or Nichole.

"Dad never liked Duke and he forbade Cassie to see him."

"A lot of good that did," Garth commented.

He was right. "Cassie started sneaking out of the house at night, and then Mom and Dad caught her."

"I can only imagine what that scene must have been like."

Karen couldn't remember her father ever being more upset. A shouting match had ensued, and it was shortly afterward that Cassie ran away and married Duke.

"She didn't ask about the cameo," Karen murmured, a bit surprised. She would have thought that was the first thing Cassie would want to know.

"Cameo? You mean the one Nichole wore at her wedding?"

Karen rested her head against her husband's arm. "It belonged to our grandmother. Grandpa brought it back from World War Two as a wedding present for our grandmother. Dad wanted Cassie to have it. Like I said, she was always his favorite." Karen did a poor job of hiding her resentment. "After she ran away, Dad gave the cameo to Nichole."

"Why not you? You're the oldest."

"I got Grandma's pearls."

Cassie had loved the cameo and their father had let her wear it for special occasions while a young teen. Karen sincerely doubted that she'd forgotten about it. She must assume that the cameo was part of what she would collect from what remained of their parents' lives. If that was the case, she was bound to be disappointed.

They were both silent for a few minutes. "Do you know what you're going to tell Lily and Buddy?" her husband asked, reminding her that she had yet to answer the question.

"Not yet. I'm going to think on it awhile."

"That's good. We want to approach this carefully."

Karen agreed. The late-night news flashed across the television screen. Was it that time already? She had an early-morning appointment with a young couple purchasing their first home. They were scheduled to sign the final papers at seven-thirty before they were due at work, which meant Karen would need to be at the office by seven.

"Are you ready for bed?" she asked Garth.

"In a bit," he promised.

Her husband was generally the first to retire for the evening, and his willingness to stay up for the news surprised her. He must have noticed her hesitation because he glanced her way. "Can I wake you?" The question held a much deeper connotation.

Karen smiled and nodded. "You can wake me anytime you want, Garth."

He smiled and then playfully growled.

How fortunate she was, Karen mused, as she headed for their bedroom, to have a husband who loved her.

Chapter 4

Cassie had a fifteen-minute break between clients and was sitting in the break room, checking her cell for messages. Earlier Rosie had connected her with her cousin Russell, who said he might be able to get Cassie a weekend job working for the catering company that serviced the suites for the Sounders' soccer games. She already had a health card from the time she worked in a fast-food restaurant while going to cosmetology school. If she got hired as a server for even two or three of their games, she'd be able to earn enough to rent a truck and drive to Spokane to collect the furniture Karen had mentioned. Her sister had made it plain she didn't want to be paying storage fees for more than two months.

Cassie had her feet braced against the chair. When she saw she had a voice message and who it was from, both feet dropped to the floor like a bag of concrete.

Habitat for Humanity.

This was it. Cassie was about to learn if she'd been accepted as a candidate for the program. She'd had to supply every bit of identification she'd accumulated in her entire life, including her birth certificate, her Social Security card, an income tax return, and bank statements. Plus she had to have worked six months with proof of income.

Megan Victory, who'd helped Cassie through the application process, mentioned that in addition to everything else, Cassie had to show proof of a savings account. Cassie opened an account with the minimum deposit. She learned that before she would be eligible to move into her new home, she'd need to have enough saved to pay the first year's home insurance premium.

Anyone applying through Habitat had to be serious about wanting a home to go through this process. Once all the paperwork was compiled and Cassie had filled out the application, she met with the family selection committee. Following the interview, she then had to be approved by the board of directors. It'd been a month she'd been waiting for their final decision.

For a long time Cassie simply stared at her phone, unable to find the courage to play the message. Her biggest fear was that she hadn't been considered a good candidate.

Teresa, the shop owner, came into the break room and grabbed a soda out of the communal refrigerator. She took one look at Cassie and paused. "You feeling okay?"

Cassie looked up from her phone and knew she must have gone pale. "I don't know yet."

"Yet? What's the problem?"

Thrusting out her arm, Cassie handed her cell to her friend. "Here, listen to the message and let me know what they say."

"Who called?"

Cassie didn't have time for explanations. "Just listen, and don't ask questions."

Teresa reached for the phone, pushed the appropriate buttons, and pressed it to her ear. Intent on watching Teresa's face, Cassie didn't notice that Rosie had come into the room.

"Mr. Greenstein is here for his haircut."

Cassie's gaze didn't waver from the shop owner. "He's early. Tell him I'll be there in a couple of minutes."

Rosie left the room and Teresa handed the cell back to Cassie.

"What did they say?" Cassie asked, doing her best to keep the quiver out of her voice.

"Well, my dear, it looks like you've been approved."

Cassie closed her eyes in order to absorb the sheer magnitude of the news. "They approved me?"

"They sure did!"

"They approved me," she repeated, louder this time, so excited that it was impossible to hold still. She leaped to her feet and pumped her fists into the air. "I'm going to have a home. A real home for Amiee and me." No more stove with no oven and nonworking burners. No more leaky bathroom faucets and a hot-water heater possessed with an evil spirit.

"They want you to stop by their office tonight after work, if possible."

"I'll be there." Cassie danced around the table, so overcome with joy that she could barely breathe. For the first time in her young life, Amiee would have stability. She would live in a neighborhood, have a sense of place and of belonging. At last Cassie would be able to give her daughter the roots Amiee had never known.

Cassie understood that this house wasn't a gift. She'd be expected to volunteer a number of hours, making her own contribution in return for this amazing opportunity. How many hours depended on what kind of house was available to her.

A foreclosure would require one hundred and eighty hours of volunteer work and not necessarily on the house that would be hers, but on whatever house needed work. Three hundred to five hundred hours was what was expected if her home was being built from the ground up.

"I told you about the conversation I had with my sister, didn't I?" Cassie cried, covering her mouth with both hands, unable to hold back her glee. This good news was almost too much for her to absorb, especially following on the heels of hearing from Karen.

"Cassie," Teresa said, laughing. "I believe you've told everyone."

"Have I?" She must have done something very right to have received two tremendous gifts in a row. First the offer from her sister and now this. Cassie longed to toss out her arms and twirl around and around as if to say her life and her heart were open and receptive to all the good things that awaited her. She'd paid her dues in misery. She'd made mistakes and learned her lesson. From this point forward, Duke and all the anguish he'd brought into her life was done. Finished. Caput.

Cassie's last appointment of the day was Mrs. Wilma Scott, who came in weekly for a wash and blow-dry. The elderly woman was close to eighty and continued to live in her own home. Raising her arms above her head had become difficult, so she had a standard appointment once a week to have her hair washed and styled. Cassie had grown fond of the older woman and enjoyed their weekly meetings.

When she'd finished, Wilma gave her a generous tip and Cassie walked her to her vehicle. "I
don't know how much longer I'll be able to drive,"
she muttered, as Cassie held open the driver's-side
door. "I suppose there will be the time when I'll
need to consider moving into one of those assisted-
living complexes. At my age it's difficult to make
significant changes, but then that's life."

"It is," Cassie agreed, as she handed Wilma the
seat belt, stretching it out to make it easier for the
older woman to snap it into place. "I'll see you
next week."

"You do good work, Cassie. I wanted to look
especially nice tonight. I'm taking my nephew
and his wife out to dinner. They have two girls in
college and can't afford an evening out, so it's my
treat."

"You're so thoughtful," Cassie told her. She
couldn't remember the last time she'd been treated
to dinner by anyone. If she could manage a dinner
out, Amiee would insist on KFC.

"John and I never had children of our own, so
I've adopted my brother's three. I enjoy spending
time with them. Thank you, Cassie. No one does
my hair better than you."

"Thank you, Mrs. Scott." Cassie closed the car
door and stepped back as Wilma pulled out of the
parking space and headed down Fourth Avenue.

As soon as she'd finished cleaning up her station, Cassie collected her purse and headed for the Habitat for Humanity offices. Her heart hummed with joy the entire way. She couldn't wipe the smile off her face. She sent a text to her daughter and promised to be home as soon as she could. But she didn't tell Amiee why she'd be late; she'd save that surprise for later.

Megan Victory glanced up when Cassie entered the office. A man stood next to Megan's desk, dressed in work jeans, with a tool belt strapped to his waist. He glanced toward Cassie and frowned. It seemed he didn't like what he saw, which might possibly be her hair. Teresa had recently cut and styled it as part of a stylist competition held at the Tacoma Dome. One side of Cassie's head was shaved close and the other side was left long and cut at an angle so that it fell forward over the side of her face. Teresa had added purple highlights to the tips of her brown hair.

"Cassie," Megan said, "meet Steve Brody."

"Hi," Cassie said, doing her best to ignore his less-than-welcoming stare.

He acknowledged her with a sharp nod and no smile.

"You'll be working your sweat equity with Steve supervising your hours," Megan explained. "Steve's a volunteer working under Stan Pearson, who's employed by Habitat."

"Five hundred hours if it's new construction,"

Steve reminded her. He looked down at her hands and her carefully manicured French nails. "You better trim those back if you expect to be of any use at the building site."

Cassie bristled and glared back at him. "Let me worry about my fingernails."

"It's called sweat equity for a reason," he returned, "with emphasis on the **sweat.** When you're working with me I expect you to work, and to work hard."

Cassie looked at Megan. "Don't worry, I'll carry my share."

Megan frowned and glanced toward the project foreman. "Steve, is there a problem?" she asked.

Steve met her look and then reverted his attention back to Cassie. "Not on my side. I apologize if I was rude. I simply want to make it clear exactly what I expect."

"I got the message," Cassie said pointedly.

"Good." He held her look an extra-long moment without flinching.

"Okay, I'm glad we've got that settled," Megan said, rising to her feet. She leaned forward and rested her palms on her desktop. "Steve, I've gotten to know Cassie over the interview process and I believe you won't have any worries. She's an excellent candidate. I don't have any doubts that she'll prove herself."

He crossed his arms. "I'll look forward to that."

Cassie was grateful for Megan's support and

thanked her with a smile. She wasn't about to let Steve Brody intimidate her. Nor would she let him walk over her. It was unfortunate that they'd started off on the wrong foot, but as far as she was concerned, the problem was his and his alone.

"I expect you at the work site tomorrow at six p.m.," Steve said, directing the comment at her. "We're working on a project for the Young family." He handed her a sheet of paper with the address.

Cassie mentally reviewed her schedule for Friday. Her last appointment was set for five for a wash and set, which meant she'd be cutting it close. Also there was Amiee to consider.

"Problems already?" Steve asked.

Cassie squared her shoulders and refused to give him the upper hand. "I'll be there at six." And she would do everything within her power to make it happen.

Steve left first, and the instant he was out the door, Cassie faced Megan. "What's his problem?"

Megan's look was full of apology. "I can't say. He's probably had a bad day. Try not to take it personally."

"Don't take it personally?" Cassie repeated. "Why would he take such an instant dislike to me?"

"My guess is that it's because you're pretty and petite. I think you might remind him of his wife."

"Someone actually married that Neanderthal?" Not a great question, seeing as she'd married Duke.

"Alicia died three years ago."

That brought Cassie up short, and she was immediately apologetic. "Oh . . . sorry."

"Alicia had cancer and did a lot of volunteer work at the store when she was going through her treatments. After she died, Steve started doing volunteer work with Habitat. He's an electrical contractor with something like fifty employees, so he's always working, either at his own business or here. Personally, I think he uses Habitat as a means of dealing with his grief. He's a great guy once you get to know him."

"Children?"

"None. From what others told me, Alicia miscarried three pregnancies. It was later that the doctors learned she had cancer, which might have been the reason she was unable to carry a baby to full term."

His wife's death might explain some of his bad attitude, but not all. "Did you ever meet his wife?" Cassie asked.

"Once at a fund-raising event. It was clear Steve was crazy about her. He's been angry with the world ever since, so when I say don't take it personally, don't."

Cassie would do her best to avoid clashing with Steve Brody, although she didn't know if that was possible.

"Kill him with kindness," Megan suggested.

"Can't I just kill him?" she joked, and they both laughed.

Megan's idea wasn't far off base, though. She would do her utmost to play nice with the bad-tempered Mr. Brody.

Chapter 5

Cassie stuck her head in her daughter's bedroom. "Amiee, time to wake up for school."

Amiee moaned, rolled over, and pulled the blanket high up, covering her head.

"Amiee." To say the twelve-year-old wasn't a morning person would be a gross understatement.

"Five more minutes," Amiee pleaded.

"I've already given you five minutes. If you don't get up right now you'll miss the bus."

"Okay, okay."

"And make your bed."

"Mom . . ."

"No arguing." Cassie wondered if the day would ever come when her daughter would cheerfully greet mornings with a smile. That was part of her problem, Cassie supposed—she was a natural-born dreamer.

About ten minutes later Amiee stumbled out of the bathroom, dressed and with her hair combed. Cassie had breakfast on the table: cold cereal, toast, and milk. She was in a rush herself. Because she had to get to the Habitat site by six, she could not run behind at all today or she'd be in trouble. Cassie was determined to make this opportunity work. Getting a real home for Amiee and her was too important to risk.

Furthermore, she had something to prove to the arrogant Steve Brody. If he didn't think she could pull her share because she had a French manicure, well, he was in store for a big surprise.

The house she was assigned to work on that evening was nearly finished. Cassie hadn't yet met the Youngs, who would eventually move into the home, but Megan from Habitat had told her about George and Shelly. At one time they'd been homeless and lived in their car with their family until they were accepted into a shelter. Slowly, a little at a time, they'd worked their way into a position to apply for a Habitat house.

The Youngs' home was nearing completion. Megan, from the head office, had explained that this evening they would be finishing the work on the roof. Frankly, Cassie couldn't think of a better spot for her to prove her worth. She'd never been afraid of heights and was ready to show Steve Big-head she had a strong work ethic.

Amiee sat down at the table and glared at the cereal. "Again?" she said, and moaned.

"Cereal is good for you. Besides, I got it on sale."

"I've had it every morning for a month. Next time don't buy ten boxes. I don't care if it was only ninety-nine cents a box. I need variety."

"Okay, fine. I'll fix you a poached egg tomorrow."

"Mom," she said, and groaned, "poached eggs are gross."

"Protein, my darling," she announced with panache. "You need protein to get those brain cells activated. And weren't you telling me you have a history test first thing Monday morning?"

As if she was being expected to eat glue, Amiee lifted her spoon and took her first tentative bite.

"You've got your homework in your backpack?"

Amiee glared at her.

"Okay, sorry I asked."

Cassie moved about the kitchen, putting away the milk and the sugar bowl as she took the clean dishes from the drainer and stacked them in the cupboard. "Remember, Rosie is picking you up on her way home from work."

Amiee glanced up. "How come?"

"Two things. The youth group at church is having pizza night and—"

Her daughter interrupted her. "What kind of pizza?"

"Amiee!" What a ridiculous question. Her daughter should be grateful for the opportunity instead of being so picky.

"You know I don't like black olives."

"I don't think you need to worry," Cassie said, shaking her head.

"Where will you be?" Amiee asked.

Cassie glanced at her wrist. Time was ticking. "I already told you. I'll be working at the Habitat house."

"Can I work, too?"

"I don't know yet, but as soon as I find out, you'll be the first to know." Her daughter had taken only a few tentative bites of the cereal.

"Time to go," Cassie announced, checking her watch. It seemed every morning Amiee left for the bus stop at the very last second.

Her daughter took one last spoonful of cereal, grabbed the toast, and reached for her backpack, which she swung over her shoulder as she headed for the front door.

"Your cell phone is charged?"

"Mom!"

"Sorry, silly question. Call me when you get home from school."

"I always do."

"Right, because I remind you every morning," Cassie tossed out, "and I do that because I love you."

"I know." Amiee headed out the door but turned

back and offered her a weak smile. "Have a good day."

"You, too."

As soon as the kitchen was cleaned, her own bed was made, and she'd applied her makeup, Cassie left the apartment for Goldie Locks. Rosie was already at the salon and had the coffee made. The scent of it filled the room. Although Cassie had had a cup at home, she reached for a mug and helped herself.

"Thank you for picking up Amiee for me tonight."

Rosie was busy at the front desk, checking the phone messages. When she'd finished she glanced up at Cassie. "No problem. And listen, before I forget, I heard back from my cousin Russell."

Cassie's hand tightened around the mug handle. "What did he say?" If she was able to get on with the caterer for the Sounders, it would mean the world to her. Earning this extra cash was the only way she could think of to collect the furniture she so badly wanted and just as badly needed.

Rosie gave her a thumbs-up. "Can you work this Sunday?"

Cassie nodded. It seemed everything had turned around for her in such a short amount of time. First she'd heard from her sister, then she learned she'd been accepted into the Habitat program, and now this. For the first time since she was a teenager Cassie felt as if she was in control of her own life. For years she'd felt like a salmon struggling to swim upstream. Now that she was out from under Duke's thumb, she'd reversed her course and flowed with the current instead of against it.

"What do I need to do?" Cassie asked.

"It's pretty straightforward. Your job consists of delivering food items to the suites, but Russell will give you the details on Sunday. He needs you to arrive early so you can fill out the necessary paperwork."

"Sure. I'll be available whenever he says."

"I told him what a hard worker you are."

"Thanks, Rosie. You don't know how much this means to me." She resisted the urge to hug her friend. It'd taken Cassie a long time to come out of the protective shell she'd built around her and Amiee. Duke had frowned upon any friendships she made—it didn't matter if they were male or female. Cassie quickly learned there was a steep price to pay if she went against her husband's wishes. The isolation she'd endured during the years she was married had been one of the worst aspects of that sick relationship. Consequently, Cassie had to relearn what it meant to be a friend and to have friends.

"Thank you," she whispered, her voice catching on the words. It was important that Rosie know how deeply Cassie appreciated the other woman's confidence in her. "I'll be the best food deliverer Russell has ever hired, I promise."

*   *   *

Cassie's Friday was harried. She gave up her lunch break, which was the price she had to pay in order to adjust to keep herself on schedule. She couldn't be in two places at the same time and she needed to be able to work on the Habitat project.

As soon as she finished with her last client, she changed into an old pair of jeans and a thin sweatshirt, ready to climb on that roof and prove to Steve that he was completely wrong about her. Hard work had never been a problem for Cassie. She didn't walk away from it or make excuses. She was willing to do whatever was necessary.

Cassie found the address for the Habitat house in South Seattle and parked her car. It was a nice neighborhood with a number of newer homes. The house was well under construction. A couple stood out front and Cassie reasoned they must be Shelly and George Young. Cassie got out of her car and walked across the dirt lot to introduce herself.

"I'm Cassie," she said.

"I'm Shelly." The other woman was tall and thin, with long, dark hair and eyes that darted around as if she was afraid of holding eye contact.

"And I'm George." The bulky, muscular man stepped forward and offered her his hand. "I heard from Steve that this is your first time working with Habitat."

"First time and first day," Cassie explained. "I

met Steve earlier . . . don't think I impressed him much." She probably shouldn't have said that, and wished now that she hadn't.

"How come?" Shelly asked, looking directly at Cassie for the first time.

She ran her fingers through her hair. "I think he dislikes the color purple."

Shelly smiled.

"And I don't think he's that keen on a French manicure." She held out her hands for inspection. "But I'm determined to work hard and prove myself to him and anyone else who thinks I'm nothing more than fluff."

"Steve's a good person," George said. "He's been with Shelly and me from the start. At first he was a little gruff, but once he got to know us he let up."

"Actually," Shelly said shyly, "I don't know who changed, if it was Steve or us."

"You have a job?" George asked.

"Hairstylist," Cassie told him, and noticed Steve had arrived.

He climbed out of his truck, slammed the door closed, and then started toward them.

"I work at Goldie Locks," Cassie continued.

Shelly bit into her lower lip. "I've been thinking of restyling my hair. It's been over a year since I had a real haircut."

"Are you going to stand around and discuss hairstyles or are we here to work?" Steve asked. Although he spoke to the three of them, Cassie had the distinct feeling the comment was directed toward her.

Cassie wanted it understood she was no slouch. "I'm here to work."

He nodded. "Good. I'm glad to hear it."

"I understand we'll be putting on the roofing material." George had placed the ladder against the side of the house and already had the roofing gun loaded and ready to fire.

Steve gave the other man a quick nod. "George, you have your assignment."

George headed for the side of the house where he'd propped up the ladder.

"Shelly, I need you to finish taping the sheetrock."

"Got it." The other woman headed inside.

That left Cassie. "What would you like me to do?"

Steve regarded her for an extra-long moment. "There's a bunch of garbage around the work site. Pick it up."

Cassie was stunned. "Excuse me?"

"You heard me," Steve said.

"You're serious? You want me to collect garbage?"

Steve released a long, slow breath. "The best thing you can do at this point is clear the lot of debris," he repeated slowly. "I realize it isn't a glamorous job, but it's a necessary one. Do you have a problem with that?"

Cassie was convinced Steve was looking to

demean her and she was determined to set him straight. "I came here to do real work," she said.

"That **is** real work," he qualified.

Cassie had been ready to climb onto the roof if asked. In fact, she'd been willing to tackle any project he gave her, but cleaning up the job site? She wanted to argue, but she could see it wouldn't do any good. "No problem at all," she said, doing her best to rein in her indignation.

"Then you'd best get started." He handed her a heavy plastic bag and headed toward the back of the house.

Infuriated, Cassie clenched the black bag and whirled around. If all he could find for her was this, then by heaven, she'd make sure the construction site was pristine by the time she left.

After the first thirty minutes Cassie had to agree that there certainly seemed to be a lot of junk lying around. She collected more than the obvious, like Coke cans and papers. She separated what she could for the recycling bin and set nails and other small screws aside. She wasn't sure what to do with them, but she didn't want to toss them, thinking it was better not to waste what could be used later.

Her cell phone rang about forty minutes later. She looked at the ID and saw that it was the Seattle shelter. That meant it was probably Maureen contacting her.

"This is Cassie."

"Hi, Cassie."

"What's up?" She didn't want to be rude, but by asking the question, Cassie let Maureen know that she couldn't talk long.

"I went for a job interview today."

"Maureen, that's great. How did it go?"

"Okay, I think. It's not much . . . I'd be working at the Safeway store, carrying out groceries. The manager was a woman and she was patient with me because I was so nervous. She said that if I was dependable and worked hard that she would keep me on and train me for other work. Lacey Wilson from the support group has a connection with her and she recommended me for the job."

"Do you feel good about how the interview went?" Cassie asked.

Maureen hesitated. "I think so, but I wouldn't have done nearly as well if Lacey hadn't talked to me first. We did a mock interview with her asking me questions. She gave me several tips, which helped boost my confidence."

"You're going to do just fine," Cassie assured her. "Take one day at a time and do the next right thing." Once Maureen had a chance to earn her own way, her self-esteem would increase to the point that she'd be better able to deal with other obstacles. In the beginning Cassie had experienced that same hesitancy, the same lack of confidence, mingled in with all the fears that went along with having walked on eggshells from the years she'd been married to Duke. When you are being told you are a useless excuse for a human being over and over, it's almost impossible not to start believing it to your very core. It had taken counseling and the support of women who had walked in her shoes before Cassie was able to come into her own. Eventually, she found the inner strength to break free of her self-imposed fears and move forward. Maureen would, too.

"The job is in the north end of Seattle, so if I am hired I'll be moving to a shelter in Edmonds, and then eventually into government housing. That means I probably won't see you for a while."

Cassie tried not to show her disappointment. "You're going to do so well," Cassie assured her friend. "I want you to know how proud I am of you, Maureen."

"I couldn't have done it without you."

Cassie pressed her hand over her heart, deeply touched by Maureen's comment. "Stay in touch, will you?"

"I will. Thank you again, Cassie, for everything you've done for me."

In reality, Cassie felt like she should be the one thanking Maureen; the other woman had helped show her how far she'd come.

"Cassie."

Her name was shouted from the top of the house. It sounded more like a bark than a summons.

Disconnecting the call, Cassie turned to find

Steve Brody standing on the roof, staring down at her. Even from this distance she could see he was frowning.

"Have you finished with your call?" he demanded.

She didn't bother to explain. "Yes."

"You have a job to do. I suggest you get to it."

She held her palms up as if she didn't understand what he was saying. "Aren't I allowed to get calls?"

"Not where you stand like a statue on the construction site and talk for fifteen minutes."

She gritted her teeth to keep from arguing. Steve had it in for her. If this was how their working relationship went, it would be impossible for them to work together.

Chapter 6

Cassie worked half a day at the salon on Saturday and then picked up Amiee at the apartment before she headed toward the Young housing site in South Seattle. Amiee insisted she was too old for a babysitter, and while Cassie agreed, she was uncomfortable leaving her daughter by herself for an entire day.

"Can we go to the lake?" her daughter pleaded, as she hopped into the car.

"Sorry, honey, not today."

"But, Mom, it's beautiful out," her daughter protested. "How many sunny days can we expect in April and on a weekend?"

What Amiee said was true. A glorious spring day in Seattle in the middle of the rainy season was rare. Blue skies and lush green foliage all around was an amazing combination. Unfortunately, Cassie had other commitments for this afternoon. "I need to put in my hours so we can get our house."

Amiee slumped down in the car and crossed her arms in protest. "Do we even know where the house is going to be?"

"Not yet, but we will before long." Megan had assured Cassie that there were several options opening up soon.

Options.

The word reverberated in her head like an echo against a canyon wall. How lovely it sounded. Options, options, options, options.

"Can I have my own bedroom?" Amiee asked, showing the first sign of enthusiasm for this project.

Cassie stopped at a red light and glanced over at her daughter. "You have your own bedroom now."

"Mom, my friends have bigger closets than what you call my bedroom."

That, sadly, was probably true. "Your new bedroom will be much bigger."

"With real closets?"

"Oh yes, with room for all your shoes and books and a desk for you to sit at while you do your homework."

"A real desk?"

"A real desk," she echoed. Cassie didn't want to make a promise she couldn't keep. Her hope was that the very desk she'd used as a girl would be among the furniture her sister had mentioned. It would mean a great deal to her if she was able to give her daughter something that came from her own childhood.

"Can I help at the construction site?" Amiee asked.

"I don't know, but my guess is probably not." Cassie had asked Megan about Amiee and learned that no one could work on the project until age sixteen or over. However, Megan hadn't said anything about not bringing Amiee to the construction site. It might be boring, but at least they'd be together and she would be able to keep an eye on her daughter. All she could do was hope that Steve Brody didn't take exception to that along with everything else.

"Then what am I supposed to do while you're working?" Amiee whined, clearly not excited about the prospect of hanging around with nothing to do.

"You'll have to amuse yourself."

"With what?"

"Did you bring a book?"

Amiee sent her a pathetic look. "You actually expect me to sit in the car and read when it's beautiful outside?"

Cassie sympathized. "It won't always be like this, Amiee, I promise. You can talk a walk and enjoy nature, or any number of things."

Her daughter's shoulders slumped forward as she went into her sulking posture.

"It won't be so terrible." Cassie wished it could

be different. She felt bad about this, but there was no help for it.

Amiee crossed her arms over her chest and made a huffing, disgruntled sound.

Cassie arrived at the work site and parked behind Steve Brody's truck. Her heart sank; she'd hoped to avoid him after their clash Friday evening. The night before, when she'd left the construction site, Cassie made sure there wasn't a speck of anything that could be termed garbage anywhere close to the lot. If Steve noticed what an excellent job she'd done, he didn't mention it. It went without saying Steve Brody was the kind of man who would be sure to point out the tiniest infraction but would be stingy with his praise. Just thinking about how critical and rude he'd been made Cassie tense.

"What's wrong?"

Amiee read her like a McDonald's menu. "See that truck," she said, and gestured toward Steve's truck.

"How could I miss it when it's parked right in front of us?"

"I don't get along with the man who owns it."

"How come?"

Cassie wasn't sure herself and didn't know how best to explain the tension between the two of them. "All I know is that we seem to clash. Whatever you do this afternoon, stay out of Steve Brody's way. Got it?"

Amiee nodded. She'd heard a similar warning

often enough when they'd lived with Duke. Even as young as two and three, Amiee had learned the wisdom of staying away from her father when he was in a foul mood.

"Is he like Dad?" she asked, lowering her voice to a whisper.

"No," Cassie said, regretting her choice of words now. "He's just grumpy."

"How come?"

Again Cassie was at a loss to explain what she had yet to understand herself. "The lady at Habitat said his wife died."

"Then he's sad."

"Yes, and that makes him grumpy," Cassie added. "Come and I'll introduce you to Shelly and George. This house is going to be their home. We're almost finished."

Amiee's eyes widened with absolute wonder as she stared at the four-bedroom house. "You mean to say this whole house will be theirs?"

Cassie struggled to hold back a smile. "Yes, the whole house."

Amiee couldn't take her eyes off the structure. "Will our home be this big?"

"Almost, only we'll have one less bedroom."

Her daughter regarded her with what could only be described as wide-eyed wonder. "Cool."

"In the good sense, right?" After being updated earlier by her daughter, she wanted to be sure this was a positive reaction.

"Right."

Cassie climbed out of the car and Amiee followed her, sticking close to her side. She wasn't more than two feet onto the property when Steve stopped her. "That your daughter?" he asked, directing the question to Cassie.

"Yes, this is Amiee. Amiee, this is Steve."

He nodded once in Amiee's direction, then asked Cassie, "How old is she?"

"Twelve."

"She can't be here. No one under the age of sixteen is allowed to be on the construction site."

"I . . . was going to stay out of the way," Amiee assured him.

Steve sighed. "Sorry. It's the rules. No one under sixteen can be here."

Shelly stood in the background, and being in close proximity, she couldn't help but overhear. "Amiee, I have a daughter around your age. I could take you over to our place and the two of you could hang. Would you like that?"

Amiee glanced at Steve and nodded.

"Thank you," Cassie told the other woman. This was by far preferable to having her daughter alone in the house or sitting in the car for the next several hours.

Cassie tagged along with Shelly to where the family was currently housed. Once she was assured Amiee was at ease with Shelly's daughter, the two women returned to the job site. "I wonder if Steve will let me do more than pick up trash today," Cassie muttered.

"He'll have to," Shelly said. "There'd be nothing for you to collect, seeing what a great job you did yesterday."

Shelly was right. When they returned, Steve met them with a gallon bucket of paint in each hand. "You're both going to paint today."

"Are you sure you don't want me on garbage detail?" Cassie asked ever-so-sweetly.

Steve responded by handing her a paint can. Cassie took it from him and was surprised by how heavy it was.

"Cassie, you're cutting out around the windows and archway in the living room," he said, and then looked to Shelly. "You can start in the dining room with the roller."

Cassie waited until he was out of the room before she snapped her heels together and saluted him, as if he were a member of the Third Reich.

Shelly broke into giggles. "What is with you two?" Shelly asked, as she slowly shook her head.

Cassie shrugged. "For whatever reason, he doesn't like me." She couldn't imagine what she'd said or done to get on his bad side, but she was solidly placed there now. It wasn't a big deal. His dislike wasn't a concern. He didn't have to like her and she didn't need to like him, either. Cassie was determined that no matter what he said, she wouldn't allow him to intimidate her. She had faced off with the master of intimidation and survived. Compared to Duke, Steve was an amateur.

Shelly had a radio, which she placed on the floor between the living room and the dining room and put it on a Top 40 station. The two women started work, singing to the music. Soon they were dancing, too, paintbrushes in hand, enjoying themselves and making the most of the song.

"Hey, you two," George said, coming inside the house and heading toward the Styrofoam cooler. "You're having way too much fun in here."

"That's because we're singing along with Uncle Kracker and you're stuck with Mr. Potato Head," Cassie said.

Shelly's eyes widened as she slid her finger sideways across her throat, telling Cassie to cut it. That was when she realized Steve had come inside with George and stood directly behind her.

Well, she hadn't said anything he didn't deserve.

"Here," George said, breaking the tension. He handed Steve a bottle of water as if nothing had happened. Then he looked toward Shelly and Cassie. "You two need water?"

"I don't," Shelly said.

"Me, neither."

The two men drank their water. Determined to prove her worth, Cassie returned to painting, using the paintbrush to cut in around the windows just like Steve had instructed. Another song came on the radio, and while Shelly didn't sing, Cassie's feet refused to hold still. At first she simply tapped her foot as she continued to paint. But all too soon her legs and hips started to sway, as it was impossible to stand still. At one point she whirled around in a complete circle and discovered Steve. He stood no more than a few feet behind her. His dark, disapproving look stopped her cold.

"Did you need something?" she asked, refusing to flinch.

"You're not using the right brush," he said, his words devoid of emotion.

"I beg your pardon?"

"The paintbrush," he reiterated, pointing to the one in her hand. "It's the wrong size. It will take you twice as much time to cover the same area with that smaller brush. Use the other one, the bigger brush, but be sure and give that one a thorough cleaning first."

Did he seriously think she'd just leave it thick with paint? Cassie's back was as straight as a telephone pole. "I happen to like this smaller brush. It fits perfectly in my hand and applies the paint smoothly and evenly."

Steve stared her down, but Cassie refused to blink. The truth was she really didn't have a preference, but she refused to let him think he had the upper hand.

"Have it your way, then."

"I will," she said, making her voice as sweet and accommodating as humanly possible. She held the same ramrod-straight pose until Steve left and returned to the roof with George.

As soon as he vacated the house, Shelly came over to Cassie. "He really doesn't like you," she whispered, as if she was afraid he would hear her.

"I told you."

"Calling him a Mr. Potato Head probably didn't help."

Cassie disagreed. "He was being a jerk, just the way Amiee said." Her daughter had the electrical contractor pegged after less than five minutes.

"He isn't always like this. Deep down, I think he must like you."

That was so far from the truth it was almost funny. "If so, he has an odd way of showing it."

"I'm serious. Try being nice to him," Shelly advised, "and see what happens."

"The thing you're forgetting," Cassie said, as she reached for the paint bucket, "is that I really don't care if Steve likes me or not."

"You're going to be working together for a long time. Those sweat-equity hours don't fly by as quickly as some people think. It's a lot of time and effort, and if you're going to be working with Steve, then you should at least make an attempt to try to get along, don't you think?"

This was quite a speech for Shelly. The other woman was shy and quiet, but she'd opened up a little bit more over the last couple days. Cassie felt that she had at least one ally.

"Steve is one of those people who takes awhile to warm to someone," Shelly added, returning to the dining room and resuming painting.

"You mean he actually has a warm side?" Cassie mumbled sarcastically.

"Both George and I were unsure when we first met him," Shelly explained, peeking around the corner.

Cassie had the feeling her newfound friend was exaggerating. "He was like this with both of you?"

Shelly hesitated.

Cassie thought so. "Not really," she answered on Shelly's behalf, returning to her own painting.

"It took him awhile to warm to us, too. It's like he's hiding inside a fort or something and won't come out until he's sure it's safe. George and I think he's really great now. Give him a chance, Cassie."

"Okay, I'll give it another try," she said, taking Shelly's words to heart, although she didn't hold out much hope.

In a gesture toward peace, Cassie switched paintbrushes and discovered Steve was right. The bigger brush spread the paint just as smoothly as the smaller one and covered twice the area. Her stubbornness, complicated by pride, had cost her a lot of extra work.

She waited until George and Shelly were ready to leave before she approached Steve. "I'll be right behind you," Cassie told Shelly. "Tell Amiee I'll be there in five minutes, okay? And if you've got a few extra minutes I'll cut your hair for you."

Shelly's eyes widened with appreciation. "You will?"

"It'll be my pleasure." Cassie felt like she owed the other woman for giving Amiee someplace to go. It looked like the two girls were going to be fast friends.

"Are you going to talk to Steve?" Shelly asked, lowering her voice.

"I'm going to try," she responded, in the same low tones.

The other woman offered her an encouraging smile. "Good luck."

Cassie was fairly certain she was going to need it.

George and Shelly drove off and Steve was picking up the last of his tools when Cassie approached him.

He pretended not to notice her until she said his name. "Steve."

Turning around, he looked at her. His face was blank, giving her no indication of his feelings.

"Do you have a minute?"

He didn't answer but waited.

"I changed brushes the way you suggested and you were right. The painting did go faster."

It would be a whole lot easier if he'd smile or give some indication that he appreciated the effort it took for her to admit this. It looked like he wasn't willing to give an inch.

"I think it would make for a better working atmosphere if the two of us could get along."

He acted as if he didn't know what she was talking about. "I don't have a problem with you. Show up on time, do the work, and we'll get along just fine."

Cassie wasn't sure what she had expected, but it wasn't this. Well, she'd tried. She'd given it her best shot. "Just FYI, I don't have a problem with you, either."

"Good. Glad we've got that settled. See you next week."

Cassie sincerely hoped matters between them would even out. She'd do as Shelly suggested, but she had the distinct feeling that next week, and all the weeks that followed, nothing was going to change.

Chapter 7

A day with her best friend was a rare treat for Nichole Patterson. With a one-year-old underfoot, she was on duty 24/7. She needed this break and lunch out with Laurie, her BFF from college. A day for herself was the perfect antidote to the new-mother blahs.

"Have a great day," Jake told her, as he kissed her on his way out the door to work. As a salesman for a growing Willamette Valley winery, he often worked long hours. They were blessed that Nichole could stay at home with their son.

Nichole stood in the doorway and watched as her husband backed the car out of the garage. Jake paused halfway down the driveway, rolled down his window, and called out, "What time will you be home?"

"I won't be too late. Five at the absolute latest.

That okay?" She felt a bit silly asking her husband such a question.

His smile was warm. "Honey, of course, and buy yourself a pair of those fancy jeans you saw online."

"Jake—"

"You deserve them," he said, cutting off her protest. "Be sure and thank Mom for me."

"I'll buy her something for watching Owen."

"No need. Mom loves it that you asked her to babysit."

It was also a blessing that Jake's parents lived close enough to watch their only grandchild on the rare occasions when Nichole and Jake went out. Unlike some of her friends, Nichole got along famously with Leanne, her mother-in-law. Having Jake's family nearby was especially important, seeing that both her parents had passed. It hurt to think that her parents would never know Owen.

Nichole met Laurie at Nordstrom at ten just when the department store was opening. They linked arms, excited to see each other. "I feel like we're teenagers again, skipping school," Laurie said.

Nichole understood—she felt the same way. It had been at least a year, since before Owen was born, that she'd taken an entire day to herself.

At one time Nichole had done all her school shopping with her two older sisters. Her parents had given her a budget of a hundred dollars for the school year. Her sisters' clothing allowance was slightly higher, based on the idea that she had hand-me-downs and they didn't.

Their mother wasn't a shopper. In fact, Nichole could remember only a handful of times that she'd gone to the mall just north of town with her mother. Mom had seemed relieved when Karen was old enough to drive so she wouldn't have to take her three daughters school shopping.

For weeks in advance of August, Nichole and Cassie read through fashion magazines and department-store fliers, making lists of what they wanted to buy, where, and at what price. Cassie was great when it came to accessorizing. She could do amazing things with a scarf, changing the look of an entire outfit. Karen was much better with makeup. Although it'd been more years now than she could remember, Nichole missed those days, missed those special times with her sisters.

School shopping was always the best. It went without saying that whatever they got would need to last them. Karen and Cassie claimed Nichole was the lucky one because she got their hand-me-downs. Nichole had quite a different opinion. She hated having to wear her sisters' old clothes and getting less money to buy new things. Her clothing allowance was always less than theirs, which to her way of thinking was completely unfair.

Cassie was the most patient of her two sisters, often bringing Nichole clothes to try on while in the dressing room. Like their mother, Karen wasn't a great shopper. She preferred to hang out at the cosmetics counter. Funny, it'd been years since she thought about their school-shopping expeditions. It was never quite the same after Cassie left, though.

"I scheduled a surprise for us," Laurie said, cutting into her musings as she steered Nichole out of the store.

Nichole glanced longingly over her shoulder. Shopping was first on her agenda. She was desperate for a new pair of jeans. Her skinny jeans didn't fit the same since she'd given birth to Owen.

Although she detested the thought, she might need to go up a size. The difference in her weight was only a few measly pounds, but those pounds seemed to have attached themselves directly to her hips.

"We'll have plenty of time to shop," Laurie insisted, dragging Nichole into the mall.

"Where are you taking me?" she asked, enjoying the adventure.

"You'll see."

The surprise was a shop that specialized in shaping eyebrows. Nichole and Laurie giggled as if they were twenty-year-old college students all over again. Once finished, they couldn't believe the difference a few hairs could make.

Every minute of this day was about as perfect as it could be. Nichole badly needed this getaway for her sanity; the demands of motherhood were above and beyond anything she'd anticipated. It wasn't that she didn't love her son with every cell in her body, but never having a moment to herself was draining. Stealing away for these few hours was exactly what she needed. This was the first time in more than a year that she felt carefree and light.

After they had their eyebrows shaped, Nichole and Laurie went in search of the perfect pair of jeans. While it was depressing to go up a size, the white rhinestone-studded jeans she tried on made her look a size smaller. Or so Laurie insisted.

"I feel guilty spending two hundred and fifty dollars on a pair of jeans," Nichole confessed, holding on to her credit card and weighing the decision.

"But didn't Jake tell you to go ahead and get them?"

"Yes." Still, Nichole hesitated.

"Do it," Laurie urged. "You wouldn't see me thinking twice if my husband suggested I buy something for myself. Besides, you deserve those jeans and you look fabulous."

That was all the inducement Nichole needed. She laid down her credit card and added a shirt that was forty percent off to go with the jeans.

"Now all you need are the shoes," Laurie coaxed.

"I couldn't," Nichole said, laughing. She felt

guilty enough after paying such an outrageous sum for those jeans.

"Jake would insist," Laurie assured her.

Her friend was right. Jake was far too good to her. He indulged Nichole's every whim. She finally had to tell him to stop buying her gifts. Hardly a week went by when he didn't come home with a little surprise for her. He insisted it was simply his way of proving that he adored her. He'd been like this ever since she gave him a son.

Both Nichole and Laurie ate crab salads for lunch, with the dressing on the side, naturally. "When was the last time you had a pedicure?" Nichole asked her friend.

Laurie set aside her fork. "You don't want to know. I swear it's been over a year. Lucy is two and is into everything. I don't have a wonderful mother-in-law like certain people I could mention—I have to pay a sitter, and you wouldn't believe what they charge these days."

"Then we're going to do it today. We passed a salon in the mall that said walk-ins are welcome." Nichole had an ulterior motive. If she did find time to shop for shoes, she absolutely refused to let a salesperson see her feet in their current condition.

They were fortunate to find two available nail technicians who could fit them in at the same time. Not thirty minutes after they'd finished their lunch, Nichole and Laurie sat side by side with their feet soaking in bubbling hot water. The chair had a pulsating massage in the back that eased the tension from Nichole's lower spine. If this wasn't heaven it was mighty darn close. She closed her eyes and luxuriated in the moment.

Just when she was certain she was about to doze off, her phone chirped. Afraid something had happened with Owen, Nichole jerked upright and grabbed her purse.

She didn't even bother to look at caller ID before she answered. "Hello."

"Nichole, this is Karen." Her sister.

"Is anything wrong?" Nichole asked, sitting up straight now, worried.

"No, not really. How are you?"

Her sister hadn't phoned just to say hi, Nichole could tell. "Karen, what's wrong?"

Laurie looked over at her and Nichole shrugged.

"I heard from Cassie."

The two sisters had discussed the rather awkward conversation already. "Yes, that was a few days ago, right?"

"Right."

"And?"

"Two things. I want to be sure you're still comfortable with what we've done?"

What a ridiculous question. It was far too late to change their minds now. "Of course I am."

"Mom wanted—"

"We both know what Mom wanted and we both

felt Mom wasn't in her right mind. You know as well as I do that in the end she wasn't anything like herself. Half the time she didn't make any sense whatsoever."

"True . . ."

Nichole didn't know why Karen would be bringing all this up now. "Karen," she said, lowering her voice, "it's too late for us to have second thoughts. The attorney has already dispensed the money from the sale of the house." She hesitated and a sense of dread came over her. "Is Cassie asking questions about the will?" It wouldn't do her any good, and both Karen and Nichole knew it. After Cassie married Duke, their father had cut Cassie out of the will. He wasn't looking to punish his precious, favorite daughter as much as protect her. It went without saying that anything of value Cassie inherited would quickly be squandered by her no-good husband. And he was right.

Later, just a few days before she died, their mother asked the two sisters to help Cassie.

"Do you think . . ." Karen paused, almost as if she was afraid to say the words.

"That Mom wanted us to share everything with Cassie?" Nichole asked, completing the thought for her sister. "I don't. I think that reaching out to Cassie and offering her Mom and Dad's furniture is above and beyond anything she should expect. As you said earlier, Cassie put Mom and Dad through hell and beyond."

"She did," Karen agreed. When Cassie disappeared, it'd been a nightmare for the entire family. Their father had been completely unnerved, unable to sleep. He lost weight and fretted endlessly. Their mother had taken Cassie's leaving equally hard. She sat at the kitchen table chain-smoking and sobbing for days on end. The police were no help. At eighteen, Cassie was considered an adult, and the decision to marry Duke was out of the hands of the law.

Nichole didn't mean to be callous, but Cassie had been out of their family for so long that it was hard to even remember what she looked like. Their middle sister hadn't kept in touch or showed any real concern when she learned of their father's death. True, she'd reached out when told their mother was ill, but by then it was far too little too late.

Nichole straightened her spine. "We made our decision, Karen, and I believe it was the right one. You said Cassie seemed happy to be getting the furniture, and she should be." That sounded heartless, she realized, but she couldn't help it. "Let's leave it at that."

Right away Nichole realized her little outburst had attracted the attention of nearly everyone in the salon. Embarrassed, she lowered her head, dreading that she might have caused something of a scene.

"I know that you're right," Karen said, after an

uncomfortable moment. "I just wanted to be sure you don't have any regrets or second thoughts?"

"None," Nichole assured her, and she didn't. She felt sorry for Cassie, but things could never go back to the way they'd been when they were kids. That time was long past. Cassie couldn't show up after all these years and just assume nothing had changed. They were different people now, with separate lives.

"She was the one who chose Duke over her own family," Karen said, as if she needed to hear it again.

"Yes. She wasn't there after Dad died or to help when Mom was so sick. Nor was she there to clean out and sell the house. You and I were the ones who worked sixteen-hour days."

"Right. I guess I was just looking for reassurance that we weren't unreasonable in what we did."

"You, unreasonable?" Nichole laughed. "You're the most levelheaded, fair person I know."

"I try to be."

"You are," Nichole said, although if Karen was having second thoughts, then maybe she should reconsider their decision herself. And she would, but not now, not when she was supposed to be spending a carefree day with her best friend.

"I'm sending Cassie an email," Karen said.

"Oh?"

"Yes. I told her I'd pay for two months' storage fees for Mom and Dad's stuff and said that was all

I'd be willing to do. She has sixty days to collect it and no more."

"It's good to set those boundaries with Cassie."

"My thought, too. What I don't think Cassie realized . . . well, actually, I failed to tell her. One of those months had already passed. In fact, five of the eight weeks are gone."

"Let her know, then. If she really wants it, she'll find a way to get over to Spokane."

"It's only fair that I tell her she has less than three weeks to collect the furniture."

"Or pay the storage fee herself."

"Should I send the email?" Karen asked.

"I don't know why you're hesitating." Nichole felt her sister was already being more than generous. It wasn't like there was anything left that was of any real value, other than maybe the piano.

Her pedicure had been finished by then, but she was so wrapped up in the conversation, she barely noticed. She said good-bye and dropped the cell back inside her purse.

Laurie glanced over at her. "That was intense. I didn't know you had another sister."

"I don't, not really. Cassie ran away from home when I was fourteen; it was like she disappeared for all these years. Now she's divorced and wants back into the family as if nothing happened. It's been weird, you know. She reached out to us once and it was all so awkward and uncomfortable.

We didn't have anything to say to one another. I haven't heard from her since."

"Have you contacted her?"

"I tried. I mailed her a Christmas card, which was returned with no forwarding address. Apparently, my sister moves around a lot."

Nichole was tense and uptight, although she tried hard to relax. "I could use a fruity drink. How about you?"

"Should we?" Laurie asked guiltily.

"We should. It'll wear off before we head home."

Laurie was game. They went into the hotel attached to the shopping mall and let a cool mojito work its magic. When they finished, they returned to Nordstrom.

On the way into the department store, Nichole passed the purses on display and stopped cold. She grabbed Laurie's sleeve.

"Laurie, do you see what I see?"

Her friend stared in the same direction as Nichole and then shook her head. "What?"

"That Michael Kors bag," Nichole whispered, as if she were speaking in church.

"Nichole, they're hundreds and hundreds of dollars."

"I know. I know. It's the alcohol talking. I'd be nuts to even consider buying it."

"Then you'd better stop looking at it." Laurie wrapped her arm around Nichole's elbow and said, "Turn your head this way and pretend you didn't see it."

"I can't **not** look," Nichole said in a breathy voice. "I would so love to own that bag. Go and check the price and then come tell me."

"You sure?" Laurie sounded skeptical.

"I think so." Nichole's head was spinning and her stomach was in turmoil.

"Call Jake," Laurie advised.

"You think I should?"

"Yes. He'll tell you you're out of your mind, and then buy it for you himself on your anniversary."

"Good idea." Nichole reached inside her purse for her phone.

Laurie walked over to the purse on display. A sales clerk was immediately there to assist her. She asked the price, nodded, and then turned back to Nichole and held up seven fingers.

"It's seven hundred dollars," Nichole told Jake, who was on the other end of the line.

"Seven hundred dollars for a purse?" Jake repeated, sounding shocked.

Nichole knew the price was above and beyond anything she should consider spending. "It's too much, isn't it?"

"Oh honey, that's a lot of money."

"I know. You're right. I'm being ridiculous."

Jake hesitated and then said, "All right, baby, buy it. You're the most amazing woman in the world and you deserve beautiful things. We'll find a way to pay for it."

"You don't mean it." Nichole was nearly speechless.

"Do it, honey. You buy yourself that purse."

That was all the incentive Nichole needed.

Chapter 8

Saturday night, Cassie turned off the light on her nightstand early. She was exhausted. She'd worked at the salon all week and then gone to the construction site and put in extra hours. It remained light until nearly eight, which helped. For most of the time, Cassie managed to keep out of Steve's way. He seemed to be preoccupied with the business at hand, which was just as well. Either that or he chose to simply ignore her.

After a hectic week, Sunday wasn't going to be a day of rest, but Cassie wasn't complaining. She was thrilled to have gotten work with the caterer for the Sounders soccer match.

"Mom?"

"Yes, honey, what is it?" Going to sleep early didn't seem likely if Amiee was in a chatty mood.

Her daughter's shadow filled the doorway leading to Cassie's small bedroom.

Amiee sighed. "What was it like when you were my age?"

Cassie sat up enough to lean on her elbow. Ever since she'd gotten the letter from her older sister, Amiee had besieged her with questions about the two aunts she'd yet to meet.

"How do you mean?" she asked. "I can tell you right now we didn't have cell phones."

"I know that. What I want to know is what's it like having sisters. Did you share clothes?"

The memories wrapped themselves around Cassie like curling ribbon atop a birthday gift. "All the time," Cassie whispered into the dark.

"Did you ever do stuff like date the same boys?"

"Never. Dad wouldn't hear of it. Karen and I were the closest in age. She's two years older."

"Your dad used to take you fishing, didn't he?"

Cassie could only wonder how her daughter found that out. "How'd you know about that?"

Amiee went silent. "You wanted to take me fishing once and Dad wouldn't let you. You tried to explain that your dad took you fishing and Dad got really upset with you, remember? He said you were putting him down and . . . and he hit you."

Cassie swallowed against the tightness in her throat. "Yes, I remember," she whispered. Trying to divert the conversation, she lightened her voice and said, "My dad took the family fishing quite a bit when I was young. We'd catch the fish, clean them, and cook them up for dinner over the campfire. Those are some of my best childhood memories."

Amiee stepped into the room and Cassie tossed aside her covers, inviting her daughter to climb into bed with her. All too soon Amiee's cold feet were tucked against her much warmer ones.

"Tell me some stories of when you were my age."

"Let me think," Cassie whispered, wrapping her arm around her daughter's thin shoulders. She'd been raised in a loving home. Her mother had been a homemaker until Nichole was old enough for school and then she'd gone to work in the school cafeteria. That way she was home in the summers with her daughters. Her mother was far less outgoing than their father, who made everything fun. Cassie hated that her last conversation with her father had been an argument. From the onset he hadn't liked Duke, and he'd done everything within his power as her father to keep the two of them apart. Sadly, his demands had exactly the opposite effect. Cassie was convinced she was in love and Duke encouraged her to meet him on the sly, which she'd done.

"Tell me about camping," Amiee urged, snuggling closer.

Talking about happier times in her childhood was certainly preferable to delving into painful memories. "Dad bought a big tent the year I turned ten," Cassie told her, pressing her head down on the pillow close to her daughter. She lowered her voice, hoping that it would lull Amiee to sleep. "I helped Dad set it up while Mom and Karen and Nichole unloaded everything from the station wagon. Mom had a folding table and a cookstove and a cooler filled with enough food for three days." It'd been a privilege to be asked to help her father, and they'd gotten the tent set up in record time.

"Were you in the National Forest or at a campsite?" Amiee asked.

"Neither. Dad knew some people who had acreage near Colville, which is a town north of Spokane. A bubbling brook that had fish ran through their property, and Dad got permission to camp out there. It was an adventure—no one else around. We had the entire field to ourselves . . ." Or so they'd thought, Cassie remembered, smiling now at the memory.

"Were you excited to go fishing?"

"We all were. Karen kept saying if she had to put a worm on the hook she refused to fish, and Nichole stood on the edge of the stream and called out, 'Here, fishy, fishy.' She seemed to think she could lure them onto the land so she could scoop up a fish with her bare hands, and then when Dad caught one she wanted to name it."

Amiee giggled. "How old was she?"

Cassie had to think about that. "There's a four-year span between the two of us, so she would have been around five or six at the time."

"Did you have fun?"

"We did until Karen woke us up, screaming hysterically."

Cassie could feel her daughter relax against her. She enjoyed hearing these stories as much as Cassie enjoyed telling them.

"What happened?" Amiee asked. "Why was Karen screaming? Did a bear come after her?" Wild animals were always a concern to Amiee.

"Not a bear; it was something else."

"Tell me, Mom, don't keep me in suspense."

"Okay, okay, remember I told you that a friend of my dad's owned this property? What he failed to mention was that he'd leased the land to a local rancher who raised cattle. And, in case you didn't know, cattle are curious animals. They wanted to find out what that funny-looking structure was in the middle of the field, so they came to investigate." Cassie struggled not to laugh out loud. "We were surrounded by cattle. They leaned against the tent and toppled the table with the cookstove, and then, to complicate everything, the tent collapsed."

"Oh no."

"Can you picture that?" Cassie asked. "Mom, Karen, and Nichole panicked while Dad and I tried in vain to get the tent back up." It'd been dreadful at the time, but the story had Cassie smothering her own giggles.

"Mom, Mom, stop . . . I have more questions."

Cassie wiped the mirth from her eyes. "Sorry. It's been a lot of years since that happened. I'd nearly forgotten about it."

"Did you ever go fishing in the brook, and did you catch anything?"

"I did," she boasted proudly. "I hooked a trout and it was a large one, bigger than any my dad caught."

"Did Karen or Nichole catch a fish?"

"No. Nichole never gave up on the idea she could catch them with her hands. Dad said Karen had to bait her own hook and she refused." The three sisters had bickered on the long ride home. In retrospect, Cassie realized Karen had been jealous of her. She'd taunted Cassie mercilessly, simply because she'd caught a fish and Karen hadn't. It was Karen's own fault, but she didn't see it that way.

According to Karen, Cassie caught that fish because she was their father's favorite, which made no logical sense. This rift between them—over Cassie being the favorite—was the cause of so much jealousy.

At age ten she thought Karen had it wrong and that her sister was being ridiculous. In retrospect, she realized her sister was right. Her father did favor Cassie. He'd found a way later that same summer to get her a piano, for one thing. And she was the only one he let trail along with him when he ran errands.

Cassie was the daughter with the good grades, the fearless one, blessed with what he called **grit.** She was like the son he never had. He taught both her and Karen how to change a flat tire, but it was Cassie he showed how to check the car engine and how to change the oil. When Cassie turned sixteen he'd promised her his mother's cameo and said Cassie could wear it on her wedding day. Instead she'd run away and married Duke just weeks before she was scheduled to leave for college.

The cameo.

Like the story of camping in the open field, Cassie hadn't thought about the cameo in years. The memory brought with it an ache—it seemed to symbolize everything she had lost when she became estranged from her family. The cameo was the most precious jewelry her grandmother had owned, and her own mother had worn it on her wedding day. She wondered which sister it had gone to after she left home.

The soft, even breaths of her daughter told Cassie that Amiee had fallen asleep. Gently, she swept the hair off the twelve-year-old's forehead and brushed her lips over the smooth skin of her daughter's cheek.

Pressing her head down against the soft pillow, Cassie closed her eyes as scenes from her childhood played through her mind like an old silent movie.

There'd been good times and bad times with her two sisters. As the three had grown older they'd had some wretched fights, but their disagreements never lasted long. At one time the three of them had been close. Even now Cassie found it hard to believe that she had gone years without talking to her sisters. Those years seemed like an entire lifetime.

Sunday morning Cassie had to be at Century-Link Field by nine. Russell, Rosie's cousin, had her fill out the proper paperwork, gave her a uniform complete with an apron, and assigned her six suites. Her job was simple enough: She was to deliver the food order each suite owner had emailed the Wednesday before the game. This was a golden opportunity and she was anxious to do everything right. She needed this job, even if it meant she had to work seven days this week. Too much was at stake.

Never having been inside CenturyLink Field before—let alone attend a Sounders game—Cassie was amazed at the size of the stadium. A light mist had started to fall, but a little rain didn't discourage the fans' enthusiasm. They crowded into the stands as an air of excitement filled the stadium. Cassie couldn't help but feel it herself.

The suites were luxurious and for the most part empty while she delivered the first round of the orders. She filled all the refrigerators with the drinks, mostly beer and soda. She noticed Russell kept close tabs on her, which caused her to work all the harder. She double-checked to make sure she had the right order in each suite.

Behind the scenes, the activity was fairly hectic.

Cassie's next job was to deliver the hot food about thirty minutes before the Sounders match officially started. Everything was going well until she entered Suite 36.

"Hello. Are you one of the servers?" A strikingly lovely blond woman approached Cassie. She was dressed in skin-tight jeans and wore a bright lime green and blue Sounders jersey.

"Yes," Cassie said. "How can I help you?"

"There's no Olympia beer in the suite. I only drink Olympia beer."

Cassie didn't recall seeing that brand of beer on the list. "I'm so sorry, please let me check. I'll get back to you as soon as I can."

"I know it sounds superstitious, but whenever I've had an Olympia when I watch a Sounders game, they win." The woman had unbelievably long black eyelashes, and her dark brown eyes were wide.

"I'll find out right away and be back in a flash." Cassie raced out of the suite, hoping to find Russell. It took her ten minutes to locate him, and when she found him, he looked at her impatiently. "Why aren't you delivering the hot entrées?" he demanded.

"A lady in Suite Thirty-six wants Olympia beer."

"What?"

"Yes, she says the Sounders could lose the match if she doesn't have Olympia beer."

Russell frowned and shook his head. "We don't carry that brand. The beverage list is detailed and specific. Tell her she's out of luck."

Cassie hated the thought of returning with bad news. "Is there a brand that's similar that I could take to her?"

"I suppose," he said with some reluctance, "but adding any additional beverages means an extra charge to the suite owner, and that has to be approved beforehand."

"I understand," Cassie said, and hurried back to inform the blond woman of what she'd learned.

When she returned, the suite was full and people were mingling around. As soon as she stepped into the room, the blonde was there. "What took you so long?" she asked impatiently. "The match is about to start."

"I'm so sorry," Cassie said, doing her best to be as polite as possible. After being married to Duke, she'd had a lot of practice looking demure and regretful. She kept her gaze lowered and hands neatly folded in front of her. "Apparently, the caterer doesn't carry Olympia beer. I do apologize."

"I thought you understood." The other woman elevated her voice and flung her hands out as though distraught.

"We carry a similar brand, but it has to be ordered through the suite owner." Her words were followed by a short silence.

"What's your name?" the woman demanded.

"Cassie."

"Cassie what?"

"Cassie Carter."

"Is there a problem?" a man asked. He stood next to the woman, but all Cassie saw was his feet.

Even then she knew. Although she kept her gaze lowered, she immediately recognized the man's voice.

Steve Brody.

Cassie wanted to curl into a tight ball and disappear. How humiliating to run into him. Though it was the last thing she wanted to do, she jerked her head up and met his eye. Squaring her shoulders, she silently stood her ground.

"This . . . this server refused to get me my Olympia beer."

Cassie longed to defend herself, but she kept silent. She had **refused** the other woman nothing. In fact, she'd done everything humanly possible to get her what she wanted.

"Is that true, Cassie?" he asked.

The blonde whirled around to face Steve. "You know her?"

He waited an uncomfortable moment before he answered. "We've met."

"Really?" The blonde gave Cassie the once-over and snorted softly.

"Come on, Britt, the match is about to start."

"But the Sounders could lose if I don't have my Olympia beer."

"The Sounders will just have to do their best without it," he said, steering Britt away from Cassie.

Relaxing her shoulders, Cassie left the suite, surprised to find that she was shaking. It was more than having to deal with that unreasonable woman. Meeting up with Steve Brody was bad enough, but then for him to show such reluctance to admit he knew her had been mortifying.

Cassie finished delivering the hot dishes to the suites assigned to her, and by the end of the day she felt like she'd walked fifty miles.

Distressed and irritated, she was eager to get home. On the way, she stopped off at Rosie's to collect Amiee.

It was after seven by the time she arrived. "How'd it go?" Rosie asked expectantly.

Cassie swallowed tightly. "Not so good, I'm afraid."

Shock showed on Rosie's face. "What happened? I told Russell you're an excellent worker and I personally vouched for you."

"I know and I'm sorry. Unfortunately, Russell said he wouldn't be able to use me again."

Amiee came to stand next to her mother. "Mom?" Her big brown eyes stared up at Cassie.

Cassie didn't feel she had any choice but to explain. "Someone complained about me. She asked me to get a particular brand of beer for her, and because I took the time to try to fill her request, I was late delivering the hot entrées to the other suites. Russell said he was sorry, but his job is to keep the suite owners happy. He couldn't risk something like this happening a second time."

"Oh Cassie, I'm so, so sorry."

"Yes, I am, too." And the worst part of it was that she'd need to face Steve Brody again later in the week.

Chapter 9

The text on Steve Brody's cell was a request from Megan Victory from the Habitat for Humanity office, asking if he wouldn't mind stopping by when it was convenient. Whatever it was, she clearly didn't feel comfortable talking via the phone.

Stop by when it was **convenient.** With his hectic schedule, **convenient** wasn't part of his vocabulary. His day was busy enough and he didn't need anything more piled on his plate. Still, if Megan asked to see him, then clearly something important was on her mind.

Steve's work with the humanitarian group had helped him deal with the unrelenting grief he'd endured after Alicia's death. If he could find a way to work from dawn to dusk, keep his mind busy and his body physically exhausted, he might distract himself long enough to find some peace. He might be able to forget the helplessness he'd felt watching the woman he loved breathe her last breath.

He wished he could say his plan worked. It hadn't. Nothing did.

Alicia was never far from his thoughts, even now, three years later. The only antidote to this pain, he discovered, was time. As the weeks and months passed he found it somewhat easier to function. He kept an emotional distance from most everyone. That was necessary because he'd learned that caring and loving put his heart at risk. He'd been badly hurt once, and he wasn't game for a second round.

The one exception had been a gentle-natured eight-year-old boy. He was the grandson of Joe Osborne, who owned a large electrical-supply company where Steve bought his materials. For whatever reason, Jeremy had taken a liking to Steve. Joe had brought his grandson onto the job site with him when Steve was there and the boy had looked at Steve with wide, adoring eyes. Even now Steve wasn't sure what the kid saw in him; perhaps he recognized the longing Steve held deep in his heart for a son one day. Whatever it was, Jeremy pestered Joe until he took the youngster to see Steve again. Jeremy had asked Steve to help him build a small wooden car for a Cub Scout event, and they'd been pals ever since.

It was through Jeremy that Steve met Britt, Jeremy's divorced mother, though he wasn't nearly as fond of her as he was of her son. Steve had dated Britt a couple times, but no way was he serious about her. The truth was he didn't feel the least bit of physical attraction for Britt. She was pretty, that was sure, but she had an edge to her that he found off-putting. The only reason he'd gone out with her those few times was because he couldn't help thinking how perfect it would be if he could have fallen for Jeremy's mother. But he didn't want to lead Britt into thinking that he was interested in her romantically, because at this point he could tell it wasn't happening.

Technically, Steve wasn't employed by Habitat— all his work was volunteer. His supervisor, Stan Pearson, was a paid full-time employee, and generally he'd be overseeing the volunteers' work on every phase of construction. However, with Steve's vast knowledge base, that wasn't necessary.

Steve was able to tear himself away from his own job site around four, which gave him only an hour to stop off at Habitat's offices before heading over to work on the Youngs' house.

Cassie Carter was scheduled to work that evening. She was an interesting character—now, there was a woman with spunk. Steve doubted that she backed down from anything. He'd never known a woman with more expressive eyes. He could see how difficult it had been for her to bite her tongue when Britt made her unreasonable demand for the beer. He gave Cassie credit, though: She'd been a picture of politeness.

Steve had been surprised to find Cassie working the Sounders game. It appeared she worked two jobs in addition to putting in her Habitat hours. She certainly didn't stand still for long.

Britt's overreaction to the fact Cassie couldn't get her what she wanted had embarrassed Steve. The minute she learned that he knew Cassie, Britt had peppered him with questions about the other woman, hounding him for information, asking if they'd ever dated. She'd come off like a jealous shrew. Steve regretted even attending the game with her.

Joe Osborne had won the use of the suite in a charity auction and had invited Steve to join him and his daughter and some other guests. Jeremy had spent the weekend with his mostly absent father and wasn't at the match. If Steve had known beforehand that Jeremy wasn't going to be there, he wasn't sure he would have accepted the invitation, although he had to admit that watching the game itself had been a lot of fun. The only downside was Britt, who'd behaved like a spoiled brat. Despite her dire predictions, the Sounders won even though she wasn't able to drink her favorite beer.

Megan Victory was at her desk when Steve arrived. She glanced up when he stepped into her office. Right away he noticed that her usual warm smile was missing.

"Trouble?" he asked.

"I'm not sure."

"What's the problem?" he asked, pulling out a chair and sitting down. Something told him this wasn't going to be a short conversation.

"You're still working with Cassie Carter, right?"

"Right."

"How's she doing?"

His response was automatic and quick. "Great. She's a good worker. I give her a task and she does it." He liked a conscientious worker with a willing attitude. Maybe they'd started off on the wrong foot, but both their attitudes had evened out since their rocky start.

"Have you noticed anything different about her lately?"

He shrugged. "Not really." Then he remembered Cassie had gone suspiciously compliant of late. It was out of character for her. True enough, she showed up on time, worked hard, but they'd barely exchanged a word all week. "Let me revise that. She's been keeping to herself a lot. I mean, she's friendly with the Youngs, but other than that, nothing. Why?"

"She was in the office on Wednesday."

He leaned slightly forward. Now that she mentioned it, Cassie hadn't been her normal self all week. He'd been busy with other matters and hadn't paid much attention. "What's the problem?"

"Cassie's feeling down and overwhelmed. She's juggling a lot and concerned about leaving her daughter alone as much as she does." Megan hesitated. "It seemed that there was a lot more bothering her than that, though. Do you know what the problem is?"

He shook his head and then frowned and asked the question that immediately came to mind. "Cassie's not thinking of dropping out, is she?" It would shock him if she did. He'd overheard a conversation between Cassie and Shelly Young when Cassie had explained how excited and pleased she was to have been accepted into the program. She claimed this opportunity meant the world to her.

"We discussed her taking a break for the time being. We'll keep her hours on file and when she feels she'd be able to return she can pick up where she left off."

Steve hardly knew how to respond. Although he didn't know Cassie well, she didn't look like a quitter to him. He'd seen other candidates come and go. One woman dropped out after the first week because it was just too hard to juggle a job and also work on the project. When it came right down to it, Steve had been happy to see her go.

Early on he had her pegged as a taker instead of a giver.

Even in the short while he'd worked with Cassie he knew she was a giver. She'd cut and styled Shelly's hair, and just that simple act of kindness had made Shelly glow with new confidence. George had gotten a free haircut, too. And from what George told him, their children had as well. Cassie had done it after working at the salon on Saturday and then putting in five hours at the construction site. She must have been exhausted. By the time he got home, Steve knew he was bone weary, and he hadn't worked near the hours Cassie had.

"You had your doubts about Cassie when you first met her."

"I've had a change of heart since then," he said quickly, still reeling with this news. It came to him that he'd be disappointed if Cassie left the project now. "Did she decide what she wants to do?" he asked, eager to know.

"No, she's thinking on it."

Steve mulled over this information. "Did she happen to mention why she's depressed?" If so, maybe getting her some treatment would help.

"Not really. How much do you know about her background?" Megan asked.

"Very little." Generally, he didn't care to know unless it related to the applicant's ability to work.

The past wasn't important to Steve. He preferred to look forward.

"She came out of an abusive marriage."

A common enough story, he thought sadly.

"As we talked, Cassie gradually relaxed and I was able to get a bit more information out of her. From what she said, she's been estranged from her family for the last thirteen years. Her ex made sure she had no contact with them."

That seemed to be a common thread in a lot of the cases he'd heard about.

"Unfortunately, in that time period both of her parents died and she wasn't able to get home for their funerals."

Steve felt bad for Cassie. In addition to his wife, his own father had passed several years back and it'd been a rough loss for him and the rest of the family. It's never easy to let go of loved ones, and he couldn't imagine what it would be like without a proper good-bye.

"Her older sister recently reached out to her. Cassie was excited and pleased to hear from her sister."

"That's nice. Families need to stick together." His own was spread all across the country. He kept in touch, but visits were sporadic.

Megan continued, "When she told me about the call, Cassie mentioned her sister had set aside several of her parents' belongings for her and her daughter. All Cassie had to do was collect the furniture in Spokane. After being away from her family all those years, it meant the world to Cassie to have this opportunity."

Steve still didn't get it. "And?"

"And she took on an extra job. It was the only way she could think to earn the extra money she'd need to rent a truck and drive to Spokane."

Steve knew all about that extra job. He'd seen her at CenturyLink Field himself.

"Apparently, someone at the match complained about her service," Megan continued. "As a result, Cassie was asked not to return. She lost the only means she had of earning the extra money she needs."

Steve briefly clenched his teeth. **Britt.** "But I thought you said these items were in storage."

"They are, and her sister has paid for two months' rental fee, which is almost up. Cassie is going to be forced to tell her sister that she can't come collect her things—the last link she has with her parents."

"That's why she's considering dropping out of the program?" Steve asked, not entirely connecting the dots.

"Oh, not really. I think it's just an example of why she's feeling so defeated and daunted by the process of trying to build a better life. And I do think she's really concerned she's been neglecting her daughter. She promised to sleep on it before she makes her decision."

"Good." All at once Steve found it impossible to sit still. He got up from the chair and started to pace the confines of the office.

"The reason I asked to speak to you, Steve, is because I need an assessment from you on Cassie. Did I misjudge her? Is she a good candidate for us?"

He didn't need to think twice. "Cassie is exactly the type of person Habitat was meant to help. She's diligent, honest, and has a strong work ethic. I'm really sorry to hear that she's considering putting her commitment on hold."

"I'm glad you have faith in her. I liked Cassie from the moment I met her. She's got a great deal going for her, but she's been through a lot. For someone who's been repeatedly beaten down, their supply of hope tends to dwindle quickly."

"Yes, it does." He remembered Alicia and the change in her when she'd given up all hope. It wasn't long after that that she died. He was so lost in thought, he almost didn't hear Megan when she next spoke.

"Sorry?" he said, and forced himself to concentrate on Megan.

"I was just talking about the Hoedown."

"Yes. What about it?"

"First of all, thank you again for sponsoring the event."

"No problem."

"It's our biggest fund-raiser and we wouldn't be able to hold it without your generous contribution."

This was the third year he'd been the main sponsor. He contributed the funds in Alicia's memory. She had only recently started to work with Habitat at their store when she was diagnosed with ovarian cancer. It was her second bout after surviving the first go-around. They'd been warned that anyone who survives stage-four ovarian cancer is at high risk for it to return. It had with Alicia—and with a vengeance. She'd died within six agonizing months.

"Fourteen Bones has agreed to provide the dinner again."

"Great barbecue," Steve said, although his mind was only half on what Megan was telling him. The other half was spinning with regret over Cassie's situation. He hated the thought of her losing out on her last family memories because of what happened with Britt. It made him realize anew that he'd made the right decision not to date her again.

"The best," Megan was saying. "And the band . . ."

"Yes?"

"The Oak Hill Boys have agreed to return."

"Their music is terrific." Last May at the Hoedown, Steve hadn't been able to keep from tapping his feet. He wasn't much of a dancer, but he'd been tempted. If Alicia had been alive she would have dragged him onto that dance floor in a heartbeat. For show he would have put up a squawk and then he would have danced the night away with his wife. Unexpectedly, a pang of loss hit him.

"What about the servers?" he asked, in an effort to divert his thoughts from Cassie.

"All lined up," Megan told him.

"It appears everything is falling together nicely." Megan was a wonder. He admired her skill for organization.

"We've already sold over two hundred tickets."

"It looks like we're going to have a full house."

"Looks that way," she concurred. "So get out that cowboy hat of yours and polish your boots."

"Will do," Steve promised, still preoccupied. "And let me know what happens with Cassie."

"I will. Thanks for stopping by. I appreciate it."

"Any time." Steve's head continued to spin as he left Habitat's office. He couldn't leave matters with Cassie the way they were. Although it hadn't been his doing, he felt a certain responsibility.

He reached for his phone and hesitated, searching his memory for the name of the salon where Cassie worked. He finally came up with the name, logged on to the website, saw the phone number, and called the salon.

"Goldie Locks. This is Rosie. How may I help you?"

"I need a haircut." He wasn't sure what he had in mind yet. Maybe he'd sound Cassie out, learn what he could. If possible, he might even be able to help.

"Is there any particular stylist you would like to request?"

Steve found himself smiling. "Yes, please. I'd like to book it with Cassie Carter."

Chapter 10

No one was more surprised than Cassie when Steve Brody was escorted to her station. She didn't know what his game was, seeking her out where she worked, but she wasn't playing.

Steve sat down in the chair and removed his hat. "I'm here for a haircut," he announced, as if she hadn't already figured it out.

She met his eyes in the mirror and asked the same question she asked every first-time client. "What do you have in mind?"

"Shorter than what it is now."

Very funny. "Do you want it trimmed around the ears?"

"Please."

She brought out the plastic cape she reserved for men. Somehow it seemed wrong to put a cape decorated with pictures of a dozen different types of high heels on a male client.

As was her custom, she ran her hands through his hair, testing the feel of it between her fingers. His was thick and healthy and only a tad long. Certainly he could have waited another week or two for a haircut. He obviously had something on his mind that had nothing to do with hair. Most likely it involved her visit to Habitat's office earlier in the week.

Without a word she escorted him to the sink in order to wash his hair. He lounged back and closed his eyes as she tested the water temperature. After wetting his hair down, she added the shampoo and, using the tips of her fingers, massaged it into his scalp. Although she performed the same task a dozen times every day, this time she felt a strange feeling come over her. Her fingers slowed as she continued to lather his hair. She grew warm all over, and her fingers tingled as she touched him. She felt completely taken aback by her physical reaction to this man whom she hoped to avoid at all costs. A longing seeped through her, feelings she hadn't dared to dwell on in a very long while. The desire to be held and kissed and loved. The desire to be cherished and appreciated.

It was a relief when she was able to rinse away the shampoo. She released her breath, bothered that she'd allowed herself to react to him at all.

Her application of the conditioner was short and over with as quickly as she could complete the task. Where in the world was this coming from? These were questions she didn't want to ask for fear of what the answers might be.

If Steve experienced any of the same sensations she did, he didn't show it. Wrapping the towel around his head, she led him back to her station. Once he was seated, she brought out the scissors and started clipping away. After a few years working in the industry, Cassie had cut countless heads of hair. She knew what she was doing and she was a good stylist. Why this man should unnerve her was a mystery and one she preferred not to delve into. She didn't like the uncomfortable feeling that stole over her.

She didn't say a word.

Neither did Steve.

Later it was unavoidable as she brought out the electric razor. "Lower your head," she told him, hoping to sound professional.

He complied.

Cassie ran the razor along the back of his neck and then around his ears. When she'd finished, she reached for her hair dryer and turned it on the low setting, blowing away any small hairs that might have clung to his neck and face. When she'd finished, she unclipped the cape and carefully removed it from around his shoulders.

In the entire twenty minutes it'd taken her to cut his hair they hadn't exchanged more than two or three sentences.

"How much do I owe you?" he asked.

Cassie told him. He stood up and removed his wallet from his hip pocket and laid down a fifty-dollar bill.

"I'll get your change."

"Keep it," he said.

Cassie's eyes shot to his. "Keep it?" she repeated, certain there was a misunderstanding.

"Yes." He hesitated, his eyes holding hers prisoner. "I heard you're considering taking a leave from Habitat."

So Cassie had guessed right. She met his look head-on and didn't answer.

"Is that true?"

"What if it is?" she said, when the silence became too uncomfortable to bear any longer. "What concern is it of yours?"

"Don't be a fool, Cassie. This is a golden opportunity for you and your daughter. Habitat is a gift. Don't blow it."

"Why do you feel qualified to give me advice?" she asked, her words dripping with sarcasm.

"Because you have what it takes to make a success of this, to give your daughter a real home and security."

She supposed she should take that as a compliment, but she didn't. "Thank you, I'll take that into consideration."

He hesitated as if he was about to say something more. "I'm telling you this for your own good. I overheard you talking on the phone recently. I don't know who was on the other end of the line, not that it matters, but I heard what you said."

"So you were listening in on my phone conversation?"

"Not intentionally," he said, ignoring her defensive attitude. "You told the person to do the **next right thing,**" he said, emphasizing the words. "That was good advice. You should take it yourself. **Do the next right thing,** Cassie, and leaving the program now isn't it."

She'd said that to Maureen, Cassie remembered, in an effort to encourage her friend. Now he saw fit to throw her own words back in her face.

"Seeing that you're handing out free advice, allow me to offer you some of my own."

His head came back. "I beg your pardon?" he said, as though incredulous. "I don't need your advice."

"I disagree. The woman you were with at the Sounders game is a real piece of work."

"Britt is none of your business," he said.

Cassie didn't have an argument. "I agree it isn't my business. Nor is my working with Habitat your concern. You felt compelled to speak your mind. The way I figure it, you owe me the same courtesy I gave you. I listened. The least you could do is the same."

He folded his arms and braced his feet apart as if he half expected her to try and run him down.

"Okay, fine, I'm waiting."

"You told me not to be a fool, and I suggest you follow your own advice. Britt isn't the woman for you."

He snorted as though highly amused. "And you know this how?"

"Because she's spoiled, demanding, and unreasonable, although, come to think of it, maybe the two of you are better suited than I thought." She followed the comment with a sweet smile.

"Very funny."

"If you think I'm joking, then you're wrong." Cassie took a deep breath and plunged ahead. "From everything I've heard about your wife, she was an amazing woman. In the time I've worked with Habitat two or three people mentioned Alicia, and each time there is this sense of great loss. Mingled in with what they had to say was an appreciation for having had the opportunity to know her and work with her. If you don't want my advice, Steve, just ask yourself how Alicia would feel about you dating Britt."

His face flushed a deep shade of red as he whirled around and stormed out of the salon. Nearly everyone in the shop froze and watched him slam the door.

"What was that about?" Teresa, the shop owner, asked, as she approached Cassie.

She shrugged. "I offered some unsolicited advice."

"You know him?"

She nodded. "He's the project manager for the Habitat home I've been working on the last couple of weeks."

"That was the Steve you're always talking about?" Rosie asked, joining her cousin.

"I'm afraid so." Cassie couldn't keep from staring out the salon window, as if she expected Steve to come back so they could finish their conversation.

"You never mentioned how good-looking he is."

"Steve?" Cassie said, downplaying her reaction to him. When they'd first met she thought he was plenty easy on the eyes, but he'd been so unpleasant to her since then that it'd sort of slipped her notice. Until that moment at the shampoo station. A moment she preferred to ignore.

Teresa simply shook her head. "Cassie . . ."

"I know . . . I know. I should have kept my opinions to myself. He felt obliged to give me advice and I was only returning the favor."

A half hour later Cassie felt dreadful. She should never have said the things she did to Steve. It was difficult enough working with him, and by letting her mouth get ahead of her brain, she'd managed to complicate their differences in what was already a problematic relationship. The worst part was the fact that she was scheduled to work with him Friday afternoon.

Later that evening, Cassie started dinner while Amiee sat at the kitchen table, poring over her homework.

"Mom?"

"Hmm?" Cassie responded halfheartedly.

"What's wrong?" Amiee said, looking up from her textbook and tucking her chin between her hands.

"What makes you think anything is wrong?" Cassie asked, doing her best to sound like that was the most ridiculous question in the world.

"Well, for one thing, you cooked me poached eggs for breakfast every day this week."

"So?" She wanted her daughter to start the day with protein, and Amiee had complained endlessly about the cereal she'd bought on sale.

"You hate the smell of poached eggs. You only cook them when you're looking to punish yourself."

"I do?" Cassie had no idea.

"I know you're upset about losing the catering job."

Amiee couldn't possibly fully understand the ramifications of that.

"Then tonight you have this down-and-out look," Aimee said. "What's the problem?"

That her daughter could so easily read her moods was a revelation to Cassie. "I was unkind to someone today and I said some things I regret now."

"Hmm." Her daughter's look went grave. "You know what you told me about unkind words. You said it was like squeezing out a tube of toothpaste and then trying to put it all back inside. Once the words are out there, they tend to stay, so think before you speak."

"I said that?" Cassie didn't remember.

"You say a lot of things, Mom. You might think I don't hear you, but you're wrong. I even write some of the stuff you say down in my journal."

This was just shy of astonishing to Cassie.

"I do it because I don't want to forget. You've forgotten a lot of the things your mother said, and I don't want to do that, so I write it down."

That was true, Cassie had forgotten a lot of what her parents had told her while growing up. "Who made you so smart?" she asked her daughter, giving her a big hug.

Amiee broke into a huge smile. "I don't know, but I think I got it from my mother."

"I'm feeling doubtful about that, after today."

"You know what you have to do, don't you?"

Cassie did know, but it wasn't going to be easy to apologize to Steve. Knowing him, he was bound to make it difficult.

*   *   *

Friday afternoon, Cassie quickly changed her clothes and went directly from the salon to the job site. Shelly and George were already there. Cassie parked behind her friends.

"Where's Steve?" she asked first thing, eager to get this over with as quickly as possible.

George answered her. "He texted to say he'll be a few minutes late."

Cassie did her best to relax and pretend nothing was amiss. For just a half second she feared that Steve had stayed away on purpose in an effort to avoid her. Maybe he didn't intend to show up at all. It didn't take long for her to realize that wouldn't be his way. He was far too pragmatic for that.

She was nervous waiting for him. If Shelly noticed, she didn't say anything. About five minutes later Steve's truck rounded the corner. Cassie's stomach was in knots. She hadn't slept well, mulling over how best to approach this.

By the time he parked, Cassie was waiting for him at the curb. She tucked her hands into the back pockets of her jeans and waited.

Steve glared at her as he climbed out of the truck and closed the door. A resounding thud echoed, causing her to retreat a step.

"Can I talk to you a minute?" she asked, as he stepped around his vehicle.

He didn't answer, but she chose to take his silence as a positive.

"I want to apologize for the things I said. Generally, I'm able to keep my thoughts to myself. I shouldn't have offered you my unwanted and unsolicited advice. And it was totally inappropriate of me to talk about your wife in that way."

He nodded, indicating he accepted her apology. She offered him a short, tentative smile.

"I suppose you're looking for me to apologize as well."

"No," she assured him. "One has nothing to do with the other."

"You sure about that?" Clearly, he was skeptical.

"Positive."

He ran his hand along the back of his neck. "Best haircut I've had in years."

"My biggest tip ever," she returned.

He smiled.

Cassie couldn't remember if she'd ever seen Steve smile, and it had an amazing effect on her. In those brief seconds Cassie saw what Rosie had seen. This was a virile, lean, red-blooded man with the capability to make women's hearts stop. To be truthful, her own heart skipped a beat and it shocked her.

"Now that this is settled I better get to work." She was glad she'd apologized and was equally glad for an excuse to escape.

She was about ten feet away when he stopped her.

"Cassie."

She turned back around. "Yes?"

"Megan phoned me this afternoon to let me know you've put aside your doubts and are going to stick with the program."

She smiled and nodded. "Someone, who shall remain nameless, offered me a good piece of advice."

He grinned again. "I'm happy you took it to heart."

"Me, too. It was the right decision."

"Okay, now, time to pick up that paintbrush and put in a few hours of sweat equity."

"Yes, sir." She saluted him like a boot-camp private, but there was far more respect in that gesture than sarcasm. To her delight, Steve saluted her back.

Chapter 11

"Who was that on the phone?" Garth asked, sitting up in bed and reading from his tablet.

Karen closed their bedroom door, her mind and heart troubled. "My sister."

"Problems with Nichole?" Garth set his e-reader on the bedside table and lifted the covers for Karen.

"It was actually Cassie," Karen explained, and slipped into the bed next to him. She scooted close to her husband, and Garth placed his arm around her shoulders, warming her with more than his closeness.

"What did she want this time?" he asked skeptically.

"Nothing. She's only asked for financial help that one time when we just weren't able to do it."

"I don't know why you insist on feeling guilty about that. If you'd given her the money it would never have ended. Every time something came up she'd come running to you to bail her out financially. I know it was hard to turn her down, but you did the right thing."

"It's more than that . . ." Garth didn't know about their last terrible fight just before she'd run away from home.

"Karen," her husband said, cutting her off. "You don't need to make up excuses with me."

"I'm not. I did what was necessary. Cassie had to know she couldn't just waltz back into our lives as if nothing had happened. We were dealing with Dad's death and I wasn't about to take on her problems, too."

"I'm not going to argue with you, sweetheart. Like I said, you did the right thing."

"I have to wonder," she murmured, her brow furrowed with consternation.

"Karen . . ."

"I know, I know. It doesn't do any good to rehash this over and over. What's done is done. When I spoke to Nichole about the inheritance, she was adamant we did everything we should have. Cassie wasn't mentioned in the will and we have no obligation to give her a penny from the sale of the house."

"It isn't the legality of the matter that concerns you, it's the moral issue. You want to be fair."

Her husband read between the lines easily enough.

"Yes." Garth always seemed to understand her best. It was as if he knew her thoughts, which were often convoluted and conflicting when it came to dealings with Cassie.

"You offered her the furniture and she was happy with that."

Happy didn't begin to describe Cassie's reaction. She'd been overwhelmed with gratitude, pleased and excited. The fact that her sister had been so grateful and appreciative of this offhanded, nearly meaningless gesture had given Karen second thoughts. The decision she'd made with Nichole didn't rest easy with her and she wasn't sure what to do about it. Karen placed a hand over her mouth to cover a yawn.

"Any particular reason Cassie called?" Garth asked.

"Yes. She needed to know for exactly how long the storage fees had been paid. I asked her when she'd be collecting Mom and Dad's things, but she couldn't give me an answer. She said she'd get them as soon as she could make the arrangements." In thinking about the call, Cassie had been vague about how and when she intended to make the trip across the state. "I told her we could give her a bit of extra time if she needed it."

"Karen, I thought we agreed. Two months and that was it."

"An extra month isn't going to break the bank,

Garth." Karen was surprised that her husband would make a fuss over this. "Besides, by the time I reached out to her she didn't have the full two months to make arrangements. I want Cassie to have something to remember our parents by."

Her husband kissed the top of her head. "You're much too kind."

"She is my sister," she reminded him.

"The sister you barely know."

That was true. Karen didn't know Cassie any longer. Although they had shared a childhood, their relationship had come to an abrupt halt the year Cassie turned eighteen. It shocked her to think she hadn't seen Cassie since she ran off and married Duke.

Garth reached over and turned out his bedside lamp. "We have a busy day tomorrow."

Karen didn't need the reminder. Her days were crammed full. In the mornings she left the house like a racehorse in the Kentucky Derby. Weekends weren't much better. It was after eleven already, and she had volunteered to accompany Lily's Girl Scout troop on a field trip to the Spokane Airport in the morning. She hoped it would take only two or three hours, tops.

Garth was scheduled to take Buddy to his baseball game, and if they were able to coordinate their schedules, then they would meet up for lunch at their favorite pizza place. In the afternoon, Karen needed to help Lily sell her quota of Girl Scout cookies. They'd gotten permission to set up a table outside the Albertsons' grocery store.

The cookie sale would well take an additional two hours out of her day, and she had yet to get the laundry going or some basic housecleaning chores. And she had no idea what she'd make for dinner.

Although the lights were off and her husband was asleep and softly snoring, Karen's mind continued to whirl like the blades of a helicopter ready to take off from the launch pad. Sunday was no better. She had yet to prepare for teaching the fifth- and sixth-grade Sunday school class, and afterward Garth's sister had invited them to dinner and Karen was supposed to bring the dessert. She didn't know when she was going to find time to squeeze baking a cake in. And on Monday there was an employee meeting before the office officially opened at eight, which meant . . .

"Mom . . ." Buddy's shout woke Karen from a sound sleep. She bolted upright and glanced at the digital readout on the bedside clock. It was barely past four.

Tossing aside the covers, Karen tucked her feet into her slippers and went to investigate. Her son was in the hallway outside his room.

"What's wrong?" she asked, struggling to hold back a yawn.

"Daisy threw up."

Daisy was their cat—or, rather, Lily's cat, although she seemed far more attached to Buddy than she was to his sister.

"It's all over my bed and it's yucky."

Great. Just what she needed to start off her morning. "Come on, I'll change the sheets for you."

"It looks like blood."

On closer examination Karen realized that Crazy Daisy had indeed thrown up and it wasn't pet food that she was seeing mingled in with Buddy's sheets. It was the remains of a mouse. Karen pressed her hand over her forehead. Daisy was an indoor cat, which meant there were mice in the house.

"What's happening in here?" Garth asked, standing in the doorway to Buddy's bedroom. "Is there a party going on? How come I wasn't invited?"

"Crazy Daisy threw up on my bed," Buddy told his father.

"You might want to take a look at this," Karen told her husband, pointing toward a readily identifiable rodent body part.

Garth walked over to the bed and his eyes met hers. "Gross."

That was putting it mildly. "We're going to need

to get someone from a pest-control service to the house," she said. "I don't have a clue when I'll have time to fit that into my week."

Garth slowly exhaled. "Don't worry about it, honey, I'll take care of it."

"The exterminator will only come on weekdays unless we're willing to pay an outrageous fee for a weekend visit and then I'll need to take a half-day off work and that's only if he arrives on time—"

"Karen," Garth said gently, and took hold of her shoulders. "I'll work at home one day next week. I'll take care of this. You don't need to do everything on your own. You have a husband, you know."

"You don't mind?" She hadn't expected Garth to be so willing.

"Waiting around for a pest-control truck isn't my favorite job, but I'll survive."

Karen sighed with relief. "Buddy, while I'm changing your sheets, you take a shower."

"Another one?" their son protested. "I had one last night before I went to bed, remember?"

"Do it anyway, and be sure and wash your hair."

"Dad?" Buddy looked pleadingly at his father.

"Do as your mother asks."

Although the cat-and-mouse incident wasn't the greatest way to start her day, the field trip with the Girl Scouts turned out to be a lot of fun. Lily was at the age when she was still pleased to spend time with her mother. Karen felt she should treasure these years, building good memories with her daughter before she hit her teens.

True to his word, Garth got Buddy ready for his softball game and left a message with the pest-control company. Having him handle this was a huge relief. Karen appreciated that he was willing to take on the responsibility. He'd been making an effort to do more lately, and she was grateful. He'd even agreed to take on the task of bill paying when they got charged for a late payment. Karen admitted she hadn't paid their Visa bill on time. Garth wasn't that great with money matters, either, but lately he seemed to have more time than she did, especially now that she'd been elected secretary for the PTA and taught Sunday school class.

"I'm hungry," Lily announced, after they left the Girl Scout troop.

"I know, honey. I am, too." In fact, Karen had grabbed an apple and that had to suffice as breakfast. She drove around the block in the downtown area of Spokane, seeking a convenient parking spot.

"Where are we meeting Dad?"

"Pizza Pete's," she replied absently, spying a space in the next block up. If the light turned green she'd have the chance to grab the spot before another car got it.

"Dad's not going to order those fish again, is he?"

"Those are anchovies. If he wants anchovies, he can order his own pizza."

Lily was pacified. "You don't like them, either."

"Nope." The light turned and Karen was able to grab the space on the street. By the time they walked into Pizza Pete's, Garth and Buddy had secured a table and ordered the pizza.

"No anchovies!" Garth answered, before she could ask the question.

"Thank you." Karen slid into the booth while Lily joined her brother in the video arcade. She'd barely had time to set her purse down when both Lily and Buddy catapulted back toward their table.

"We need more quarters," Lily announced breathlessly.

Karen reached for her coin purse and dug out eight quarters, giving four to each of her children. As quickly as they'd arrived, the two departed.

"How did Buddy's game go?" Karen asked, looking up at her husband.

"They lost."

"Really?" His team, up to this point in the season, had gone undefeated.

"Thirteen to ten; it was a great game. Buddy was disappointed, but I think it was good for him. His team will learn more from the loss than another win."

Garth was like this. No matter what the situation, he continued to have a positive attitude. It was one of his most attractive attributes and why she loved him as profoundly as she did.

"What are your plans this afternoon?" she asked.

"It's time I started working in the yard. On the way home, Buddy and I will get lawn fertilizer and some organic plant food."

Their yard was badly in need of attention. Karen couldn't remember the last time she'd weeded the flower beds. Last year it was late July before she'd had a chance to plant the annuals, and by then the season was nearly half over. "Good idea."

"I'm thinking it might be time to teach Buddy to mow the lawn."

"Garth!" Their son was far too young to handle a mower.

Her husband laughed. "I was teasing."

Their pizza arrived and they were quickly joined by their two children. Garth had ordered one large family-size veggie pizza, which was Karen's favorite. He preferred pepperoni and sausage.

"Where's the sausage?" Buddy asked, staring down at his plate. "This pizza has tomatoes on it."

"All pizza has tomatoes, Buddy."

"In the sauce, maybe, but these are right on top where I can see them."

"You can take them off if you want."

Buddy lifted one thin slice of tomato as if it were a dead mouse in his bed.

Garth shared a smile with Karen. It was moments like this that she loved most, together as a family.

They parted outside the pizza parlor, Garth and Buddy heading off to the local hardware store while Karen and Lily went to Albertsons. If Lily sold her allotment of cookies, Karen would be home in time to lend a hand with the yard work.

Cookie sales outside the grocery were less brisk than Karen had hoped. By the time she returned home, she felt like she'd run a marathon. Garth and Buddy were just finishing up in the yard and putting away the lawn equipment.

"What's for dinner?" Buddy asked, as soon as Karen was out of the car. She hadn't given dinner another thought since last night.

"Hamburgers," Garth answered on her behalf.

Where was her head? Karen had just spent three hours at the grocery store and hadn't even thought to run in and get something for dinner.

"I didn't take any burgers out of the freezer," she confessed to her husband.

"Not to worry, I did. It's warm enough for me to light up the grill."

This initiative on his part was a change, and one she wasn't about to question. "Perfect. Thanks, sweetheart."

While Lily ran into the house to change out of her Girl Scout uniform, Buddy jumped on his bike to join his friend James. Karen walked out to the street to collect the mail. As she returned to the house, walking up the driveway, she sorted through the catalogs and junk mail. She stopped abruptly when she saw a notice from the bank.

She brought the mail into the house while Garth brought out the barbecue grill from the shed, where they kept it in winter, and washed it off. Holding on to the envelope, she set the rest of the mail on the kitchen counter and opened the notice from the bank.

Their account was overdrawn. Money had been automatically transferred from their savings account to cover the deficit. What was going on here?

Karen didn't say anything when Garth came into the house. Instead she just handed him the single sheet and let him read the notice for himself.

"Oops," he muttered. "I guess I'm not as good at this bill paying as I thought."

"Didn't you get a text from the bank?" she asked. Garth's phone number was the one listed for the account.

"If I did, it slipped my notice."

"Is there a fee attached to this?" she asked.

"I don't know," Garth confessed. "I doubt it. We've never bounced a check before . . . well, technically, we didn't now."

"Only because we have a healthy amount in our savings account."

"Thankfully." He kissed her cheek and opened the refrigerator for the meat.

"I'll make a macaroni salad to go with those burgers," she said, and got going on a cake for tomorrow night, too.

Chapter 12

Cassie had been in a blue funk when she'd spoken to Megan at the Habitat office. Losing the part-time job with the caterer had been an emotional hit that sent her reeling. But even before Steve showed up at Goldie Locks she'd decided against taking a hiatus. Their discussion, if she could call it that, as well as the apology after, had cleared the air between them. They'd sort of made peace with each other. Cassie had put in her hours that week, going directly from the salon to the construction site for an hour or two nearly every day. Shelly and George's home was close to completion. The inside was all painted and the flooring was nearly finished.

On Sunday Amiee had a day planned with her best friend, Claudia, who was having a birthday party, which gave Cassie six hours to dedicate toward the Habitat project.

In addition, with Megan's urging, Cassie had signed up to work at the Hoedown on the third Saturday in May, serving food and seating the guests. The time spent volunteering at the fundraiser would count toward her five-hundred-hour obligation. A lot of the volunteers, including Shelly, talked about the Hoedown and what a good time everyone had, and Cassie was actually looking forward to it.

She enjoyed working with Shelly. They were putting the finishing touches on the trim in the master bedroom right then.

"Everything going well in here?" Steve asked, stepping into the room to check their progress.

"Moving like a runaway freight train," Cassie assured him.

"Then slow down. There's no need to rush."

"Aye, aye, Captain," she teased.

He smiled and returned to the kitchen, where he was laying down linoleum with George.

"Steve says that at the pace we're progressing, George and I might be able to move in two or three weeks."

"That's wonderful news." Cassie had a piece of good news herself. Habitat had purchased a vacant lot in the same school district where Amiee attended classes, which might mean she could stay in the same school even when they got their new house. This was especially gratifying after all the moves her daughter had made in her young life. What Cassie longed for most was to give Amiee love and a deep sense of security—uprooting her every few months had been traumatic for her daughter. It had gotten better after Cassie left Duke, but only slightly. The thought of a permanent home for her and Amiee was more than she ever dreamed possible.

"Cassie, would you . . ." Shelly asked.

Cassie turned around, but as she did, her foot slipped on a splotch of wet paint. Before she realized what was happening, she took a tumble. She heard the sleeve of her jacket tear and then felt a pain sharp enough to make her gasp.

Shelly raced across the room. "You okay?"

"I think so." Cassie was more stunned than hurt, although she could see blood gushing down her arm.

"It doesn't look like it. Stay here," Shelly shouted in a panic. "Don't move."

"I'm fine, Shelly," Cassie insisted, although her arm really did sting. She couldn't get a good look at it but could feel it was bleeding badly. Worst of all, her jacket was ruined. It wasn't like she had a closet bursting with a huge wardrobe. She should never have worn it.

"Cassie's hurt." Shelly shouted for Steve, and Cassie heard the panic in her friend's voice.

It didn't take a minute for Steve to find her.

Shelly stood protectively over Cassie. "I told her not to move."

"Good." Steve got down on one knee next to Cassie. "You did the right thing."

His face was grim and she half expected a lecture. "Better let me see what you did to yourself," he said. Looking over his shoulder, he asked Shelly to get the first-aid kit.

"I'm okay," Cassie insisted, embarrassed by all the fuss.

"I'm better qualified to judge that." The jacket sleeve was torn already, and he ripped it wide open to get a better view of the injury.

Shelly returned and handed Steve the first-aid kit.

"Thanks," he said, as he opened it and removed a thick wad of gauze, which he pressed against the cut.

"There's a lot of blood," Shelly commented, her eyes brooding and serious. Because it was on the back of her arm, Cassie couldn't get a good look at the cut.

"It looks deep," George murmured, standing next to his wife. He, too, wore a look of concern.

Shelly's face was grim.

Steve sighed and announced, "I'm afraid you're going to need stitches."

Even without the ability to look, Cassie was sure the cut couldn't possibly be that bad. "It'll be fine.

Just wrap it up so it quits bleeding and I'll be good as new. It hardly hurts—if you put a bandage on it I'll go back to work."

"You're going, all right," Steve insisted. "You'll go directly to the ER."

"Steve," she protested.

His hard gaze met hers. "I would think by now you'd know better than to argue with me."

She could put up a fuss, but Cassie recognized all the complaining in the world wouldn't do her any good. "All right, if you insist."

"I do." With a gentleness she didn't expect from him, he helped her to her feet. He gave her a few moments to steady herself and kept his arm tucked securely around her waist.

By the time he got Cassie settled inside his truck, her arm was throbbing with such intensity that she was forced to grit her teeth to keep from moaning. The drive to the hospital seemed to take an excruciatingly long time. Neither spoke. By the time they arrived, Cassie was beginning to feel light-headed. Steve parked close to the entrance.

"Stay put. I'll come around and get you."

She waited until he collected her and slid out of the vehicle, but her knees nearly buckled when her feet hit the pavement. Right away Steve's arm was around her, holding her upright.

The waiting room seemed to be packed. To her surprise, she was called in almost right away. Steve might have had some influence, but that didn't seem possible. Or perhaps she was worse off than she realized.

"The paperwork?" she asked.

"Don't worry, I'll take care of it."

The physician was a woman who, after examining the cut, gave Cassie a shot for the pain.

The last time Cassie had been in a hospital had been a life-altering moment. The physician had been a woman then, too. Cassie had had yet another "accident" because she was so "clumsy." That was what Duke had told the attending physician. Her arm was broken and both eyes were black and blue. The female doctor had questioned her extensively. She knew, and Cassie knew she knew. The look in the other woman's eyes told Cassie she'd figured out that this was no accident.

Then Duke picked up on it, too. As soon as the cast was on, her husband had jerked Cassie off the examination table and dragged her away. As they fled the hospital, Cassie saw security chasing after them. She suspected the physician had already contacted law enforcement. What Duke didn't know was that the doctor had managed to slip Cassie the phone number of a women's shelter. It was to that very shelter that Cassie had escaped a few weeks later.

Steve remained in the waiting room while she was being attended to by the medical staff. The cut was deeper and larger than she realized and required twelve stitches.

When she was finished, the nurse escorted her to the waiting area, where Steve was pacing. He stopped when he saw her. Their eyes connected and Cassie thought she might have seen a look of relief in him.

"I'm good as new," she told him, her reassuring smile wobbly at best.

"Glad to hear it." He led her out of the hospital and across the parking lot to his vehicle, and carefully helped her inside. She grimaced at the pain the effort caused her just climbing into his pickup.

"Did you get a prescription for pain?" he asked, and held out his hand expectantly. "Give it to me."

"Why?" she asked.

"Because I'll get it filled for you."

Cassie's head was swimming. "Oh, I don't have much cash and—"

"I'll worry about that later." His tone told her this wasn't a subject he was willing to discuss.

Too weak to argue, Cassie closed her eyes and braced her head against the side window. He stopped off at the drugstore.

Cassie remained in the truck as Steve went inside to collect her meds. She leaned her head against the window and remembered when her sister had been badly cut. Cassie had been about fourteen when Nichole ran through the sliding glass door. Their mother was at the grocery store and Karen was with friends, so Cassie was the only one home and had nearly panicked. The sight of all that blood had horrified her, but she'd kept her cool and called 911. Wrapping her sister's arm in towels, she did what she could to comfort Nichole and assure her she wasn't going to die, although at the time Cassie had serious doubts. Karen walked in a couple minutes later and took one look at Nichole and burst into tears, which terrified Nichole all the more. The ambulance arrived and took Nichole away. Karen, who had her driver's license, followed along with Cassie. Unfortunately, their mother returned from the grocery store to find the kitchen a bloody mess. It was a day Cassie would long remember.

After Nichole was stitched up and returned home, Cassie and Karen stayed with her the rest of the afternoon, reading to her and telling her how brave she was. They promised to let her use their makeup. That afternoon, Nichole lay with her head on Cassie's lap, and just before she fell asleep she thanked Cassie for saving her life.

Cassie must have dozed because when she opened her eyes she realized they weren't anywhere close to the Habitat house. "Where are you taking me?" she asked, perplexed.

"Home."

"But my vehicle is at the site."

"Don't worry, I've asked one of my men to pick

it up and drive it to your place. I'll take him back afterward."

Cassie hardly knew what to say, and when she did speak her voice sounded scratchy and uneven. She wasn't accustomed to anyone being this accommodating or helpful. "Thank you."

He stopped at a red light and looked at her. "You're welcome, Cassie." His voice was warm and gentle, and just hearing the tenderness in him made her feel like weeping. She would never allow him to see her get emotional. That would be too embarrassing. She'd learned when she'd been married to hold back tears. Seeing her cry only made Duke angrier.

That Steve was familiar with her address came as a surprise. She hated the thought of him viewing her dinky, dingy apartment and planned to leap out of the truck and escape the minute they arrived.

Steve pulled up in front and parked. "Thank you again," she said, opening the passenger door.

"Hey, just a minute. I'm coming in with you."

"You are?"

"No choice. I need to wait for Lenny to drop off your vehicle so I can drive him back."

"Oh, right." She dug the key out of the bottom of her purse and unlocked the door, wondering what he would think once he entered her humble lodgings.

She was being silly, Cassie reminded herself. Just

plain silly. If she had lived in a nice apartment, then she wouldn't need housing from Habitat.

As soon as she was inside he opened the cupboard doors until he found a glass, filled it with water, and held out a pain pill. "Take this and then lie down."

She stared at him, trying to decide if she was going to put up a fuss or do as he demanded. Having a man tell her what to do went against the grain. She'd come too far to have another male dictate her actions.

"Cassie?" Steve stared at her quizzically.

Once again she realized she didn't have the energy to put up a fight. Taking the pill out of the palm of his hand, she reached for the water glass in his opposite hand and swallowed down the pain medication and another pill, too. The doctor mentioned it was to help ward off infection.

Cassie laid on top of her bed and Steve covered her with an afghan he found in the living room. She was determined to prove to him she was made of sturdier grit than this. Napping in the middle of the afternoon was unheard of for her.

The next thing Cassie heard were voices. Right away she recognized Steve's; his friend had arrived. The next voice wasn't that of a man, though. It belonged to Amiee.

Amiee was home. Something must have happened, as it was far too early. Her daughter wasn't due back until five that night and it was only . . . she looked at her wrist. It was after six. Impossible.

"Amiee." Cassie tossed off the blanket and sat upright. The room started to spin and she waited, afraid she'd stumble if she got off the bed now.

"Oh hi, Mom," her daughter said ever so casually. "Steve's here."

"Steve?" He should be long gone by now.

"Steve," Amiee repeated. "You remember Steve, don't you?" Then, glancing over her shoulder she asked, "Are you sure she didn't bump her head?"

"I know who Steve is," Cassie muttered, pressing her hand to her forehead. The room hadn't quit spinning. "What I want to know is why he's still here."

"Mom, that's rude, especially when he brought dinner." She lowered her voice. "And it's KFC."

It hadn't taken Steve long to locate the path that led directly to Amiee's heart.

"I saved you a leg."

"Nice of you," she said, coming out of the bedroom, placing her arm against the doorjamb in an effort to regain her balance. Whatever was in that pill Steve gave her had a kick to it.

"It was very nice of me," Amiee insisted. "The legs are my favorite part."

Pressing her free hand against her forehead, Cassie saw Steve sitting at the kitchen table with a ten-piece bucket of KFC resting in the middle, with all the trimmings that went along with it. "You didn't need to stay this long," she told him.

"I didn't want your daughter coming home and finding you in bed and injured without anyone else here."

Cassie was about to tell him Amiee would be far more worried discovering a man in their apartment, but she let it pass.

"How are you feeling?" he asked, coming to his feet.

"I don't know . . . What's in those drugs, anyway? They knocked me for a loop."

"Are you in pain?"

She had to stop and do a quick self-inventory. "I don't think so."

"Good."

"My car?" It might not be much, but it got her where she needed to go.

"Parked outside."

Amiee beamed at him. "Steve took care of everything. He's really cool, Mom."

"Don't get a swelled head," she told him. "It's the KFC. My daughter has a weakness for fried chicken."

He grinned and looked almost boyish. "I figured as much."

"Thank you again." He had gone above and beyond any expectations.

He was halfway to the door. "No problem."

"Yes, thank you, Steve," Amiee piped in.

His gaze connected with Cassie's. "Call if you need anything."

"I will," Amiee assured him before Cassie could.

He left then, and the moment the door closed her daughter whirled around. "Mom, is that the same guy we didn't like before? Because he's changed, and he's awesome."

"I like Steve," Cassie said, downplaying her feelings. "He's a friend, nothing more, got it?" The last thing she needed was her daughter picking up a hint of romance between her and Steve.

"Mom," Amiee whispered, as if this was a huge secret they needed to keep under wraps. "He bought me an entire bucket of KFC."

"Yes, honey, I know."

"I didn't ask for it or anything." She made it sound as if Steve had cooked the chicken himself. "This is exactly the kind of guy you should marry . . . you know, if you ever want to marry again."

"Amiee! Don't be ridiculous."

"Hey, it was just a suggestion," her daughter said, gesturing with both hands before she reached for another piece of chicken.

Chapter 13

Steve Brody's mind was full of Cassie. All day she'd been front and center in his thoughts. He wondered how she was feeling, if there was any infection, and hoped she'd taken the day to rest.

In fact, he was thinking about Cassie on his way to the cemetery and nearly missed the entrance. He made the turn just in time, and was shocked to realize his head had been on another woman on his way to visit his wife's grave site.

It'd been two weeks since he'd last visited Alicia's grave. Generally, he stopped by every few days or so. It was important to him that it be kept neat and that she had fresh flowers. True, he'd been busy, but he was always busy and made time anyway. It shook him that he'd let two entire weeks slip by. He parked in the same spot as always and climbed out of the truck.

He knelt down on one knee over the gravestone. Then he brushed aside grass clippings from the freshly mowed lawn so that her name could be clearly read. The flowers he'd delivered on his last visit had been removed, so he filled the container with the fresh ones he'd brought with him. Alicia had always loved red tulips, and they were in season.

"There's a woman I met," he said, standing now, his hands hanging awkwardly at his side. "She's stubborn as a mule . . . I met her at Habitat and I've been thinking about her a lot." He paused, unsure he should even mention Cassie. "She had an accident recently and I drove her to the ER."

He remembered how Cassie had tried to insist that she was fine and that all she really needed was for him to bandage her arm. The pain hadn't hit her yet, and when it did she went pale and silent. Not once did Cassie let on that she was in agony, but he could see it in her eyes and the way she clenched her jaw to keep from groaning.

She had intensely disliked being at the hospital, although the staff were wonderful. Steve had hated it, too. While sitting in the waiting room, he'd been flooded with memories, the very ones he was trying to put behind him. Alicia had been in this very hospital. By the time Cassie appeared, her arm bandaged, he was more than ready to leave.

Once again his mind was on Cassie. He focused his eyes on Alicia's gravestone, feeling somewhat guilty to be at his wife's grave site and thinking about another woman. They'd been close, Alicia and him, and his life felt empty without her. She'd been gone three years now and the ache wasn't as piercing as it had been that first year, but the closeness he felt toward her remained. Alicia would always be a part of him, even if she wasn't with him physically.

"Her name is Cassie," he whispered. He buried his hands in his pockets and then stood silent for a couple minutes. Before he left, he squatted down, placed his fingertips against his lips, and then placed them on her name then he returned to his truck and drove away.

What he'd told Alicia was true. His head had been full of Cassie for a long time now. Being that he was the one responsible for the construction site, he felt it was his obligation to check in and see how she was doing. That was the excuse he gave himself as he pulled up in front of Cassie's apartment. He sat in his truck for several minutes, silently debating if dropping by unannounced was in his own best interest. A phone call would do just as well, but he had the urge—okay, the need—to see for himself how Cassie was doing.

Her daughter answered the door and her eyes lit up like a kid on Christmas morning when she saw it was him. "Hi, Steve," Amiee greeted him, as if they were the best of friends. "Mom's home." She held the door wide open for him to come inside.

Steve could see Cassie standing by the stove. It looked as if she was cooking dinner. Right away he noticed how pale she was. It was the same pained look he recognized from the day before when he drove her to the hospital.

For a long moment they did nothing but stare at each other. Steve felt Amiee's eyes travel from him to her mother and then back to him.

"What are you doing here?" Cassie asked, and looked none too pleased to see him.

This woman didn't do a lot to build up his ego. "I came to check on you, seeing there's a liability issue here."

Right away Cassie frowned. "Liability issue? Do you seriously think I would sue Habitat?"

The fire he'd so often seen was back in her eyes. "No, but it's a logical concern."

"Logical?" she repeated, snickering softly.

He was making a mess of this. He might as well be honest before he dug himself in a hole too deep to climb out of. "Actually, I stopped by to see how you're doing."

"Mom worked today," Amiee told him. "Most everyone takes Mondays off, but not Mom, because she needs to make extra money so we can drive to Spokane—"

"Amiee." Her mother cast her daughter a look that immediately silenced the twelve-year-old.

"Okay, okay, but I thought Steve should know."

"You were at the salon?" He couldn't begin to

imagine how painful it must have been for Cassie to repeatedly lift her arm while dealing with her clients. He'd assumed she would take the day off due to her injury, and he couldn't believe she hadn't. Didn't she know that she should give her body at least one day to recover?

"She wouldn't take her pain pills, either, because she said she needed a clear head," Amiee blurted out, and then turned to face her mother, her hands braced against her hips. "You can be mad at me if you want, but Steve needs to know. He told me to make sure you took the pain pills and got lots of rest and you didn't. You wouldn't take the pills and you were up half the night, and I know because I heard you."

"Amiee," Cassie said, her face flushed with embarrassment. "Give it a rest, will you?"

"Steve would want me to tell," her daughter insisted, squaring her shoulders as if to say she'd be willing to accept her punishment.

Steve couldn't take his eyes off Cassie. "You must be exhausted."

Stubborn woman that she was, Cassie didn't confirm or deny her condition.

"Come sit," he said, making sure his voice was even and low. When she didn't move right away he walked over to her, took her by the hand, and then gently led her to the sofa. Looking over his shoulder, he instructed Amiee, "Get me some ice."

"Okay." Eager to be of help, Amiee hurried

to the refrigerator, opened the freezer door, and brought out an ice-cube tray. "Now what?" she asked, looking to Steve to supply the instructions.

"Put the ice in a plastic bag and bring it to me wrapped in a towel."

The fact that Cassie wasn't fighting him was all the evidence he needed—she had overextended herself too soon. Amiee dumped the ice into an empty bread bag and returned from the bathroom with a clean towel. "Here," she said proudly.

Gently Steve set Cassie down on the sofa, lifted her arm, and wrapped the towel and ice around the upper part of her arm. "Feel better?" he asked.

She nodded and closed her eyes. It seemed her entire body relaxed as she pressed her head against the back of the sofa.

"Should I get the pain meds?" Amiee asked, eager to assist.

"No," Cassie protested. "They make me sleepy."

Steve clenched his jaw, and when he spoke he did his best to hide his irritation. This woman was beyond stubborn. "In case you haven't figured this out, your body needs to rest in order for you to heal."

On hearing him, Amiee raced into the bathroom and returned with the prescription bottle and a glass of water. "Listen to the man," she said, as she handed her mother the pill and a glass of water.

Cassie didn't put up a fuss.

"What's your mom's favorite meal when she has a special treat?" he whispered to Amiee.

"A Whopper. I like KFC."

Steve hid a smile. "I sorta got that impression already."

Amiee grinned and lowered her voice. "I had a thigh for breakfast this morning and it was almost as good as it was last night."

His decision made, he said in the same low tone he'd used earlier, "Put away whatever it was your mother is cooking and then the two of us will make a food run."

Amiee's eyes brightened. "Really?"

"Really," he echoed.

The twelve-year-old looked absolutely delighted. "I told Mom she should marry someone like you and you know what she said?" She didn't wait for him to respond. "She said men like you don't marry women like her. I said she was wrong and then she said she didn't want to talk about it. She gets grumpy like that sometimes." As she spoke she removed the pan from the stovetop and took out two hot dogs from the boiling water and stuck them in a small plastic sandwich bag before setting them in the refrigerator.

"You ready?" he asked, thankful Cassie was already dozing.

"If you married my mom, could I get a mini iPad?"

"Ah . . ." Steve was rarely at a loss for words, but Amiee had completely flummoxed him.

Amiee hesitated. "I shouldn't have asked you that, right?"

He placed his hand on her shoulder. "It's a whole lot premature."

"Don't tell my mom, okay? She'd be upset enough to lay an egg."

He grinned. "It'll be our secret."

By the time they returned, Cassie was sound asleep. Amiee tiptoed over to her mother. "Should I wake her?"

"No, let her sleep." He'd stop by tomorrow and make sure she'd changed the bandage.

Amiee looked uncertain. "Mom would want that Whopper."

"She can eat it when she wakes up." Steve spread the afghan over Cassie, tucking it in over her torso. If Amiee wasn't there to witness it, he would have kissed her forehead.

Amiee watched every move he made. "This is where she slept last night, too."

The ice had melted and the fact she didn't feel the bag leaking on her arm was a testament to how exhausted Cassie must be. The tenderness that swelled in him was hard to explain.

"I'd better head out," he said.

"Should I have Mom call you when she wakes?" the kid asked hopefully.

"No, that's fine. Let her rest." He'd better get going before Amiee started looking at pictures of wedding dresses for her mother.

"Okay." Amiee sounded disappointed as she walked him to the front door. "You can stop by anytime," she assured him.

"Even if I don't bring KFC?" he teased.

"Oh sure," she said, taking him seriously. "But if you do happen to have a bucket with you, all the better."

Steve headed out to his truck and couldn't keep from chuckling.

Chapter 14

For the whole following week, Steve refused to allow Cassie on the construction site. It both angered and frustrated her—at this rate, it would take years to get in her hours. While Cassie might not have had any contact with Steve, he communicated with Amiee on a regular basis. Cassie overheard their phone calls, which her daughter did her best to keep secret. She let Amiee believe she didn't have a clue what was transpiring between the two.

From what Cassie could make out, Steve was checking up on her, making sure she was taking her meds and not working too hard at the salon. Actually, the injury was pretty much self-limiting. Cassie had overdone it that Monday and had paid a steep price. By the time Steve arrived she'd been ready to collapse.

On Monday, eight days after the accident, Cassie was starting to feel more like herself. It was a gorgeous day in the Pacific Northwest. The sun was out and the temperatures were in the mid-seventies with a light breeze. Amiee finished with her homework in record time without Cassie even needing to ask, which came as a surprise. She assumed her daughter wanted to get out into the gorgeous sunshiny day with her friends, but she hung around even when her homework was done.

Cassie was thinking about mixing up a big salad for dinner when someone knocked on the front door.

"I'll get it." Amiee tore out of her room like a prisoner set free. She opened the door and then a high, overly loud voice said, "Oh hi, Steve, what a surprise to see you."

Cassie didn't know what these two had concocted, but she was fairly certain she was about to find out.

Steve came into her apartment with his fingertips tucked in his back pockets. "How are you feeling?" he asked, his eyes on her.

"She's in a much better mood," Amiee answered for her mother.

Cassie tore her gaze away from Steve long enough to glare at her daughter. "I can answer for myself, thank you." That said, she returned her attention to Steve and announced, "I'm in a much better mood."

He grinned, and once more it came unbidden to her how sexy he looked. She really shouldn't be thinking these kinds of thoughts about him and at the same time was completely helpless to stop.

"I'm glad to hear that," he said casually. "Are you up to a little outing?"

"Mom and I would love—"

Cassie cut her daughter off with a single look. "What do you have in mind?" she asked, as if the possibility existed that she might have other plans.

"I know you heard about the building lot Habitat recently purchased not far from here."

Cassie could feel her heart starting to race. "I did hear something about it." Megan had casually mentioned it, but Cassie had been afraid to press for more details. She was only one of several people on the waiting list for new homes and it seemed wrong to ask for this piece of land when there were surely others on the list ahead of her.

"Being it's such a nice afternoon, I thought you might like to take a look at that lot," Steve said.

Amiee folded her hands like she was in deep prayer, and she looked to Cassie, her eyes wide and appealing. "Please, Mom, can we at least look at the property?"

Cassie had no intention of refusing. "I think we could squeeze it into our busy schedule."

Unable to hold back her glee, Amiee jumped up and down, clapping her hands.

"If you can behave yourself," Cassie added under her breath.

"I'll be good, I promise," Amiee assured her.

"It's a go?" Steve looked to Cassie.

"It's a go."

He led the way outside and waited while she locked the apartment door.

Steve drove a car this time, a four-door sedan that looked as if he'd just driven it off the show-room floor. She'd only seen him with his truck. He must have read the question in her eyes because he opened the passenger door for her and stepped aside before explaining, "This was Alicia's car."

"Oh." This was the first time he'd mentioned his dead wife.

Amiee hopped into the backseat and made loud sniffing sounds. "Wow, this car even smells new."

"It's over three years old," Steve said, as he slid into the driver's seat. "Alicia didn't get a chance to drive it much and I mostly drive my truck."

Cassie didn't need to worry about carrying the conversation. Amiee chatted with Steve like they were longtime friends. She filled him in about her week at school, chatting about a difficult math test and her friend Claudia, who was no longer her BAE. "I hope you don't mind me telling you these things," she said, stopping in the middle of her long-winded story of why she'd downgraded Claudia.

"Not at all," Steve assured her. "This is fascinating."

"Mom insists on hearing every detail of my day," her daughter added, as if burdened with the telling. "It was something Mom and her sisters did at the dinner table with their mom and dad, so now Mom makes me give her a minute-by-minute report of my day."

Steve took his gaze off the road long enough to make eye contact with Cassie. He arched his brows and she was left with no choice but to explain. "I wanted more than a one-word reply when we chat at dinner."

"See what I mean?" Amiee said, sighing with the weight of such a heavy burden.

"Got it," he said.

It didn't take more than ten minutes to reach the property, which was on the west hill of Kent. Steve had barely put the car in park when Amiee threw open the backseat passenger door and leaped out with all the urgency of someone avoiding an explosion.

"This is it?" her daughter cried, already halfway onto the lot.

"This is it," Steve echoed, following her onto the land. "And it's all yours."

Cassie had a hard time taking it in. The lot was huge, much bigger than anything she'd ever hoped or imagined. Slowly she joined her daughter. The back part of the lot had several trees tucked up against a fence. Steve followed her. "What kind of trees are these?" Cassie asked. She reached up and examined a small bud.

"Apple. Two apple trees and a plum."

Cassie sucked in a deep breath. "Fruit trees."

"Mom, we can make applesauce. Claudia's grandmother served us applesauce she cooked herself. It was so much better than what we buy at the store."

"I bet it was."

"Can we?"

"If we get enough apples, then yes, we could do that."

In her enthusiasm, Amiee hugged the tree. "Give me apples," she told the tree. "Lots and lots of apples."

Cassie caught sight of Steve doing his best to hide a smile. He glanced down at the ground and softly chuckled.

Although there were neighbors on each side of the property, they both had fences up, so she had a clear idea of the lot size. It seemed immense. "Will there be room for a garden?" she asked Steve.

"Would you like that?"

Afraid her voice would betray the emotion that came over her, Cassie nodded. Her mother had kept a huge garden and it'd been her and her sisters' job to weed it every summer. The three of them found ways to make games out of the task. Karen had taken delight in chasing her with a huge worm. Cassie had run through the sprinkler in order to avoid her sister and screamed loud enough to send her mother running out of the house.

She looked up and noticed Steve was talking to her. "I'll check with Stan and see if we can situate the house in such a way that you have ample room for a garden."

Cassie never dreamed it would be possible to own a home with enough space to grow vegetables. A lump filled her throat, making it impossible to speak. In an effort to hide the emotion, she walked around the property, counting the steps, barely absorbing how fortunate she was.

"Do you know any of the neighbors?" Amiee asked, and then before Steve could answer, "Any girls my age? What about boys?"

"Sorry, I haven't met any of the neighbors," Steve told Amiee. He turned his attention to Cassie. "Well, what do you think? Do you like it or would you rather wait for another lot to become available?"

"She likes it," Amiee cried. "She likes it. We both do."

With her throat clogged with what could only be joy, Cassie was more than happy to have her daughter speak for her.

"Cassie?" Steve looked to her for the answer.

She swallowed against the thick lump, met his gaze, smiled, and nodded. Thankfully, she didn't have to say anything more, as another car pulled up and parked behind Steve's vehicle.

A man climbed out. He looked vaguely familiar to Cassie, although she didn't remember where she'd seen him before. He walked directly up to Cassie and extended his hand.

"Stan Pearson," he said, by means of an introduction. He nodded at Steve.

"Stan will be the construction manager for this project," Steve explained.

Cassie's spirits sank and she was barely able to disguise her disappointment. "You won't be working on the house?" When she'd first met with Habitat, Megan had told her Steve would be heading up her project. She remembered that vividly because after their first meeting she'd intended to ask if there was anyone else. She hadn't wanted to work with him. And now . . . well, it wouldn't be the same without him.

As if reading her thoughts, Stan explained. "Steve will be here. He's a volunteer, but he knows as much about construction as I do, if not more. I'll basically leave everything up to him, while I supervise the progress on another home. That said, I'll be by now and again to check up and see how things are going, the same way I did with the Youngs' property. Technically, I'm the construction manager, but I sort of leave everything in Steve's hands."

So that was where Cassie had seen Stan before. She remembered Steve and him conferring a number of times.

"I'm a paid employee," Stan went on to explain, "and Steve's a volunteer, although he sometimes puts in as many hours or more than I do."

"You'll be at the Youngs' on Friday, won't you?" Stan's question was directed at Cassie.

She looked to Steve, not understanding. It made sense that after a week away from the construction site she'd missed out on something.

"There's a dedication ceremony," Steve explained, and then, looking to Stan, added, "Cassie's been out all week. She's the one I mentioned who cut her arm."

"Oh right. I forgot about that. How's it healing?"

"No problem," she said, wanting to make light of her injury "It was only a scratch."

Steve frowned. "Twelve stitches is hardly a scratch."

She ignored him. "Steve wouldn't let me on the job site," she said, frowning back at him.

"Good. We don't want you reinjuring your arm," Stan said, and then, as if looking for a way to change the subject, he added, "I brought along the house plans to show you and your daughter. This is very similar to the Youngs' plan."

"You already have plans?" Amiee cried, crowding in next to Cassie. "How many bedrooms?"

"Three," Stan answered.

"Three," Amiee cried. "Bedrooms?"

"We always build a minimum of three bedrooms," Steve explained to her daughter.

"What about if it was one person moving in—would they still get three bedrooms?"

"They would," Stan said, picking up the conversation. "We do that for resale value. If and when the home is sold, the chance of selling it is much greater with that third bedroom."

Stan took a tube out of the backseat of his car, uncapped it, and rolled it out across the top of his vehicle, anchoring it with the windshield-wiper blade on one side and his hand on the opposite corner.

"Look it over, Amiee," Steve advised, as the girl squeezed in front of Cassie and Steve.

"How many square feet?" Cassie asked, as she looked over the floor plan.

"Twelve hundred. These aren't big homes."

"Did you happen to notice the size of our apartment?" Cassie asked, half joking. Twelve hundred square feet would feel like a mansion by comparison.

"We just recently added garages," Stan was saying. "We're putting the washer and dryer in there."

"We get a washer and dryer, too?" Amiee was nearly beside herself, rubbing her palms together with sheer joy. "Mom, did you hear? Our own washer and dryer."

"I heard."

As if this was more than she could imagine, Amiee asked, "What about a stove with more than two burners and an oven that actually works?"

"All yours," Steve assured her.

Amiee closed her eyes and tilted back her head. "Have I died and gone to heaven?"

Steve chuckled and looked at Cassie. "Is she always like this?"

"I'm afraid so."

Clearly amused, Stan collected the design, rolled it up, and reinserted it into the tube. "I'll see you Friday, then?" he said, looking at Cassie.

"I wouldn't miss it."

Stan drove off and the three of them were left standing by the curb. Steve waited until Stan's car had disappeared around the corner before he spoke. He looked at Cassie. "Do you two like Mexican food?"

"Love it," Amiee said, before Cassie could open her mouth to answer.

"Cassie?" Steve apparently wanted to hear it from her.

She shrugged. "Sure."

Amiee slapped her hands against her sides. "Oh come on, Mom, it's your favorite and you know it, well, other than a Whopper."

So much for playing it cool. "What have you got in mind?" she asked. Steve seemed to be smiling a lot lately, she noticed.

"There's a great Mexican restaurant in downtown Kent."

"The Lindo?" Cassie knew it well. The food was amazing.

"You've been there?" Steve asked.

Cassie nodded. "Once for a beer with the girls from the salon."

"You have?" Amiee sounded aghast. "You never said anything to me."

"There are some things I don't mention," Cassie told her daughter.

Amiee looked to Steve. "Can I order a cheese enchilada?"

"Of course."

"Two cheese enchiladas?"

He chuckled and nodded.

"I'm not being greedy, am I?"

"No," he said. "You're hungry, and as it happens, so am I."

Chapter 15

"Mom," Amiee shouted from her bedroom. "Can I please wear makeup?"

"When you're thirteen." Cassie stood in front of the bathroom mirror, applying eyeliner.

"M-o-m." Her daughter dragged out her name, making three distinct syllables out of a word that contained only one.

"What?"

"You're treating me like a kid."

This was an old argument, and one on which Cassie wouldn't relent. "You are a kid."

"But this dedication ceremony is a big deal."

"Tell you what," Cassie said, adding mascara to her eyelashes. "When our home is dedicated, you can wear mascara and blush."

Amiee stood in the doorway to the tiny bathroom. "You're killing me. I hope you know that. Claudia's been wearing makeup since fifth grade."

"Good for her."

Shaking her head with disgust, Amiee asked, "Why are you like this?"

"Are you going to argue with me all day or are you going to get ready to leave?"

A frown darkened her face. "Okay, okay, but on the inside I'm still mad."

"Not my problem," Cassie said, giving herself one last look before she turned away from the mirror. Her hair had grown out enough that she could cut it back to what it'd been like before Teresa had entered the styling contest. The purple highlights were gone and she was almost back to her normal bob. She hoped Steve would notice.

No, she didn't. It didn't matter if he noticed or not. She hadn't had it cut for his benefit. At least that was what she kept telling herself. They were friends. He hadn't so much as held her hand, which was perfectly fine by her. With the two of them working on the Habitat house, anything personal could get messy. He was smart enough to recognize that and so was she.

"I'm ready," Amiee announced impatiently. "What's taking you so long?"

"We're on our way." Cassie locked up the apartment and mother and daughter walked together toward her car.

"Do you think Steve will ask us out to dinner

after the ceremony?" Amiee asked with what could be interpreted only as hope. The kid thought far too much about her stomach.

"I can guarantee you he won't."

"Mom," Amiee cried. "What have you done?"

"What have I done?" she repeated.

Amiee looked aghast. "Don't tell me you broke up with Steve?"

Cassie definitely needed to find a means of curtailing her daughter's imagination. This could get highly embarrassing. "Amiee, the two of us would need to be involved before we could break up. Steve won't be asking us to dinner because there will be food after the ceremony. Shelly invited us both to stay. I asked if I could bring a dish and she said her extended family was taking care of everything."

"Is it Mexican food?"

"I don't know for sure, but probably." Cassie knew Shelly's mother was Hispanic.

Seemingly pacified now, Amiee asked, "Was Steve invited?"

"I'd be surprised if he wasn't. And listen, honey, please don't embarrass Steve or me, okay?"

Ever expressive, Amiee's head came back as if stunned. "Embarrass you how?"

"By mentioning that Steve brought us dinner and took us to the Lindo or anything else involving the two of us."

Her daughter looked at her and then slowly

shook her head. "If that's what you want." She sounded highly put out.

"I do, and I'm thanking you in advance."

By the time Cassie arrived there was barely a parking spot to be had. Both sides of the street were lined with cars. The entrance to the house had a big red ribbon with a bow, and tables had been set out front that were piled high with a variety of colorful dishes.

Shelly, George, and their children stood on the small porch. They had a daughter around Amiee's age and a nine-year-old son. The family was dressed in their finest clothes. Cassie knew that Steve had helped Shelly and George move furniture into their new home earlier in the week. Cassie had spent a couple evenings with Shelly, helping unpack boxes.

The night was lovely, although slightly overcast. Family, friends, and the Habitat staff and volunteers milled around. Cassie caught sight of Steve but didn't make a point of seeking him out.

Amiee, however, felt no such restraint. She rushed to his side and started chattering away as if it'd been weeks since she'd last seen him. Cassie had no option other than to rescue him from her daughter.

"Why is everyone waiting?" Amiee asked Steve, as Cassie approached. "Shouldn't they cut the ribbon? That's what this is all about, isn't it?"

"The priest hasn't arrived yet." Steve's eyes went straight to Cassie's and he smiled. "Hi," he said.

"Hi." His intense look flustered her and she quickly added, "I hope Amiee isn't bothering you."

"Not at all," he assured her.

Cassie felt his gentle gaze sweep over her. "I like your haircut."

"Thanks." She flushed slightly and raised her hand to the back of her head before she took her daughter by the shoulder and gently steered her away from Steve.

Father Colchado arrived. He stood with the Young family and delivered a beautiful blessing, praying over the home, asking God to stand guard over this house and this beautiful family. Before the ribbon was cut, George said a few words.

"Shelly and I need to thank a number of people who were instrumental in this project. First we want to thank the local chapter of the Kiwanis Club for making this home possible for our family. Although Shelly and I have been married thirteen years, this is our first home. It gives me such pride to bring my family into this house, knowing that I helped build it with my own two hands. Shelly, too. My wife, I learned, is as good at construction as she is at making homemade tortillas.

"We both owe a debt to Steve Brody. We couldn't have done it without him. Steve was with Shelly and me every step of the way. He was patient and generous with his time."

"And I want to give a special thanks to Cassie Carter," Shelly added shyly.

"Yes, Cassie, too," George added, "plus all the other volunteers who stepped in and worked alongside of us to give us this home."

Wearing a huge smile, George looked to his wife, who held the scissors. "You ready?"

Shelly beamed and nodded. "Ready."

Shelly cut the ribbon and it fell away. Everyone cheered and applauded, and a sense of joy and excitement filled the air as people exchanged hugs. George led the first group in for a tour.

Cassie and Amiee followed the crowd into the house.

"This is what our house will look like when it's built?" Amiee asked Cassie, staying close to her side and eyeing each room.

"Yes."

"Mom," she whispered, in what sounded like awe, "what are we going to do with all this room?"

"Oh, I think we'll find a way of filling it up." Cassie hid her amusement. By almost anyone's standards this was a moderately sized home, but to Amiee it seemed huge.

After the blessing and the tour, Shelly and her family brought out paper plates and plastic forks and set up chairs around the yard. A line quickly formed for the buffet. By the time Cassie and Amiee went through, there weren't any places left to sit.

Cassie paused and scanned the area and then saw Steve motion to her. "I'll put the tailgate down on the truck and you and Amiee can sit there," he suggested.

She hesitated and then realized she was being foolish. "That would be great. Thanks."

"I don't know if Mom wants me to tell you this or not, but I think you're cool," Amiee said, giving him a huge grin.

"Why, thank you." The tailgate was high off the ground, and Steve took Amiee by the waist and effortlessly lifted her up. He looked at Cassie and raised his eyebrows.

"I weigh a bit more," she assured him.

Steve laughed under his breath and said, "I think I can manage." While Amiee held Cassie's plate, Steve placed his hands at Cassie's waist. She automatically set her hands on his shoulders as he lifted her off the ground.

He held her at eye level for just a moment longer than necessary, and in that brief space of time, their gazes locked. She read in him pain and longing and then wondered if what she saw was a reflection of what was in her own eyes. He blinked and it felt as though a shaft of electricity shot through Cassie. She sucked in her breath, convinced Steve felt it, too. When he set her down on the tailgate it was all she could do to breathe normally again.

"Aren't you going to eat?" Amiee asked Steve.

The spell was broken, and frankly, Cassie was grateful. Though if Steve had chosen to kiss her right there in front of all these people, she wouldn't have objected. In fact, she would have welcomed it. The shock of how badly she wanted his kiss unnerved her almost as much as the fear of making a public spectacle of herself.

"I'll get a plate now," Steve said, and he, too, appeared relieved that the moment was over.

The few minutes he was away gave Cassie time to compose herself. If Amiee noticed anything was amiss, she didn't mention it.

Steve returned in short order with his plate loaded down with Shelly's and her mother's cooking. The crowd had dwindled to about half of what it had been for the dedication ceremony. Steve leaned against the tailgate as he ate, crossing his ankles.

"I heard you helped move the Youngs' furniture," Cassie commented, thinking that was a safe subject.

"Yeah, they didn't have that much. We were able to make it all in one trip, which was easier than making three or four smaller loads." He hesitated and jerked his head up to stare at Cassie.

"What?" she asked, taken aback by the change in him.

"The truck."

"Yes?"

"I have a big truck for business. I don't use it that often, but when I need it it's there."

Cassie still didn't get the connection. "Then I imagine you've helped other families move."

"Yes, and furthermore, I can help you. Didn't I hear that you have a load of furniture that needs to be brought to Seattle from Spokane?"

Cassie pressed her hand against her heart, sure it was about to pound straight through her chest. She'd given up hope of ever having the opportunity to collect her parents' things. The time was fast approaching when she would have no option but to let it all go.

"Cassie?"

"Yes . . . yes, I do, but once all the furniture is in Seattle, I don't have any place to store it." This was another complication that had plagued her.

"I can keep it for you," he volunteered. "I have a warehouse and it wouldn't be a problem to set aside whatever you have there. Why don't you see if we can do it this weekend?"

Cassie was overwhelmed. She hardly knew what to say. "I can't ask you to do that."

"Mom," Amiee cried, "why are you being so stubborn? Of course you can."

"Of course you can," Steve echoed.

"But it's short notice and my sister—"

Steve removed his cell from where it was clipped on his belt and handed it to her. "Call her and find out."

"But Amiee's got an all-day track meet tomorrow—"

Her daughter cut her off. "I can go with Claudia and her mom; they won't mind."

Steve raised his eyebrows. "Well?"

She couldn't refuse his generous offer, not when he'd made it effortless. She should be grateful. What was it her mother used to say about looking a gift horse in the mouth? Why she would even hesitate was beyond her own understanding.

"I'll phone my sister," she said.

"Aren't you going to thank Steve?" Amiee asked.

"Yes, of course. I'm grateful, Steve, really." But if that was the case, it certainly didn't explain why her stomach had twisted into tight knots.

Chapter 16

When Steve came to collect Cassie at six on Saturday morning, Amiee was already up and dressed for her track meet. Cassie felt guilty about leaving her daughter on the day of her big meet. Amiee was fine, but Cassie had lingering doubts.

"Call me as soon as you finish," she insisted.

Amiee rolled her eyes. "Mom, just go already, it's no big deal."

"It's a big deal to me," Cassie told her.

Amiee brushed off her mother's concerns. "I'm not even that good. The only reason I turned out for track is because Claudia did."

Steve glanced at his wrist and Cassie realized he was anxious to get on the road. With a five-hour drive across the state, making the trip there and back in a single day was bound to be exhausting.

Even now she was overwhelmed by the generosity of his offer.

Cassie started out the door and then turned back. "I don't know what time I'll be home."

"Mom!" Amiee protested again, tossing up her arms in frustration. "Would you just go?"

"Okay, okay."

Once outside, Cassie was struck by how huge Steve's truck was. She knew he owned his own electrical contracting business, but she hadn't realized how large his company was. If he had both a truck and a warehouse at his disposal, then he was far and away more successful that she'd imagined. Steve opened the passenger door and helped her inside the cab.

Neither spoke on the way out of Seattle. When they hit I-90, Steve glanced over at Cassie. "Do you mind if I ask you a personal question?"

She wondered what had prompted this, and carefully considered her response. "You can ask, but I reserve the right to refuse to answer."

"Fair enough." He waited while he changed lanes, moving over to the far right-hand side of the interstate as cars whizzed past. "When you cut your arm and removed your jacket I saw several scars. Can you tell me how you got them?" He didn't look her way, and Cassie was grateful.

She weighed her answer and decided to tell him what she told others. "Those scars were my stupid tax."

"I beg your pardon?"

"That's what I tell the women I mentor at the shelter."

"Your ex gave you those scars?" He sounded incredulous.

"If I'd stayed with Duke I would be dead now." She was convinced of that beyond a shadow of a doubt. "There were times when I wished he had murdered me." She paused when she read the shock in his expression.

"You can't possibly mean that."

She was serious. "After a person has been beaten down time and time again they lose the will to live, to fight back. As outrageous as it seems now, there were times when I felt I deserved to be beaten."

"What?" He didn't bother to hide his shock.

"If only I'd paid more attention . . . if only I'd asked first . . . if only I was a better cook."

Steve clamped his mouth shut and she could see that her words had upset him. "No woman deserves to be beaten, Cassie."

It'd taken Cassie far too long to come to that same conclusion. "I agree, which is why I call it my stupid tax." She regretted that she hadn't been able to volunteer much time to the shelter these days—every spare moment she had went toward working off her hours. Once her home was built, she'd go back. She missed it, missed meeting the women there, missed showing them proof positive that they, too, could make it on their own.

"I hope your ex is in prison," Steve said between clenched teeth.

"I wouldn't know, and furthermore, I don't care, as long as he stays out of Amiee's and my life."

An hour outside of Seattle they exited the freeway at the top of Snoqualmie Pass for a restroom stop and a cup of coffee. "Alicia and I made this trip often," Steve casually mentioned, as they headed back on the road.

He rarely mentioned his wife, and she suspected the reason was the pain it caused him.

"She loved visiting the Yakima Valley and doing wine tours in the summer months."

"And you?"

"I loved Alicia. That last summer, we both knew she didn't have long to live—five, six months at the most—and so we squeezed in as much time together as I could manage. My business suffered, but I can't regret a single minute I spent with her that last year."

"I wish I'd known her," Cassie told him. "I have the feeling we would have been friends."

"I wish you'd known her, too," Steve whispered. "It's been three years now, and it seems like only yesterday that she was with me."

No one needed to tell Cassie that when Steve loved it was with his whole heart. Any woman he loved would feel cherished.

"My one regret," he said, speaking into the void, "was the fact that we never were able to have children. People tell me how difficult it would be for me as a single father. I wouldn't care."

Cassie couldn't imagine her life without Amiee. "Alicia must have had a big heart. She's the one who got you involved in Habitat, isn't she?"

Steve nodded. "She spent countless volunteer hours at the office and the store. She was passionate about giving families a hand up. People loved her. You can't imagine how huge her funeral was."

They passed a sign saying they were nearing Spokane. They'd talked for so long that Cassie didn't realize how close they were—the miles had sped by with barely a notice. All at once Cassie's heart started racing at a frantic pace. Her palms grew sweaty and she found it difficult to breathe. For a moment she thought she was going to be sick.

"Steve," she whispered, her voice in a panic. "I need you to find a spot to pull over."

He glanced away from the road. "What's wrong?"

She felt all the blood drain from her face. "I don't know . . . please, just pull over."

"Okay, hold on." He pulled off the interstate and found a spot off the road and put the truck in park.

Cassie opened the passenger door and leaped down. Her head started to spin and she reached out and placed her hand on the side of the truck in order to keep her balance.

Right away, Steve was at her side. "Cassie, what's wrong?"

She was familiar with this feeling. It'd come over her far too often while married to Duke. "I'm afraid," she whispered.

Steve frowned. "Afraid of what?"

"You won't understand." Leaning against the truck now, she covered her face and took in deep gulping breaths in an effort to gain her equilibrium.

"Explain it to me." His voice was gentle, encouraging.

Cassie hardly knew where to begin. "I'm seeing my sister for the first time in more years than I can remember. I was eighteen and in love for the first time in my life. My father in particular didn't want me seeing Duke. So Duke convinced me our only option was to run away and get married. Karen found out that I'd withdrawn my graduation money out of the bank—I think she might have guessed what I intended to do. We had a huge fight. She said I was stupid if I couldn't see the kind of man Duke was, and I said she was jealous because she was so ugly and such a loser no one had ever fallen in love with her. We hurled some hateful accusations at each other . . . We haven't seen each other since that night . . . I said things I regret and, well, I . . . I don't think she's ever forgiven me."

"That was a lot of years ago, Cassie," Steve said, in the same gentle tones he'd used earlier. "I'm sure she must regret what happened, too."

Cassie had hoped that would be the case, but

there'd been precious little contact from either of her sisters, and what there had been was stilted and awkward. When Cassie reached out to her sisters she'd gotten a less-than-welcoming response. Neither Karen nor Nichole seemed interested in connecting with her.

"Surely you've seen your family since you've been back?"

Cassie dropped her hands, straightened, and shook her head. "No. Not since the night I ran away with Duke. One of the first things he did was move me as far away from my family as he could take me. I wasn't allowed to have contact with them . . . The last time I was in Spokane, I was a teenager."

"But I thought you said your mother recently died."

"She did."

"You weren't at the funeral?"

Clenching her stomach, Cassie held back a sob. "No . . . I had no way of getting to Spokane; I was thousands of miles away. Mom and I talked and we made peace . . . but that isn't the case with my two sisters."

"Your younger sister lives in Spokane, too?"

"No, Nichole and her husband are in Portland." Both her sisters had done everything right. Cassie was the black sheep, the outcast, and she didn't know if that would ever change. She longed for a deeper relationship with her sisters, but to this point she'd seen no evidence either Karen or Nichole were interested.

"Don't your sisters realize everything you've been through?"

"No." That Steve would ask the question showed he had little concept of the complicated relationship Cassie had with her siblings. She didn't want to explain further. As it was, she'd said more than she intended.

"But—"

Cassie could see he wasn't going to let this drop. "They don't know," she said, her voice shaking. "They don't realize . . . They seem to think it was my choice to stay away. They're angry for what I put my parents through. My father died far younger than he should have . . . Mom, too, and they believe my running off with Duke contributed to all that. The truth is, it probably did." All at once it came to her what she needed to do. She had the answer to all this.

Her head came up and she cried, "Steve, leave me here."

"Leave you on the side of the road?" He shook his head as he spoke. "I'm not doing that. What are you thinking? There's nothing around here for miles."

"Not here here, but somewhere close. We could find a diner or something, and I'll stay there and wait for you."

"Wait for me while I do what?" He frowned, clearly perplexed.

"While you meet my sister."

His automatic response was to shake his head. "No way. Sorry, but I'm not doing that."

Her heart continued to pound so hard her ribs ached. "You don't understand. Please. I don't know that I can do this."

"You can and you will," he insisted. "Where's the gutsy girl I met that first day in the Habitat office? The one who challenged me every time I turned around?"

"That same woman is shaking in her shoes."

"Cassie," he said, and placed his hand on her shoulder. "You're stronger than you think."

"Says who?" She certainly didn't feel any of that resolve or courage now.

"I do," Steve challenged. "You're one of the strongest women I know. You escaped a brutal marriage. You took your husband to court and stood up to him. If that wasn't enough, then you started over with nothing in order to make a new life for yourself and your daughter. In my book that takes courage; that takes a strong woman."

Cassie straightened. She had done all that and more.

"And you did it on your own, Cassie. You didn't have anyone to lean on, did you?"

She shook her head.

"That's what I thought."

"You're a good mother to Amiee."

Cassie was almost able to smile. "The kid's got a mouth on her."

"Really?" Steve said, feigning surprise. "I can't imagine where she got that."

She did smile then, although the amusement quivered at the edges of her mouth.

"You can do this, Cassie. I know you. After everything you've endured, this is a piece of cake; it's nothing."

"You haven't met my sister," she said, slowly expelling her breath.

"Is she anything like you?"

Cassie thought back to the days she'd shared a bedroom with Karen. "We're nothing alike . . . Karen was the organized one and I was the slob. Because Karen couldn't stand my messes, she took masking tape and divided the room in half and I wasn't allowed to cross the line."

Steve grinned.

"She resented the fact that I got top grades and I barely needed to study. School always came easy to me. If I'd gone to college . . . I had a full-ride scholarship. My parents were so proud."

"You gave it up when you married Duke?"

Cassie nodded, not wanting to explain that she'd been pregnant and blinded by love. The scholarship was only a small sacrifice compared to everything else she'd lost because she'd been young and foolish. She'd lost her self-respect. She'd lost all contact with her family. She'd lost all self-esteem and pride. Loving Duke had come at a high price, one she'd repeatedly paid through the years. Her stupid tax for sure.

"Did Duke . . ." Steve hesitated, almost as if he could barely speak the words. "Did he ever hit Amiee?"

"No. He knew . . ."

Steve frowned waiting for her to continue.

"He was well aware I would do whatever it took to protect my daughter, and if that meant doing him bodily injury I wouldn't hesitate. I swore to him if he ever laid a hand on her, he would pay and the cost wouldn't be cheap." He'd slugged Cassie for her impertinence, but somehow her threat had gotten through to him. One misplaced slap, one blowup aimed at their daughter, and he'd need to sleep with one eye open for the rest of his life.

Cassie had meant it, too. The beatings had gotten much worse after she'd made that stand. People asked why she'd stayed in the marriage, why she'd put up with the abuse. Those who wanted to know weren't familiar with the human psyche. One reason was that Cassie felt she didn't have any choice—Duke had convinced her that she'd never make it on her own. The crazy part was she'd believed him. She might have failed if not for the support and encouragement of the women at the shelter. Because of them she felt an obligation to give back in kind for all the help given to her.

"Feel better?" Steve asked.

Cassie nodded.

"You ready to get back on the road?"

"In a minute." She drew in several deep breaths and tried to quell her pounding heart.

"Let's walk for a bit," Steve suggested.

"Okay." They followed a dirt road for several feet, walking side by side in silence. "I . . . I don't know what I'll say to Karen."

Steve leaned down and grabbed hold of a long stem of grass, which he placed in the corner of his mouth. "My guess," he said, "is that your sister is wondering the same thing. She's probably just as nervous."

Not Karen—her sister was always so put together. What Cassie had in brains and talent, her two sisters made up for in beauty. Karen had been nominated for the homecoming court her senior year of high school. And while Nichole was barely in her teens when Cassie left, it was apparent she would grow out of that awkward stage and be just as lovely as Karen.

"I can't see Karen as nervous."

"I'll bet she is," Steve continued, chewing on the long stem of grass.

Cassie remembered how awkward the first conversations with Karen had been shortly after their father died. Her older sister had sounded as uncertain as Cassie felt. Just recently, since they'd started communicating again, it'd gotten a little better; they'd both lowered their guard bit by bit, and yet it continued to be firmly held in place.

After several minutes, Cassie slowly turned around and started back toward the truck. Steve followed. He didn't ask her any further questions, didn't coax or cajole her.

"Ready?" he asked, when they reached the truck.

Cassie inhaled a deep breath and nodded.

He opened the passenger door and Cassie climbed in. Steve was right. She could do this. She would do this.

Chapter 17

Nichole Patterson set out her husband's favorite lunch on a floral place mat. She poured him a tall glass of iced tea and then waited for Jake to return from his golf match with his buddy Dave. He'd been spending a lot of time with Dave lately—not that Nichole minded. Ever since the birth of their son, Jake had been especially loving. She simply adored her Michael Kors purse, although she felt a twinge of guilt now and again when she saw it. If Jake hadn't insisted, she would never have purchased anything so extravagant for herself. Jake enjoyed spoiling her.

The door off the garage opened and Jake walked in. "Hi, honey," he said and brushed his lips across her cheek. Owen sat on the floor, playing with his toys, which he had spread out across the hardwood. Jake reached for his son and lifted him high in the air and kissed his chubby cheek.

Owen squealed, dropped his toy, and flung out his arms before Jake handed him to Nichole.

"You made me lunch," he said.

"Yes, a sandwich, and I've got the soup on the stove. How was your golf game?"

Jake pulled out the chair and sat down. "Great. I ended the round only two over par."

Nichole hoped that their son inherited his father's athletic abilities. Owen showed a lot of promise—he'd started walking at nine months and was into everything. She had to be on constant guard when it came to their son, which meant she had little free time—not that she minded. This was what it meant to be a mother and she enjoyed her role.

"Is tomato soup okay?" she asked, setting Owen in his high chair. She handed him a handful of Cheerios, his favorite cereal, to keep him occupied while she went to the stove to dish up Jake's lunch.

"Perfect." Jake reached for the floral napkin that matched the place mat and spread it on his lap.

"Karen called this morning to tell me she'd heard from Cassie." She delivered his soup to the table. Pulling out a chair, she sat across the table from her husband.

Jake pushed his sandwich aside in order to make room for his soup. "The prodigal sister you hardly remember?"

"Oh, I remember Cassie, all right. It's sort of crazy, you know. It was like she died after she ran off with Duke. She put my parents through hell: Mom worried herself sick and Dad was never the same. He used to sit and stare at the piano. Once I saw him in his chair, looking at the piano with tears glistening in his eyes. She made some bad decisions and then looked to us for help. Remember when she called, needing money?"

Jake took a big bite of his sandwich before he nodded. "It looks like she's mended fences with Karen, though."

"Not really." Nichole was following Karen's lead when it came to Cassie. "But I think this is a move in the right direction."

Jake frowned and reached for his spoon. "Was Cassie looking for money again?"

"No, no, nothing like that. Cassie reached out to come and collect the leftover things from my parents' house."

"What did I tell you?" Jake said, wagging his index finger at her.

Nichole frowned, not remembering. "What did you tell me?" Jake looked so sexy when he thought he was right about something. Those three little lines at the bridge of his nose would crinkle up with that "you know I'm right" look she adored. His eyes were the most incredible blue-gray, and thankfully, their son had inherited them.

"I told you," Jake reminded her, "that if you put

a time limit on how long the family would hold all that stuff, then your sister would magically find a way to collect it."

Actually, Nichole didn't remember her husband saying that. She was the one who'd mentioned it to Karen over the phone, suggesting she give their sister two months and no more. It sounded a bit dictatorial now, and she regretted being so harsh.

"Cassie's driving over to Spokane today with a friend. It'll be the first time Karen and Cassie have seen each other since their big fight right before Cassie married Duke." Nichole had been in the room at the time and put a pillow around her head so she couldn't hear.

Jake grew thoughtful. "Karen must be nervous?"

"Really nervous. She hardly sounded like herself." After talking to her oldest sister, Nichole almost wished she could be in Spokane with her. She'd enjoy seeing Cassie again, too, she thought, then took a breath, realizing the desire had caught her unaware. Cassie had been out of her life for so long Nichole hadn't thought there was any emotional attachment left. Well, other than the guilt she felt for the role she'd played in Cassie's disappearance.

"We used to fight all the time."

"You and Cassie?"

"All three of us. When Karen was a senior she felt like she should have her own bedroom. Karen and Cassie were constantly fighting over clothes and boys and everything in between. Dad took Cassie's side. She was his favorite and we could tell. Mom championed Karen. After one big shouting match, Dad decided Cassie would share my bedroom."

"You had your own room?" Jake arched his eyebrows playfully.

Nichole rushed to explain. "I was so much younger than Karen and Cassie. It only made sense for me to have my own room and have them share, since they were close in age. But I wasn't happy about this new arrangement. To make matters even worse, Cassie was bossy and she kept the light on all night reading. She told our mother it was homework but it wasn't. She was reading romance novels. I took one of her 'textbooks' to Mom and then it was all-out war between me and Cassie." She smiled at the memory of some of the antics they'd pulled on each other. Nichole had switched out Cassie's expensive shampoo for salad dressing, and in retaliation Cassie had destroyed Nichole's homework.

Jake continued eating his lunch and didn't seem to notice she wasn't eating, which was fine. She didn't want to make a point of the starvation diet she was on. Nichole was determined to lose the baby weight she'd gained with Owen. It was as if Jake read her thoughts, because he looked over at her empty place mat and frowned.

"Where's your lunch?"

"I'm not eating."

"Why not?"

Nichole leaned slightly forward. "You haven't said anything about my weight, and honey, I want you to know I'm grateful. I've gained a few pounds since the baby."

Once more her husband's eyebrows shot up. "You have? Where?"

"Mostly my hips. When Laurie and I went shopping, I had to buy my new jeans in a larger size. Laurie tried to comfort me. She says it's what happens after we have children, but I got on the scale and while those few pounds might not be much, I feel them."

"Honey, stop." His look was intent and full of love. "I haven't noticed a single pound, and it wouldn't matter to me what you weigh. I love you, and in my eyes you're beautiful just the way you are."

He was saying exactly what she needed to hear, what she had hoped to hear.

"Now eat. I don't like the idea of you starving yourself. It isn't necessary. You're perfect."

"Jake." She felt like crying. How was it she was so fortunate to have married such a wonderful man? "I appreciate what you're saying, but I'd feel better about myself if I was able to shed this weight."

Jake set his lunch aside and grew thoughtful. "Do you want to join one of those diet centers?"

"I don't know . . ." Nichole wasn't sure what to do. She'd considered joining a weight-loss program, but it would be difficult with Owen in tow.

"What about one of those weight-loss spas," Jake suggested, his eyes brightening with the idea. "You could go away for three or four days, lose the few pounds that are bothering you, and be done with it. Like I said, you're perfect just the way you are, but if the excess weight is causing you concern, then do something about it."

Nichole couldn't believe her husband would suggest anything this . . . drastic. She couldn't go off on spa vacations—it wasn't like they were rich. Yes, there was her inheritance, but that was to be invested for the future, not squandered on unnecessary expenses. "I've read about those spas," she said, sighing. "Jake, they're ungodly expensive."

"Are they?" He seemed surprised. "Let's check it out." He left the table long enough to retrieve his briefcase. He set it on the table and brought out his impossibly small laptop, lifting it open and turning it on.

While the idea of a spa was extravagant, she couldn't help being curious. Scooting her chair next to her husband, she watched as he typed in a few pertinent words for an Internet search. Within seconds they had a list of weight-loss health spas from one end of the country to the other.

Jack scrolled down the list. "What about this one in Arizona?"

Nichole looked at the price. "Jake, this is too much."

Her husband shook his head. "Is there a price tag on what brings my wife happiness?"

"I couldn't spend that kind of money!" While it was more than generous and loving of her husband, Nichole, in good conscience, couldn't do this.

"Yes, we can," Jake insisted. "I'll call the spa and get all the details, then we can decide."

Still, Nichole wasn't sure. "I wouldn't want to go alone, and Jake, just look at those golf courses." The greens were lush and verdant. Jake would be in golfer's heaven.

Her husband released a regretful sigh. "Oh honey, I wish I could, but there's no way I could take that amount of time off work. The spring release has been announced and this is our busy season."

"You're always busy, Jake."

"I know, and I'm sorry, I truly am, but all these extra hours go with the territory. I'm in sales and I have to be available to my accounts. You understand, don't you?"

Nichole did understand. It didn't make her life easy for him to be away so many hours of the day, but that was the price she had to pay to be a stay-at-home mom for Owen.

Their son was nearly asleep in his high chair. It was already past his nap time, so Nichole collected him in her arms. He fussed a little, then nestled in and closed his eyes.

"Why don't you take Laurie with you?" Jake suggested.

It was a great idea, but Laurie would never be able to afford this. Nichole wasn't sure they could, either, at least not without digging into her inheritance.

"Let me see if I can work a deal with the manager," Jake said, smiling broadly. "It's what I do all day, sweetheart."

Still she hesitated. "What about Owen?" It wasn't like she could take their son with her.

For the first time Jake hesitated and then said, "I can manage Owen. I mean, really, how much trouble could one toddler be?"

Nichole squelched a laugh.

"My mother and I will work something out," he added. His eyes grew soft as he looked toward Nichole, holding their son in her arms.

Nichole's head was spinning. While Jake insisted those few pounds didn't matter to him, she had a sneaky feeling they mattered a lot, otherwise he wouldn't have suggested a fancy spa. Still, she wasn't sure this was what she should be doing.

Nichole bit into her lip again as she weighed out the pros and cons. A part of her was leaping up and down, excited. Her more practical half couldn't stop calculating the price tag.

After a few moments, she said, "Let me talk to Laurie."

"Of course." Jake brightened with enthusiasm. "I'll call now and find out what kind of deal I can get for you."

Again she paused. "Okay. I'll put Owen down for his nap."

She wasn't away more than ten minutes. When she returned she heard Jake on the phone.

"Three days would probably be better," Jake glanced up, saw her, and then gave her a thumbs-up sign.

This was happening so fast, but Jake was like that. When he had an idea, he didn't hesitate. As soon as he was off the phone with the spa people, he announced, "I called my mother and she said she'd be happy to take care of Owen during the day. At night I would have quality time with my son."

"You could manage?"

"Of course I could."

"This is the deal," Jake said excitedly. "Five days. One day to fly in. Three days at the spa and then one day to fly home. Five days in total."

Nichole didn't know what to say. "Five days. What can I say? You're the most wonderful husband in the entire universe. Thank you for this,

Jake. thank you so much." Now all she had to do was find a friend to accompany her. Preferably Laurie.

"I think this spa trip will do us both a world of good," he said, smiling.

Nichole wrapped her arms around her husband and they shared a long, deep kiss.

Chapter 18

By the time Steve parked the truck in front of Cassie's sister's house, she was shaking. Her fingers had lost all feeling from the tight grip, her hands were clenched so hard. Her breathing was shallow and her heart beat at the speed of a racehorse. For just an instant she was afraid she was about to pass out.

"Cassie?"

Steve's voice came at her as if he was shouting from the bottom of a well. "You okay?"

She shook her head.

"You can do this."

Easy for him to say. Emotions swirled around her.

"Cassie?"

"Let's leave right now. I can't . . . I can't."

Steve hesitated and seemed ready to do as she

asked, when the front door to the house opened and her sister stepped outside. Karen stood at the top of the porch steps, watching, waiting.

"Is that your sister?" Steve asked.

Cassie's eyes connected with Karen's. She hadn't been sure what to expect. Unresolved anger? Judgment? Disgust? What she hadn't anticipated was the same hesitation and doubt she was experiencing herself.

It took her a moment to realize Karen was just as tentative and just as unsure as Cassie was. Steve had said as much, but she'd discounted his words, convinced he was wrong. Karen was the one who had her life together; she was married to a great husband and financially secure, with two terrific children. From the time Karen was young, she'd done everything right: graduated from college, been a good daughter. She'd been the one who had taken care of their parents when they were ill and had even been the executor of their estate.

"Cassie?"

Once more Steve broke into her thoughts. She turned back to look at him and saw the question in his eyes.

"What would you like me to do?"

The shaking hadn't subsided. "Stay close to me, okay?"

"If that's what you want."

"Please," she whispered, finding it difficult to speak. It demanded more courage than she knew she possessed to open the passenger door. It was up there with leaving Duke, with nothing but her daughter and the clothes on their backs.

Steve hopped out of the truck cab and came around, offering Cassie his hand.

The gesture surprised her until she realized she'd been sitting frozen in the truck with the door open. Cassie stared at his hand for a long time before she placed her own in his. He gave it a gentle squeeze as if to remind her she was stronger than she realized. At the moment, that fact was in serious question. Once she stepped out of the truck, she feared her knees wouldn't support her.

"Cassie." Karen stepped down from the small porch and slowly approached her.

"Hello, Karen."

They stood about three feet apart.

"You've changed," Cassie whispered, as if surprised her sister was no longer twenty. She'd matured into a woman.

"You've changed, too."

Cassie smiled and nodded. True to his word, Steve remained close to her side.

"I barely recognized you. If I'd seen you on the street I might have walked right past."

Cassie had to wonder if the years had changed her that much. "It's me," she whispered, having a hard time getting the words past the tightness that gripped her throat.

"You look . . ."

"Different," she supplied. And she was. The girl who'd fled in the middle of the night shared little with the woman Cassie was now. And those differences were much deeper than what showed on the surface.

"You look great." Karen was beautiful. Her thick, dark hair was cut short, and it set off her cheekbones. Nichole was the dirty blonde of the family, and even when she was in her pre-teens, she'd pleaded to bleach it.

For the first time, Karen tore her gaze away from Cassie and looked at Steve.

Cassie realized Karen was waiting for an introduction. "Steve Brody, this is my sister, Karen."

Karen broke eye contact with Cassie long enough to shake Steve's hand. "Thank you for driving my sister home."

Home.

The word echoed in Cassie's mind. Spokane had been her home at one time, but that had been a lifetime ago. She'd left as an innocent teenager, convinced she was doing the right thing by marrying the father of her baby. How incredibly naïve she'd been.

"Come in," Karen said, as if suddenly remembering her manners. She led the way into the house. Garth stood just inside the front door, watching and waiting. He introduced himself to Steve and the two men exchanged hearty handshakes.

"I wasn't sure what time you'd arrive," Karen

said, and rubbed her palms together with what looked like nervous agitation, "but Garth and I held off on lunch."

"You fixed lunch for us?" Cassie looked to Steve and offered him an apologetic smile. It was well past one o'clock and she hadn't given a single thought to lunch. He must be half starved by now, and yet he hadn't said a word. Nervous as she was, embroiled in dread and fear, she hadn't once considered that he might be hungry.

"Actually," Garth explained, "I've got the barbecue going and I thought we'd rustle up a few hamburgers."

Steve nodded enthusiastically. "That sounds fantastic. Need any help?"

"Sure." Garth headed through the kitchen and toward the sliding glass door that led to the backyard.

Cassie's gaze was drawn to the photographs on the fireplace mantel. The picture of Lily must be recent—it showed a young girl in braces, doing her best to smile with her mouth full of wires. Buddy had bright freckles floating across the bridge of his nose. Of the two children, Buddy resembled his father's side of the family. Cassie knew how excited her father must have been to finally have a boy, a grandson. She imagined that Buddy and his grandpa had been tight.

"I'm sorry the kids aren't here to meet you," Karen said. Then she added, as if she felt she needed an excuse, "Lily's with the church group, doing volunteer work at a low-income housing project, and Buddy's attending a Boy Scout function with his troop. The kids are constantly on the run. Was it like this when we were young?" Karen asked.

"I doubt it," Cassie said, thinking of those long hours running around the neighborhood.

"Me, too. You had piano lessons, and otherwise we were free-range kids and that was about it." Then she added, "Do you still play piano?"

The question was almost worthy of a laugh. "No." A piano was well beyond her means. At one time Cassie had loved playing for her father when he got off work. He'd said hearing her play the old church hymns helped him relax. Cassie half suspected it'd been a lie meant to encourage her to practice, but she'd enjoyed those special times with her dad.

"We saved the piano for you," Karen commented, as she led the way into the kitchen.

"You saved it for me?" Cassie could barely believe what her sister was saying.

"Well, yes. You were the only one who played. The music gene completely skipped over Nichole and me. The piano is in the storage unit with the rest of the furniture. Unfortunately, it will probably need to be tuned—"

Cassie's hand flew to her mouth and she choked back a sob. It'd been years since she last played, years since she'd even thought about playing the piano.

"Cassie?" Karen gave her an odd look. "Is that okay? I thought you'd probably want the piano."

"Yes, yes," she rushed to tell her sister. "I just didn't expect that you'd keep it . . ."

"Of course we would."

In an effort to cover the intensity of her reaction, Cassie asked, "What else is in the storage unit?"

Karen took a plate of sliced tomatoes, onions, and dill pickles out of the refrigerator and set it on the kitchen countertop. "It's been months since we cleared out the house and I really don't remember all that's in there. There's the sofa and matching chair, but those are relatively new, so you won't recognize them. A couple lamps . . ." She paused as though trying to remember what else was inside the storage unit.

"A bedroom set?" Amiee would be glad of that.

"Yes, but it's pretty beaten up. I almost gave it away. There's probably a bunch of stuff that won't interest you. Take what you want and then Garth and I will haul the rest to Goodwill or Saint Vincent de Paul."

Cassie nodded, still overwhelmed with the thought that her sisters had saved her the piano.

"I made Mom's recipe for potato salad," Karen said, as she took out the hamburger buns from the bread drawer.

Beset by memories, Cassie realized she hadn't

done a thing to help with the meal. "Karen, thank you . . . really, thank you for everything. Please, tell me what I can do to help with lunch."

"Okay. You can take these buns out to Garth—he likes to have them grilled. Garth loves to barbecue. Work has been slow for him the last couple weeks and he's been home early enough to get dinner started. We've used the barbecue nearly every day this week." Karen chattered away.

Cassie wanted to say something, anything to help ease this tension, but was afraid whatever she said would bring up memories best laid to rest. She carried the hamburger buns outside and found Steve and Garth talking as if they'd known each other for years. Garth flipped the burgers and took the buns from Cassie without breaking stride in their conversation.

Steve shot Cassie a look filled with questions. She could tell he was wondering if everything was going okay between her and her sister. She sent him a smile to reassure him that all was well, although that was a slight exaggeration.

When Cassie returned to the kitchen she saw that her sister was busy dumping a bag of potato chips into a bowl.

"I thought we'd dish up in here and then eat outside."

"Sure." Feeling at loose ends, Cassie looked around for a way to help.

"The iced tea is in the fridge if you want to bring that out."

"Glad to." She needed to do something to occupy her hands.

"I hope you brought pictures of Amiee," Karen said, as if looking to fill the silence.

"I did," Cassie assured her. "I'll show them to you later." What she wanted to tell her sister was how eager Amiee was to meet her family. Aunts, uncles, and cousins. She wanted her sister to know how Amiee hounded her for stories of her childhood and questions about the three sisters. But she said nothing, fearing anything more than a polite response would topple this fragile peace.

Karen sliced several hard-boiled eggs and artistically arranged them on top of the bowl of potato salad just the same way their mother had once done. "Do you mind if I ask you something?" Her sister sounded hesitant.

Cassie braced herself, knowing Karen was about to bring up Duke.

"Do you have any contact with him?" her sister asked, avoiding eye contact.

"None."

"What about child support for Amiee? I hope he's helping you financially."

Cassie nearly laughed out loud—that was a joke if there ever was one. If she hadn't been blinded by hormones and love, Cassie might have recognized the sign that Duke was not the kind of man you could depend on. Her father certainly had. It wasn't until after they were married that Cassie discovered that Duke had never been able to hold down a job for more than a few weeks at a time. Child support! What was it their dad used to say? "You can't get blood from a turnip"? Duke was either too drunk to work or too high on drugs to be of much use to anyone. Even when he did manage to find employment, his quick temper and drinking habits invariably caused him to get laid off or fired, often within a matter of a week or two. Once he was fired after a single eight-hour shift. Cassie remembered that specifically because Duke had blamed her and she'd been beaten for her imaginary efforts to sabotage his promising career as a dishwasher.

Karen studied her, her eyes round and sad. "Cassie, why did you stay away so long? Didn't you realize how desperately Mom and Dad missed you?"

She carefully weighed her response. She could explain the truth, dredge up the horrors of her marriage, but she hesitated. She feared Karen might not believe her, might think she was looking for sympathy, or worse, bring up their last fight and how right she had been about everything. "I missed everyone, too," she whispered, and then added, "desperately."

If Karen knew the truth, the natural question

would be why Cassie had stayed with Duke. This was a question Cassie had asked herself a thousand times. Others asked, too, and there was no easy answer. She stayed because she didn't feel it was an option to leave. She had no job, no money, no friends, no connections. She was completely dependent on Duke, and for more than her and Amiee's physical well-being. Emotionally she was tied to Duke, but those ties were like barbed-wire fencing, ties that brought her nothing but pain. Still, she hadn't been able to find the courage to leave, not until it became a life-or-death situation. She was sure this would be beyond Karen's scope of understanding.

"Why did I stay away?" Cassie repeated her sister's question, unsure how to answer. Rather than attempt an explanation, she said, "I don't know . . . why do any of us do the things we do?"

Karen continued to regard her, and a brooding frown came over her. "I ask myself that same question sometimes. Why do we do the things we do?" she repeated slowly.

Cassie was taken aback by how serious Karen had become. "Do you have regrets, Karen?" She did, and hoped this would open the way to a conversation about their last argument.

The frown left as quickly as it came. "Well, we all have regrets, don't you think?" her sister asked lightly, as if having second thoughts about wading into such painful territory.

Cassie held her breath, hoping she was doing the right thing, then said, "I regretted the argument we had shortly before I left with Duke," Cassie whispered. There, it was out. She took a deep breath while she awaited Karen's response.

Her sister shrugged off the comment. "Like I said, we all have regrets."

She seemed not to want to dredge up the ugly accusations that they'd flung at each other that day. As if looking for a way to change the subject, Karen glanced up.

"Who's Steve?" She tossed a look over her shoulder at the two men on the patio.

"He's a friend." This question was tricky.

"Are you two involved?"

"Involved how? Romantically?"

"Well, yes."

"No," Cassie said, leaving no room for doubt. "Nothing like that." Because she knew that wasn't likely to satisfy her sister's curiosity, she added, "He's a volunteer with Habitat for Humanity and we've been working together for the last month or so. I can promise you there's absolutely nothing romantic between us."

Karen raised her brows so high they nearly met her hairline. It was clear she didn't believe Cassie.

"It's true," Cassie insisted. "Steve lost his wife a few years back and he's pretty much still hung up on her." Her ego would like it if Steve was interested, but Cassie hadn't seen any real evidence.

Certainly nothing physical. Yes, he'd been kind, generous, and thoughtful after they'd finally gotten over that initial friction, but that didn't constitute romantic interest.

The sliding glass door leading to the patio opened and both men walked inside. Garth carried a platter of hamburgers with buns.

"Lunch is served," Garth said, and set the plate down on the counter. "Can we eat now? I'm starved."

Chapter 19

Considering the stilted conversation between Cassie and her sister before lunch, the meal went relatively well. Cassie would be forever grateful Steve was with her. He steered the conversation away from any topic that would have caused her discomfort. Mostly Karen and Garth discussed their children, a subject that was safe. Cassie showed them pictures of Amiee, which Karen stared at for a long moment before handing them back.

"She looks like you," Karen said, after an unusually long moment.

As if seeking a way to cover a sudden awkward silence, Cassie talked about working with Habitat, and Steve quickly mentioned that Cassie was actively involved in the building process.

"You'll have to come and see the house once it's finished," Steve suggested.

Karen looked to Garth, who set his hamburger aside and nodded. "That's something to consider."

They finished their meal, and Cassie helped her sister put away the leftovers. Steve and Garth cleared off the patio table and cleaned the barbecue.

When she was alone again with her sister, Cassie braved asking the question. "Will you really come once the house is completed?" she asked, her back to her sister for fear of what she would read in Karen's eyes. No matter what Karen said, Cassie wanted her family to know she wanted them in her life and yearned to be part of theirs.

"When will that be?" Karen responded. "I mean, we'll come, I suppose, but you have to remember the kids' activities keep us pretty busy."

Cassie knew she was hedging. "I'll remember," she said, fighting down the disappointment.

"Winter is less busy than this time of year," Karen added.

"We're breaking ground next week," Cassie explained. "We hope to have the house completed by early spring."

"You mean you haven't actually started?" Karen looked surprised.

"Well, not on our home. I've been putting in my hours helping other families."

"Oh." That was her only comment as she dried her hands on a kitchen towel.

Garth returned to the house. "Is everyone ready to head out for the storage unit?" he asked.

"Ready," Cassie assured him.

Karen and Garth rode in one car while Steve and Cassie followed behind in the truck.

As soon as they were alone, Steve asked, "Everything went okay with your sister?"

"Yes. It was fine." It was about as good as she'd let herself hope for. Karen was being polite, if not particularly warm. She didn't seem interested in recrimination. Or maybe that would come later. At least the two were talking. Cassie waited for a moment and then glanced over at Steve and watched a quirky smile come over him. "You aren't going to tell me I told you so?" she asked.

"Do you want me to?"

"No . . . but thanks for the encouragement, I needed it." She doubted he realized what a huge step meeting with her older sister had been. It was the first move toward reconciliation with her family. It came to her how badly she needed her sisters, how dreadfully she missed being with them. Standing in the middle of her sister's kitchen, she had decided to do whatever was necessary to reconnect with her family. Apologize for past mistakes, swallow her pride, anything.

"Garth is a decent guy, easy to talk to," Steve was saying.

"What did you talk about?"

Steve hesitated. "Man stuff."

"In other words, nothing you want to tell me."

His face blossomed into a huge grin. "You got it."

"So be it. I won't pry."

They drove up to a storage facility close to the Spokane airport in an industrial neighborhood and parked out front. Garth had the key and paused before turning to look at Karen. "Did you put an additional lock on here?"

"Me?" Karen pressed her hand to her chest. "No."

Garth straightened and spoke to Karen. "You did pay for two months in advance, didn't you?"

Waiting outside the unit, Steve stood behind Cassie and placed his hands on her shoulders. His touch felt warm against her skin and a tingling sensation went down her arms. She wasn't sure what to make of the gesture and told herself it probably meant nothing.

"Let me check with the office," Garth grumbled. "I just hope someone's available on a Saturday afternoon."

"There should be," Karen called after him. Garth hurried toward the front of the facility, walking at a clipped pace. Karen looked embarrassed and apologetic. "I have a feeling there's been a misunderstanding. Garth recently took over the bill paying and we've had a few minor glitches."

"It happens," Steve said.

"Garth is generally responsible. I don't think

things are going well at the office . . . he wanted to take a load off my shoulders, but I'm not sure having him tackle the bill paying is working out the way I'd hoped."

Garth returned within ten minutes with another man, who removed the lock. As soon as he left, Karen asked her husband, "What happened?"

"I assumed you'd paid this in advance." He turned toward Cassie and Steve. "I'm sorry about this, but it's all taken care of now."

"I feel bad for causing you all this trouble. I realize I took far longer than I should have to come."

"No problem," Garth said. "The fault was mine."

The unit wasn't big enough for her to walk inside. Right away Steve and Garth started loading the contents of the unit into the truck. Thankfully, the truck had a lift, otherwise it would have been nearly impossible to get the piano inside.

When Steve rolled the upright Baldwin out of the unit, Cassie stepped forward and reverently ran her hand along the top. Right away tears gathered in her eyes, though she managed to swallow them down. The emotion she felt seeing the piano was almost as powerful as what she'd felt when she first saw Karen standing on the porch steps.

The Baldwin reminded her of the innocence she'd lost and the connection with family, especially her father. She'd left all that behind when she'd run away with Duke. Struggling to hold back the tears, Cassie pressed her hand over her mouth, embarrassed by the feelings that flooded through her.

"Cassie." Right away Steve was at her side, concern in his voice.

Cassie said, "It's . . . nothing." She was grateful her sister was occupied elsewhere and didn't see her eyes welling up.

Steve's look told Cassie he didn't believe her, but he went back to moving things into the truck.

Rather than take the time to sort through all the boxes, Cassie had Steve and Garth load up the contents of the entire unit. With the two men working together, it didn't take long.

When they'd finished, Steve tucked his hands into his back jean pockets. "You ready to head back to Seattle?" he asked Cassie.

She'd already taken up his entire day, and she could tell he was anxious to get back on the road.

"I'm ready." She looked to her sister and Garth. "I . . . appreciate this," she whispered. Without giving thought to her actions, Cassie impulsively reached out and hugged her sister. "Thank you."

At first Karen didn't return the hug, but then she did, squeezing Cassie tight and close. "It was good to see you."

Cassie nodded. "You, too."

When they broke apart, she noticed that Steve was already in the truck. "I'd better go." Leaving was far more difficult than she'd anticipated. A large part of her yearned to stay, to turn back the clock to the time she was a teenager. She'd give anything to step back through the years and be smart enough to trust her parents' wisdom. Knowing what she did now, she'd gladly accept their help. Reliving the past wasn't an option, though. Cassie could only continue down the path she'd chosen all those years ago and do the best she knew how. Like she'd said to Maureen weeks earlier, she would do the next right thing.

Steve rolled down the driver's-side window. "Cassie, you ready?"

She nodded and then climbed inside the cab and waved to her sister and Garth. It took only a few minutes to reach the freeway on-ramp. Steve was silent, and Cassie was glad because normal conversation was beyond her. She kept her head turned away as she struggled to hide the tears that rained unchecked down her cheeks. As hard as she tried, she found she couldn't restrain the feelings of regret. She'd lost so much and hurt her family and herself. Though they might be back on speaking terms, it didn't seem like they would ever find it in their hearts to forgive her.

Steve must have sensed her anguish, because he gently patted her knee. Unable to stop crying, Cassie blindly reached for her purse and grabbed a tissue to blow her nose.

"I'm sorry," she whispered, mortified that he would see her openly weeping.

"Don't apologize," he whispered. "Cry, Cassie, let it out; there's no need to hold it inside any longer."

She broke then, doubling over. Cassie rested her face on her knees as she dissolved into deep, heart-wrenching sobs that echoed through the truck's cab. After a moment, she felt Steve's hand on her back, and then gently stroking her head, offering her comfort.

Cassie felt the truck veer to the right and looked up to notice that Steve had pulled into a rest area. He drove the truck to the far side of the parking lot generally reserved for truckers and came to a stop.

Her sobs had turned into shoulder-shaking hiccups as she tried her hardest to bring her emotions under control. She wasn't having much success as she searched for another tissue.

"Cassie," Steve whispered, and unbuckled his seat belt and reached for her, bringing her into his arms, holding her close. If he hadn't been so gentle or so kind she might have been able to resist him. Steve whispered to her, but she didn't hear a word, only the soothing sound of his voice breaking through the pain.

He tucked his finger under her chin, tilting her head back, and then he was kissing her. His mouth was warm and soft as he held her as close as possible in the front seat of the truck.

It was as if he wanted to absorb her body into his own and swallow the pain for her. Cassie looped her arms around his neck and even while the tears continued to rain down her cheeks, dripping onto her chin, she responded to him, opening her heart. Soon their kissing took on a more intense quality until they were both nearly panting and breathless. Reluctantly, Steve pulled away and braced his forehead against hers as he drew in several deep breaths.

Neither spoke. Even if she could have, Cassie wouldn't have known what to say. She was sure Steve felt the same way. After several minutes, he gently kissed the top of her head, broke away, and started up the truck's engine. Cassie was more in control of herself now and wiped her face clear of the tears as she straightened and leaned her head against the passenger-side window.

They must have traveled an hour before Steve spoke. "Garth asked me if you were concerned about the cameo. I didn't know what to tell him."

The cameo. Cassie bit into her lower lip and explained. "My grandfather gave a cameo to our grandmother when they married. As the oldest child, my father inherited the cameo. It's a family treasure and Dad wanted me to have it . . . I don't know what happened to it after I left."

"Garth said Nichole has it."

"Then she should keep it . . . I was the one who left."

A fresh tear escaped and rolled down her cheek.

"I'm sorry . . . I probably shouldn't have said anything."

"No, I'm glad you did . . . I did wonder about it." Her father had been wise not to give it to her. Duke would have taken and sold anything she had that was of any value. He was in constant need of money, though he'd spent whatever he got on himself. If not for government assistance, Cassie was convinced she and Amiee would have starved.

"I told Stan I'd give him a call when we were about an hour outside of Seattle," Steve mentioned sometime later. "He said he'd meet us at the warehouse and help me unload the truck. I'll be able to lock up your things so you won't need to worry about anyone getting into them."

"Thank you," she whispered. Finding the words to voice her appreciation failed her. Steve had done so much already. "As soon as the house is built I'll get it out of your way."

"It won't be in the way, Cassie."

"I don't want to be a burden; you've already been so kind."

Steve snorted. "Don't mistake me for a saint, Cassie Carter, because trust me, I'm not."

When they reached the summit over Snoqualmie Pass, they stopped for a bathroom break. When Cassie exited the restroom, she saw that

Steve was on the phone. He disconnected the call as she approached.

"Stan will meet us in an hour," he announced.

Cassie climbed back into the cab. Steve joined her but didn't start the engine. His hands gripped the steering wheel. "Listen, if I was out of line back there, kissing you, then I apologize."

Cassie could feel her face heat up. "You weren't out of line."

Her answer seemed to relieve him. Reaching over, he took hold of her hand and gave it a gentle squeeze.

"You're a good woman, Cassie."

"I was an extremely foolish one."

"You were young . . ."

"And stupid."

He shook his head as if to discount her words. "Quit beating yourself up over something that happened thirteen years ago."

"I'm trying."

"Try harder."

Cassie smiled for the first time since leaving Spokane. "When did you get to be so dictatorial?" she asked, and then realized what she'd said and added, "No need to answer that. You've always been bossy."

"Have I?" he joked.

"Yes! Don't you remember the first day we met? We clashed right away. Your arrogance rubbed against my stubbornness. To say we started off on the wrong foot is putting it mildly."

He grinned then, too. His hand covered hers and his fingers curled around her own. "I've since had a change of heart."

"Me, too. You aren't so bad, you know."

Steve chuckled. "Interesting that you should say so, because I was thinking the same thing about you."

His phone rang. "Must be Stan," he murmured as he reached for it.

It wasn't.

Although Cassie couldn't make out the other side of the conversation, the voice was clearly female and just as clearly upset. The woman continued on for several seconds before Steve had a chance to speak.

"Listen, Britt, I had a commitment today. I'm sorry that I missed the softball game, but I can't be at every single one."

Britt.

That was the name of the woman from the suite who'd complained when Cassie couldn't get her the brand of beer she wanted—the woman responsible for Cassie losing the job. All at once she understood why Steve had been so willing to help her collect her parents' things. He felt guilty, and driving her to Spokane had simply been his penance.

Her heart sank as an uncanny sense of disappointment bore down on her. This day wasn't about helping her. It was about absolving the guilt Steve felt over what his girlfriend had done. No wonder he was worried about the kiss.

Chapter 20

That night Cassie decided not to go to the home site and work with Habitat on Sunday, as she'd been away from Amiee the whole previous day. Although she was mentally and physically exhausted from her trip to Spokane, she found it difficult to fall asleep. No one needed to tell her what was wrong, or what plagued her.

It was all about her meeting with her sister. And if she was being honest, it was also about Steve's kiss.

All night her mind dwelled on the conversation with Karen and how in the end she'd reluctantly hugged Cassie. When she allowed her mind to drift away from Karen, Cassie was confronted with the disturbing memory of the phone call Steve had gotten from Britt. It seemed clear that he was still involved with the other woman. In retrospect, Cassie was embarrassed by how fervently she'd responded to his kisses. Then again, the entire thing could be excused by the simple fact that she'd been completely overwrought.

It didn't explain why Steve had chosen to kiss her just then, but she was relatively certain he would rather it hadn't happened. In thinking back she remembered that he'd apologized, saying he felt he might have been out of line. She understood now that his real concern was that she might have read more into their exchange than was warranted, and frankly, she had. She was falling for him and it scared her half to death. Having already made one disastrous mistake in love, she wasn't eager to make a second.

When it came to relationships, Cassie was sadly lacking as a judge of character. Steve seemed so stable and responsible compared to Duke, whose life had been in constant upheaval. But then again, Duke had seemed great at first, too. Her mind turned and turned.

"Mom, are you awake?" Cassie woke to find Amiee sitting at the end of her bed.

Sunlight streamed in from the window. Cassie sat up, leaned on one elbow, and rubbed the sleep from her eyes. "What time is it?"

"Past nine."

"You're joking."

"Why would I joke? Are we going to church this morning?"

Cassie tossed aside the covers, shocked that she'd slept so late. It'd taken hours for her to fall asleep, and the last time she'd looked at the clock it had been nearly three. "Yes, of course."

"Are you working at the house later?"

"No." She leaped out of bed and grabbed a shirt and a pair of pants on her way into the bathroom. "I want to spend the day with you."

Right away Amiee brightened. "Are we seeing Steve?"

Cassie froze and glanced back at her daughter. "No. What makes you ask that?"

Her daughter shrugged. "Because we almost always see Steve on the weekends."

"No, we don't. Now hurry and get ready for church."

"Okay, okay. Can we have pancakes for breakfast?"

Her daughter was constantly thinking about her stomach. "If we have time."

"We don't. What about after church?"

"Okay, whenever."

"At IHOP?"

"Amiee . . . we can't afford to eat out."

"Just this once, Mom. Please." Amiee placed her hands in a praying position and pleaded as if this was a matter of national security. "I won't ask again for a really long time. Just this once. I'm so in the mood for blueberry pancakes with that special flavored syrup they have."

"Okay, okay."

"Really?" Amiee rubbed her palms together as if she could barely contain herself. "You mean it? You aren't going to change your mind, are you?"

"Yes, I really mean it."

Her daughter hurried into her tiny bedroom and dressed in record time.

By the time they arrived at church for the nine-thirty service, the music had already started. Amiee immediately joined her friends for the first part of the service and just before the sermon was excused for her Sunday school class. The kids filed out of the sanctuary looking gleeful to escape.

Cassie and Amiee met up following the service, and Amiee was quick to remind Cassie of their earlier discussion. "You ready for pancakes?" her daughter asked, even before they reached the car.

"Ready."

"You're not taking this out of my allowance, are you?" Amiee asked, as her eyes narrowed suspiciously.

Cassie laughed. "No, but now that you mention it, maybe I should."

"Mom!" she protested.

Because she had been upset when Steve dropped her off, Cassie had skipped dinner. By the time they were seated and handed the huge IHOP menus, Cassie found she was ravenous.

Both Amiee and Cassie ordered pancakes— Amiee's with blueberries and Cassie's with whole grains. It'd been far too long since Cassie had spent quality time with her daughter.

Amiee talked nonstop through breakfast, animated and excited. She'd decided that in the new house she wanted to paint her new bedroom a pale teal and wanted blue curtains. Not navy blue but sky blue. She thought the kitchen should be yellow, but she was willing to compromise. Cassie enjoyed listening to her daughter's enthusiasm. Amiee was as excited to have a real home as Cassie herself.

"Can we go to a movie, too?" she asked.

"Not when the weather is this beautiful," Cassie said. The theater would have been the perfect place for her to hide, although she wasn't sure who she wanted to hide from. Possibly from herself?

"The beach, then. Remember how we went to look for seashells . . . That was a long time ago, though."

"Not that long ago, just last year."

"Mom," Amiee said with what sounded like limitless patience. "A year is a long time."

"Is it?" Cassie asked, playing dumb. Shortly after they'd arrived in the Seattle area, Cassie had taken Amiee to West Seattle and the beach there. Technically, it was Puget Sound, but it was as close to the ocean as Amiee had been since an infant in arms. Her daughter had raced up and down the beach, the wind ruffling her hair, as happy as Cassie could ever remember seeing her. At the end of the day, they'd accumulated four pockets full of seashells. Cassie had always wanted to return, but life had gotten complicated and busy. So much for the best intentions.

They climbed back into Cassie's wreck of a car. Amiee sat in the front seat beside her. "Can we stop by the house?"

"The house?" Cassie repeated, a bit confused. "Do you mean our apartment?"

"No, our house or what will be our house. I want to see the yard again."

"There's nothing to see," Cassie reminded Amiee. "It's a section of land, nothing more."

"But it's going to be our home."

"One day."

"Mom, please."

Cassie hesitated and then relented. Considering she'd left Amiee alone so much because of her work with Habitat, Cassie thought it was a good idea for her to have a tangible sense of the goal of this sacrifice. It would help her to understand it wouldn't always be like this.

As soon as Cassie turned the corner leading to the property, she saw Steve's work truck. He was at the site. Right away her heart bounced into her throat, making swallowing difficult.

"Is that Steve?" Amiee asked, peering out the window. "Mom, it's Steve," she said, answering her own question.

"It looks that way," Cassie muttered. She wasn't

up to seeing him again this soon after her emotional breakdown.

"Who's that with him?" her daughter asked.

Cassie saw that he was with a young boy. Apparently, he'd brought him to help clear away debris from the property. A pile of branches was bunched together in the middle of the yard, as if he planned to light a bonfire.

Before Cassie could stop her, Amiee rolled down the window and shouted his name. "Steve. Steve." Then she proceeded to wave frantically at him as though she needed to be rescued.

On hearing his name, Steve glanced up, smiled, and then started walking toward Cassie's car.

Cassie pulled to a stop, and Amiee leaped out of the car and eagerly raced toward him. Cassie groaned inwardly and waited as Steve approached.

He paused momentarily to say something to Amiee, then continued walking toward Cassie. He leaned into the open window on the passenger side, folding his arms. His smile was warm.

"I didn't expect to see you today."

She hadn't expected to see him, either. Of course, sooner or later she would have needed to face him again. Maybe sooner was a good thing. She'd spent half the night trying to figure out what to say.

"It was Amiee's idea to stop off and see the house. I tried to explain that there was no house," she said, laughing, "but she wanted to see the lot, at least."

"No house **yet,** you mean."

"That's what Amiee said." Her gaze flew to her daughter, who was making friends with the boy. He looked to be about six or seven. "Who's your friend?" she asked.

"Britt's son." Steve must have read the look in her eyes. "About that phone call from Britt."

"What phone call?" she asked, realizing she sounded childish but unable to stop herself.

"Britt phoned when we were just outside of Seattle—"

"Steve," she said, stopping him. She reached over and put her hand over his forearm. "Listen, you don't owe me any explanations. It doesn't matter if you're involved with her or not. It's none of my business."

A frown darkened his face. "None of your business?" he repeated.

"Well, yes. We're nothing more than friends."

"Friends?" he repeated, and arched his brows.

He wasn't making this easy. She decided to be direct. "Yes . . . okay, I'll admit matters got a bit out of hand after Spokane, but I was distraught. It didn't mean anything."

"It?" he repeated, again.

"The kiss." She hated that he forced her to say it.

"Kisses," he corrected.

"Whatever." She wanted it understood that she

knew it wasn't a big deal. It happened. It'd been an emotional moment.

"So you'd rather be friends?" he asked, his frown easing up only slightly.

"Of course. Wouldn't you?"

He didn't respond, just looked at her thoughtfully.

The boy squealed with delight and Amiee took off, chasing after him. Steve glanced over his shoulder. "Jeremy's a great kid. Alicia couldn't have children and . . ." He paused as if he'd said more than he'd intended.

"Jeremy needs someone like you." Just from the way the boy looked at Steve, Cassie could tell he idolized him.

"He does. His father is mostly out of the picture. I try to spend time with him once a week or so."

Cassie opened her car door to climb out and the door creaked. Steve frowned and shook his head. "It's amazing this car still runs."

"It's served me well," Cassie said, in the car's defense.

"You need a new one."

"Well, that's not going to happen anytime soon," she said.

"Mom, Mom." Amiee came racing back to Cassie. "Steve is going to build a fire and burn all this wood. Can we roast hot dogs with him and Jeremy?"

"Ah . . ." She looked to Steve.

He shrugged as if it was up to her. "You're welcome to stay if you want."

"We wouldn't be intruding?" This was supposed to be his time with Jeremy.

"Not really. The more, the merrier."

"Can we, Mom, can we?" Amiee pleaded.

Despite all her claims to the contrary, Cassie felt herself drawn in by the idea of spending time with Steve. "Okay."

Amiee and Jeremy cheered wildly. They hugged enthusiastically and then raced around in tight circles. The little boy had certainly captured her daughter's interest. Cassie hadn't realized how well Amiee related to younger kids.

Steve handed Cassie a rake and she started cleaning up the yard, adding leaves and twigs to the bonfire pile.

"Are you sore from moving all that furniture?" she asked, as she gathered an armful of debris to deposit on the pile.

"A little," he confessed. If he admitted that, it must mean he was aching from head to foot.

Keeping her head lowered, Cassie told him, "I'm really grateful for your help, Steve. I couldn't have done it without you." She wasn't just referring to him driving there, and she hoped he knew it.

"Not a problem." He brushed aside her appreciation. "It was something I wanted to do."

"Because of Britt." The words were out before

she could censor herself. She added, "Because of what happened at the Sounders game?"

He didn't answer right away. "Partially, I suppose but I . . ." He let the thought trail off without finishing.

They continued working side by side for a few more minutes in companionable silence. Then he said, "I won't be around this next week."

"Oh?" She experienced an instant sense of loss. She'd miss seeing him, although she couldn't very well admit as much.

"I'm going to be working out of town for the next couple weeks."

"But Saturday's the Hoedown." She wanted to bite back the words the minute they left her mouth.

He smiled. "No worries, I'll be back in town for the Hoedown next Saturday."

"I wasn't worried," she was quick to say, although it was a lie.

He chuckled. "I could tell."

"I understand your construction company is one of the major sponsors." She continued raking, as if getting every last twig and leaf was of immense importance.

"We are. You'll be there, right?"

"I'm working at the event." It would be a fun way to work off a few equity hours.

"But you won't be working the entire time, will you?"

"I . . . I don't know. I don't think so."

"When you're done with your shift, maybe you could save a dance for me . . . you know, us being friends and all."

Cassie grinned. "Yes, I suppose I could manage that."

"Good." He continued to rake, but with far more enthusiasm than he had earlier.

Chapter 21

Tuesday evening Karen tossed her car keys into the basket just inside the garage door. Garth was busy in the kitchen fixing dinner—God bless him! For the last two weeks, he'd been home by the time she arrived. Seeing that he was salaried, his shorter hours hadn't made a difference in his paycheck, thankfully.

"Hi, sweetie," Garth said, looking up from the salad he was mixing. "How was work today?"

"Busy." She reached over and grabbed a radish, munching it. "What about you?"

Garth expelled a sigh. "Okay, I guess. I'm still working on the Weyerhaeuser account."

Karen kissed her husband's cheek and reached for another radish. "You've been working on that same account for months." He'd never talked much about work, and most of the time she had to pry information out of him.

"The job is winding down now, which is good and bad."

"Any new work on the horizon?"

"Some." He continued to slice the tomatoes.

Garth's job as a consultant for one of the large lumber companies had been demanding in the past. The company had gone through a slump over the last few years as less and less timber was harvested in Washington state, but thankfully there'd always been enough work to keep her husband in a job.

"What's for dinner?" Karen asked, glancing toward the stove.

"Spanish rice."

"Buddy's favorite," Karen said, smiling. Garth had served it twice in the last couple weeks, and with Buddy going through a growing spurt, there were rarely leftovers.

"I want to call my sister before we eat," Karen said, as she slipped out of her heels and wiggled life back into her toes. "There's enough time, isn't there?"

Garth glanced up. "You're calling Cassie?"

"Nichole. I haven't told her about the weekend yet. I was avoiding her calls—I guess I just needed time to digest it all."

"I thought after your sister left that you said you wanted to make an effort to connect more often."

"I do," she said.

Her husband braced his palms against the kitchen counter and his look grew intense. "You haven't been sleeping well the last couple nights since Cassie's visit."

Garth was right; she'd been uneasy ever since their visit with Cassie. When she'd learned Cassie was coming to Spokane, she'd been determined to remain aloof and distant. Karen had never been able to forget the huge fight they'd had shortly before Cassie disappeared. Her sister had said things that Karen would never be able to forgive. Cassie must have shared her feelings, since nothing else explained the cold silence for the last eight years. When they did hear from Cassie again it hadn't been to apologize. She'd made no reconciliation efforts. Instead she'd been looking for a handout. She was in trouble and needed help. Well, where was Cassie when their parents needed her? Nowhere to be found—that was for sure.

As Saturday had approached, Karen had grown anxious. She wanted to meet Cassie, take her to the storage unit, and send her on her way. Garth had been the one to suggest they at least offer Cassie and her friend lunch. Karen had reluctantly agreed.

And then Cassie arrived. One look assured Karen that her sister was as nervous and anxious as she was herself. Karen had steeled herself, hoping to get this meeting over with as quickly as possible.

Yet Cassie was nothing like what she'd anticipated. Oh, she looked basically the same . . . only different. She'd come a long way from that rebellious, headstrong teenager she'd once been. Her sister seemed so much more mature and wise, humble and gracious. When Cassie broke into tears at the storage unit, emotion she tried desperately to hide, Karen had fought back tears herself.

"Are you going to suggest Nichole reach out to Cassie?" Garth asked, cutting into Karen's thoughts.

"I . . . I don't know yet."

Karen got her cell from her purse and sat down in the living room. She dialed Nichole, and sitting back in the chair, she crossed her legs and waited. While the phone rang, Garth brought her a tall glass of iced tea, with a thick slice of lemon on top, and she smiled at him.

Nichole answered on the second ring. "Hey!"

"Hi, Nichole."

"I've been hoping to hear from you. How did it go with Cassie?"

Karen hardly knew where to begin. "It went . . . okay." Even now she wavered, uncertain of her feelings. She was conflicted, sad, weary, and she stifled the urge to cry.

"What was she like?"

"Well, she's obviously grown up like the two of us. I can see so much of Dad in her. She's definitely got his eyes."

"What about . . . everything else?"

This was a far more difficult question to answer. "She's not angry or defiant any longer, determined to prove how she's right and everyone else is wrong. My memories of her revolved around how angry she was, how eager to argue with Mom and Dad, especially over Duke. She'd always been so smart, and then, after she met Duke, she became a completely different person."

"I remember her that way, too. What's she like now?"

Karen searched for how best to respond. "She seems much more . . . humble."

"Cassie, humble?"

"She's thankful for every little thing," Karen rushed to explain. "We had lunch ready for her—"

"You cooked lunch? I thought—"

"I know," she said, cutting her off. "Garth thought it was the least we could do. The truth is I was sure she would have eaten before they arrived and it would be moot."

"Was it awkward having her there?"

It had been, especially in the beginning. "We were both on edge. You know, other than a few short, painful phone conversations, I haven't talked to her in years."

"So what did you have to talk about?"

"Mostly we talked about our kids. She was eager to hear every detail I had to tell her about Lily and Buddy. She showed me pictures of Amiee and you wouldn't believe how much her daughter looks like her . . . and Dad. She mentioned that Amiee is full of questions about her cousins. From what she said, we're the only family Amiee has. I asked about Duke's side, and from what Cassie said, she never met any of his relatives. Odd, don't you think? Anyway, she said they aren't in contact anymore."

Karen had realized later that in her nervousness at lunch she'd missed a lot, and was able to read a bit more between the lines. "She didn't talk much about Duke, but I have the feeling this marriage wasn't a happy one from the very beginning."

"Yet she stayed."

"Yes, she stayed." Karen couldn't help wondering what price she'd paid for her pride. It was more than obvious that Cassie had come out of the marriage with nothing.

Nichole was quiet for a moment, as though taking time to absorb the conversation. "Did Cassie ask about . . . anything?"

By "anything," her sister seemed to be asking about far more than the cameo or the inheritance. "No, nothing. She was overwhelmed with gratitude with what we gave her. It meant the world to her to have the very things neither you nor I considered important."

"The piano was worth something, but we both knew she would want that."

"I'm glad we decided to give it to her." Karen's

throat clogged with the memory of how happy Cassie had been to see the piano. It was right in front when Garth opened the door to the storage unit. Cassie's reaction had been immediate and overwhelming.

"We hugged before she left." That was a slight exaggeration. Cassie had reached out and hugged her. It took a moment before Karen had hugged her back. They'd both struggled with tears. Karen had been determined to keep an emotional distance from Cassie, and yet brick by brick that wall was beginning to be dismantled.

"You hugged. So what happens now?"

"I don't know yet," Karen hurried to explain. "But I think we need to be open to Cassie. We don't need to rush into anything. We should take this slow, a little at a time. Perhaps you could phone her."

"Me? What about you? You're the one who's communicated with her most. I hardly know her."

"The thing is," Karen said, "we don't know her and she doesn't really know us, either, but I think it's time we changed that."

The sliding glass door slammed and Buddy came into the house, automatically going to the refrigerator. He opened it up, reached for the pitcher of iced tea, and drank straight from it.

"Buddy!" Karen shouted, appalled at their son's behavior. She looked for Garth and saw that he was no longer in the kitchen.

Her son whirled around, obviously surprised to see her. "Oh, hi, Mom."

"I've got to go," Karen told Nichole, frowning at her son.

"Okay." Nichole sounded eager to get off the phone herself.

"Call me soon and we'll talk more about what comes next with Cassie."

"I'll be in Arizona."

"Arizona?"

"I'm going with Laurie. Jake arranged for us to stay at this exclusive spa. I'll be away five days. I still can hardly believe it."

"Wow! Have fun."

Nichole sighed. "We plan to. I swear I'm married to the most wonderful husband."

"We both married good men," Karen added. Her thoughts instantly went to Cassie, and she wondered what had happened with Duke. Karen wasn't entirely sure she wanted to know. Perhaps one day Cassie would tell her.

"We'll connect soon," Karen said, as she ended the call. "Have a great time in Arizona."

By the time she set down the phone, Buddy had put the pitcher back inside the refrigerator.

"Where's your father?" Karen asked.

Buddy, his face red and sweaty from a game of neighborhood baseball, shrugged. "He was on his cell like you."

Karen went in search of Garth and found him in the far end of the backyard, pacing by the fence line, his head bowed and shoulders hunched, and deep in conversation. He looked up when Karen approached.

"I have to go," he said to whoever was on the other end of the line. "Yes, yes, I understand, but there's nothing I can do about it now. I'll call you in the morning." Her husband didn't look the least bit pleased. His face tightened as he listened. "Okay, okay," he said, and snapped the phone shut. For a moment it looked as if he was about to toss it down on the grass in a fit of anger.

Garth was an easygoing sort of guy, and to hear him this upset was a rarity.

"Everything okay?" Karen asked.

Garth shook his head. "It's just work."

"Problems?"

"You could say that," he muttered, and then surprised Karen by reaching for her and wrapping his arms around her and holding her close as if he needed someone to cling to.

"Garth?" she asked, because it was obvious that something was terribly wrong.

"It's nothing. Just leave it, okay?"

This, too, was uncharacteristic of her husband. Karen hugged him back and after a few minutes they returned to the house with their arms around each other.

Buddy had set the table without being asked, which was a shocker, thought Karen, smiling. "Where's Lily?"

"She's got dance class this afternoon."

Garth froze. "It's not my turn to pick her up, is it?"

"No, you drove last week," Karen reminded him.

Garth released a slow exhale. "I'm telling you I need a personal assistant to keep track of whose turn it is to drive in all these carpools." He brought out the salad he'd mixed and set it in the middle of the table.

As if on cue, the front door opened and Lily came in and dropped her backpack just inside the door. "I had the worst day of my entire life," she complained with a loud groan. "Michael turned twelve and got a Facebook account and the first thing he did was post a horrible picture of me and now people are sharing it."

"Oh boy. It looks like you could use a hug," Garth said to his daughter.

"Oh, Dad, a hug isn't going to help."

"Sure it will," he countered. "A hug always helps."

Karen dished up the Spanish rice and removed the green beans from the microwave.

"Spanish rice again?" Lily complained.

"Hey, hey, count your blessings. We could be

having liver and onions. That's what my mom always made."

Lily's head came up and she grimaced. "That is just gross."

"Count your blessings," Karen repeated, as the four of them sat down at the table for the evening meal and joined hands.

The banter around the table was lively. It wasn't until later that Karen realized that Garth had had very little to say. As they readied for bed that night, she noticed how withdrawn he'd become. Whatever had happened at work had deeply bothered him.

Both read for a half hour or so before turning out the bedside lights. As soon as it was dark, Garth reached for her.

"I love you, Karen."

"I know. I love you, too." She nestled her head against her husband's shoulder. But it was a long time before she went to sleep, and she knew it took just as long for Garth, too.

Chapter 22

Steve hated the thought of leaving town for even one day, let alone five. Normally he looked forward to these short business trips even if he was troubleshooting a job. Not this time.

The simple truth was he hated to leave Cassie. While she might choose to deny it, something strong and powerful was happening between them. He hadn't stopped to analyze it, mainly because it felt too good. It was as if his heart had come alive again. After Alicia died, for all intents and purposes it seemed as if he had as well—at least emotionally. For the first year he'd had to will himself to get out of bed each day. It felt as if there were heavy weights attached to his feet and his heart.

It didn't seem right that the world kept on going as if nothing of significance had happened. He fought it, struggled with depression, let business matters lapse when he should have been paying more attention. Thankfully, Stan had his back and did for Steve what Steve seemed incapable of doing for himself.

It was partially because of Stan that he'd gotten involved with Habitat for Humanity. His general manager had left Brody Electrical for a full-time position with Habitat, working as a project manager. Stan had half dragged Steve to the first job site. Steve hadn't been a willing volunteer until he saw how hard these families worked to have a home to call their own.

Alicia had strongly believed in the work of Habitat and had volunteered countless hours herself. For the last two and a half years, working with Habitat had been his salvation. He'd been able to pull himself out of the black hole of grief and loss by investing in others. Stan trusted him to run the housing projects from start to finish, stopping by every now and again to make sure the building was coming along as it should.

Then Steve had met Cassie. They'd clashed in the beginning, and looking back, he realized why. Right away he knew she was a threat to his shriveled-up, dried-out heart. It'd been only in the last year that he'd been comfortable in this new role life had given him. He wasn't big on change, and then there she was with her purple hair and a chip on her shoulder, challenging him at every turn. She didn't back down and she made sure he understood that she wasn't going to let anyone, in particular a man, railroad her.

He'd been attracted to her, almost from the first, and then he'd decided to drive her to Spokane. Even now he wasn't sure what had happened on Saturday. It'd never been his intention to kiss her. But to witness this strong, independent woman dissolve into heart-wrenching sobs had shaken him. When he'd pulled into the rest stop he'd meant to only hug and hold her, to comfort her. Before he could stop himself, they were kissing. Rarely had anything felt as good or right as to have Cassie in his arms.

Now it was Wednesday and the feeling of holding her still lingered with him. She'd tasted of sweetness and goodness and everything he held dear. This was a woman who had walked through fire and instead of coming out scorched and bitter was as refined as gold.

Seeing her Sunday had been an unexpected bonus, although he had to admit she'd shaken him with her talk of just being friends. He got it. He really did. She was scared. Frankly, so was he. This was as new to him as it seemed to be to her.

The truth was he'd planned to give them both a bit of breathing room. Sunday morning he'd picked up Jeremy and intended to take the boy to a park where he could ride his bike, which they'd done. Later he'd gone to the plot of land that would one day be Cassie's home because—

this was a bit embarrassing—it was a way to feel a connection with her. Jeremy had enjoyed building a fort with dead branches from the property, and so they'd lingered there.

And then Cassie arrived with Amiee. Right away happiness had stolen over him, and while the early afternoon had been overcast and cloudy, it felt as if the entire day had suddenly brightened and grown unexpectedly sunny and warm.

While Steve wasn't sure where the relationship between him and Cassie was headed, he was content to let it take him where it would. In time she'd come around. He was willing to be patient. Maybe going out of town was good—it would give her some time.

"Steve," his foreman said, breaking into his thoughts.

Steve shook his head, shocked that he'd been lost in his own world. "Yes, sorry."

"Do you have another appointment?" Charlie Lane asked. The job was with Grand Coulee Dam in eastern Washington, wheat country. They were a small company compared to the other bidders, and Steve had considered himself fortunate to get the contract. He had a good estimator who'd brought in a highly competitive bid. Now, however, Steve's company was losing money and it was the fault of the supplier. Steve had gone in to troubleshoot the project and stay long enough to make sure the job was back on schedule before he headed back to Tacoma for the Hoedown on Saturday night.

"Another appointment?" Steve asked, repeating the question. "What makes you ask?"

"You keep looking at your watch."

He was looking at the time, wondering how long it would be before he could talk to Cassie. He had forced himself not to call her for the last three days—she seemed to need some space, and he didn't want to scare her off. All he could do was hope that she missed seeing him as much as he missed being with her.

Originally he'd intended to wait out the entire week. Then that morning he'd woken with a strong desire to hear the sound of Cassie's voice. If he called, he would need to wait until early evening, when he was sure she'd finished work at Goldie Locks, and then give her a couple extra hours in case she was putting in her time with Habitat.

"I have a phone call to make," Steve explained.

"Do you want to wait to go over these schematics?" Charlie asked.

"No, now is good."

By the time Steve was back in his run-down hotel room, he felt like a compulsive smoker who'd put off having a cigarette until the end of the day. Sitting on the edge of the bed, he reached for his cell and noticed that his fingers actually shook in their eagerness to connect with Cassie.

Her cell rang three times with no answer, and

Steve was convinced it was about to go to voice mail. Should he leave a message? Or should he wait and try again later? Before he could decide, the line connected.

"Hello."

This wasn't Cassie. It didn't seem possible that he had the wrong number. "Amiee?"

"Oh, hi, Steve." The twelve-year-old sounded bright and cheerful, happy to hear from him.

"Where's your mom?"

"She's in the shower. I can get her if you want. She never takes long because the hot water turns cold real fast."

"I can call back later."

"No, don't, because she's been in a real funk ever since you left. You're her BAE, you know."

"Her what?"

"BAE. **B**efore **A**nyone **E**lse."

Steve couldn't help it—he broke into a huge smile. "Really?"

"Yeah, she's eaten oatmeal for breakfast three days straight and she hates oatmeal. Hold on a minute and I'll tell her you're on the phone."

Steve heard the sound of Amiee setting down the phone and then, a minute later, her calling her mother. "Mom, your phone rang and I answered it."

A short silence followed in which Cassie asked who was calling.

Amiee answered, "Steve." Another silence followed before Amiee picked up the phone. "Mom said she'd be here right away. She told me to talk to you until she gets dried off."

"So how's school?" he asked.

"Okay, I guess. My friend Claudia asked me to go to a concert with her and Mom wants to listen to the group's lyrics before she'll agree to let me go. All bands use swear words, you know. If she insists there be no swearing I'll never go to a concert for my entire life."

"I agree with your mom on that one," Steve told her.

"You adults stick together, don't you?" She didn't sound angry as much as resigned. "Here's Mom."

He smiled when he heard Cassie say his name breathlessly. "Steve?"

"Hi, there." He could almost hear Cassie's heart pounding. What she didn't know was that his own was just as loud in his ears.

"Hi, Steve."

He didn't really have a good excuse to call. "How are things going on your end? Have you been to the building site this week yet?"

"Every day. Everything is coming together so quickly. The foundation got poured this afternoon. I wasn't really able to help much, but I stayed close by. All the while I kept thinking, **This is going to be Amiee's and my house!** I find that unbelievable." She said this all in one giant breath.

"The work is only just getting started."

"Stan was there, supervising everyone."

Steve had personally asked his best friend to fill in for him. Stan was a good man and Steve trusted him to see that the work was up to his own high standards.

"Shelly and George stopped by, too. They've finished their equity hours but came anyway."

"They're good people." He savored hearing the joy in her voice.

"How are you doing?" she asked. "I hope you were able to resolve whatever the problem was at work."

"It's all good." He didn't dare admit he was lonely and bored. "Were you busy at work?"

"Three haircuts, a color job, plus two perms, so yes, you can say I was busy, which is good. I'm building up my clientele, which helps with my finances. Once I have regular customers I'll be able to make a decent living and I won't need to worry so much."

"You're a good stylist, Cassie. In fact, I was thinking I should book another haircut."

"You don't need to do that. I'd be happy to cut your hair anytime."

"Tell him, Mom." Steve could hear Amiee pleading with her mother in the background.

"Tell me what?" he asked.

"It's nothing."

"Cassie." He whispered her name low and deep. "Tell me."

He heard her exhale as if bracing herself. "I heard from Duke . . . a letter."

Cassie's ex-husband, the bastard who'd beat her. "He knows where you live?" God help him if he learned Duke ever came near Cassie again. He didn't know what he would do, and whatever it was would probably land him in jail.

"No . . . he has no way of knowing where Amiee and I live. The letter took six weeks to reach me. Duke wrote to the neighbor lady, an older woman who was more his friend than mine, but a friend. Doris took the letter to the women's shelter and they forwarded it to me."

"And?"

"Duke's in prison for manslaughter charges. He'll be there for a very long time."

"Good. So what did Duke want?" If he wanted Cassie back, the brute would have a real fight on his hands.

"He said that he loved me and Amiee."

Steve snorted with disbelief. "You don't beat the people you love."

"I know."

"Are you going to write him back?"

"No. I've learned my lesson. I can't believe a word he says and I won't put myself or my daughter in a position to be hurt again."

"Smart decision."

"But Duke did say one thing that gave me pause. Hold on a minute . . . let me step outside."

Steve heard some movement as Cassie had stepped outside of her apartment.

"Are you still there?" she asked. "I just wanted to go out here where Amiee can't overhear."

"I'm here. Tell me what's got you concerned." The muscles in his neck were tense.

She hesitated. "Duke asked about Amiee . . . he said he's done a lot of stupid things in his life but the only good thing was marrying me and fathering Amiee. He said he understood if I didn't want anything more to do with him, and I don't. Duke is completely out of my life."

"Yes?" said Steve.

"Toward the end he believed every bad thing that had happened to him was somehow my fault. If he lost his job, he blamed me, if he stubbed his toe, I had somehow caused it to happen. If I stayed I'm convinced he would have . . ." She sighed. "Oh, never mind."

"He would have murdered you," Steve finished for her.

"Yes." Her voice became a broken whisper. "If I hadn't fled the night I did, I believe Duke would be in prison for murdering me. I'm as convinced of that as I am of standing right here talking to you."

"Then why would you even consider having anything more to do with him?" Steve asked, fighting back outrage.

"Not me. Amiee. He said he loves his daughter

and wants her in his life. He pleaded with me to allow him to at least write her."

Steve hesitated. "Do you know what you're going to do?"

"No, I have no idea. I protected Amiee . . . she was too young to fully understand what was happening between her father and me. Even when we were living in the shelter, she asked when we could go home again. She said she missed her daddy."

Steve knew he wasn't in a position to give her advice on this question. It was a decision Cassie had to make on her own.

"I'm so glad you called," Cassie whispered. "I've been upset the last few days over this. I needed a friend to talk to, a sounding board."

Friend. Steve was beginning to hate that word.

"And I'm glad you confided in me. You can trust me, Cassie. I won't let you down."

She didn't say anything for a long moment, long enough that Steve wasn't sure she'd heard him. "Cassie?"

"Thank you," she said.

Chapter 23

Nichole and her best friend, Laurie, landed in Phoenix Friday afternoon and stood in line for a taxi that would deliver them to the Phoenician Garden Hotel and Spa. It was ninety-eight degrees, in stark contrast to the mid-sixties and rain drenching Portland, Oregon.

"I am going to soak in this sunshine," Nichole said, as she dragged her suitcase out of the airport and toward the taxi line. She closed her eyes and raised her chin, letting the warmth wash over her upturned face. "I can't tell you how much I need this break."

"Me, too," Laurie agreed. "Thank you so much for bringing me! I can't believe that Jake was able to get us the prices he did."

"He's the best," Nichole said. Laurie's gratitude

was touching, but this long spa weekend wouldn't have been nearly as much fun alone. And it would be fun, even if she already missed Owen. He'd cried when she'd left him with her mother-in-law, but Leanne had been delighted to have this special time with her only grandchild. Nichole had half expected Jake to regret arranging this, but he'd been in good spirits that morning when he'd dropped her off at the airport. They'd hugged and kissed before he had to hurry to the office.

Their turn for the taxi finally came, and none too soon. Standing this long in the intense sun had become uncomfortable, though Nichole laughed at herself, given that she'd been uncomfortably chilled just a few hours ago. Nichole gave the driver the name of the spa and off they went.

When they arrived, the outside of the hotel was everything the Internet site had promised. The valet opened the cab door, and even before they could ask, a bellman wheeled a cart to the car and collected their luggage. They were escorted to the front desk, where a clerk greeted Nichole.

Nichole was agog. She turned a full circle, gazing at their lush surroundings. The lobby was luxurious and inviting, with marble floors and pillars and deep-cushioned chairs and sofas.

Standing at the front desk, Nichole and Laurie signed themselves in. Within a matter of minutes they were handed their room keys and personally escorted to the elevator.

"This is unbelievable," Laurie whispered, as they arrived at their room. She plopped down on the bed, her arms spread-eagled as she was nearly buried in the lush white bedding.

"It's even better than what I expected," Nichole agreed. She walked to the window and looked out over the view of the expansive swimming pool with its Caribbean-colored water. The area surrounding the pool was a thick green lawn with small white tents set up as areas of shade. Several sun worshippers took advantage of a refreshing dip in the water, cooling themselves off from the heat.

"Let's go down to the pool," Nichole suggested. She'd call Jake and let him know that they'd arrived safely. Later, she'd check on Owen, too, and see how Leanne was faring. Nichole didn't want Leanne to feel she took her generosity for granted. She wanted Leanne to know how much she appreciated her willingness to look after Owen. Although Nichole was reluctant to admit it, it felt incredibly strange to be away from her son. They were together 24/7 and he'd become her entire world.

As soon as they unpacked their suitcases and changed into their swimsuits, they were out the door. First thing the next morning, their spa time would start, and Nichole could barely wait. Her goal was to get a good start on chipping away at this baby fat—she really wanted to get rid of it before she got pregnant a second time.

They ordered lemon drops, which were the perfect complement to their afternoon. They lazed out by the pool, dipping in to cool off, and later retreated to one of the cabanas with two padded lounge chairs. Laurie napped, and while her friend dozed Nichole reached for her phone and called her husband. Jake answered right away.

"Hello, my darling," she said, her heart bursting with love and appreciation for her husband.

"Hi, sweetheart. I take it you've arrived safe and sound."

"We did. The sign at the airport said it was ninety-eight degrees, but it hardly feels that warm."

"Low humidity," Jake said.

"Laurie and I are by the pool with our drinks. This feels so decadent; you shouldn't spoil me this way, Jake."

"You, my beautiful wife, deserve to be spoiled."

Nichole smiled.

"Okay, sweetheart. Listen, I'd better get back to work. Will you call me tonight?" Jake asked. He sounded distracted.

"Of course. You aren't going to be working late again, are you?"

Jake expelled a long sigh. "I might not have a choice. You know what it's like here at the winery, with the spring release."

Nichole did. "Don't work too hard." Her husband gave a hundred and ten percent at his job.

"Bye, my love," she whispered, before disconnecting.

As she hung up, her phone pinged with a text message. It was from her sister, Karen. She read the few words and frowned.

"Trouble?" Laurie asked Nichole.

"It's my sister. She asked if I'd called Cassie yet. We've talked a couple times since Karen saw Cassie, and she's been encouraging me to get in touch with her." Nichole had been putting it off. She wasn't sure why, other than the fact that she didn't know what to say. Her memories of Cassie were tainted by that last dreadful summer when it seemed their entire family had imploded because of her. Nichole had been only fourteen at the |time.

What she'd never told anyone, not even Karen, was that Nichole had found Cassie's journal and read it. She'd found the entry in which Cassie wrote that Duke had made love to her for the first time. She'd said how badly it had hurt, but that it was better the second time. Then she'd read a later entry where Cassie had written that she feared she was pregnant. When she returned the book, she must have put it in the wrong place, because Cassie knew someone had moved it.

And she knew who'd read it, too. The look she gave Nichole said as much: a look of disgust and anger that cut Nichole to the quick.

It was the very next night that Cassie ran away with Duke.

Nichole's throat tightened. She'd never said a word to anyone else for fear she was the one who'd caused Cassie to leave. And she'd always been hurt that Cassie didn't trust her enough to not tell their parents. Cassie had left a note saying she was pregnant, so in the end, Nichole never had to say anything about the journal. Her parents and sister never knew it had been no surprise to her.

Nichole looked up and noticed Laurie studying her. "You okay?"

"Sorry . . . I was. What were we talking about?" She knew exactly what the topic had been.

"Your sister. Karen wanted you to call Cassie, but why doesn't Cassie contact you?"

"Good question." When she first moved to Seattle, Cassie had reached out to Nichole. The conversation had been brief and tense. Nichole hadn't known what to say and it seemed Cassie didn't, either. Cassie had congratulated her on being a new mother, and soon afterward the conversation had dwindled to an embarrassed silence as they each searched for some way to connect. Nichole had felt that if she asked Cassie any questions about her life now, Cassie would cut her off again. At the same time she had too much pride to show a lot of interest in the sister who'd not bothered to stay in touch for years. They hadn't talked since.

Laurie asked a couple more questions, which Nichole answered with one-word replies. She didn't want to talk about Cassie, didn't want to dredge up the past, especially when it was so unpleasant.

After several futile attempts at conversation, Laurie brought out her e-reader. Nichole reclined the lounger and decided to nap—her day had started early and she was tired. She closed her eyes and let her mind wander, but her thoughts went straight to Cassie.

Cassie had been with her when Nichole, at age ten, had gotten badly cut when she fell through the sliding glass door. She could still remember it vividly—once she saw the amount of blood, Nichole had panicked. Cassie had been calm and reassuring, taking care of everything, including calling the paramedics. Afterward, at the hospital, once Nichole had been stitched up, Cassie had started to shake and had tears in her eyes as she confessed how frightened she'd been. Nichole would never have guessed it.

It was Cassie who'd helped her understand geometry, too. Her sister had patiently sat at her side and explained it in a way that made sense, far better than their math teacher ever had. It was Karen who'd taught her about makeup, but Cassie was the one who helped her put together cool outfits. She also helped her do her hair.

The memories unsettled her and Nichole sat

up, intent on putting Cassie out of her mind. It was now after Owen's nap time—she'd call her mother-in-law.

Leanne answered on the second ring. She sounded a bit breathless, as if she'd been chasing after her grandson. "Is Owen wearing you out?" Nichole asked, concerned.

"I prefer to think he's keeping me young," Leanne told her with a soft laugh.

"I bet after a day with Owen you're wondering why I need to lose weight. You'd think I'd be as skinny as a toothpick," Nichole joked. "But I want to lose these ridiculous five pounds before Jake and I have a second baby."

"You're going to try to get pregnant again soon?" Leanne asked, not bothering to hide her delight.

"We've talked about it." She wasn't sure she should have said anything just yet—it was really Jake's place to share this with his family. Nichole liked her in-laws, but she hadn't bonded with them the way she would have liked. Leanne was nice but oblivious—Jake's father had run around on her for years. Nichole and Jake hadn't been dating long when she'd first heard the rumors.

"Another grandbaby would be wonderful," said Leanne.

Nichole hoped for a girl, because Jake and she intended on having only two. Having the two close like this was a necessity; if she was going to be home full-time when her children were little, she wanted to have them close in age, so she could go back to work before too much time had passed. Her degree was in French literature, which hadn't proved to be much of an employable skill, but Nichole was determined to find a way to make use of it. She loved all things French. She wasn't sure how to do that just yet, but she'd figure it out.

They ended the call and Nichole reached for her own e-reader, although she wasn't sure it would hold her attention. Laurie lounged next to her, reading as well. This was the sign of a strong friendship, Nichole thought. They were content to be together without having to chat the whole time.

Nichole's phone dinged with another text message. She reached for it and sighed with exasperation. "Karen again," she announced, before Laurie could ask. "She's waiting for an answer."

"She's going to be a pest until you call Cassie, so just do it," Laurie advised.

Her friend was right. Karen wasn't going to let up until Nichole reached out to Cassie. She needed to put aside her dread and just do it, like Laurie advised, so she could enjoy her vacation.

Karen had included Cassie's cell number with the text, which saved Nichole the hassle of finding it. Her hand shook slightly as she pressed the button that would connect her with her sister. While the phone rang, she rummaged through her brain, searching for how best to start the conversation.

"Hello." Cassie sounded hesitant, unsure. Nichole wondered if her number was saved in her sister's phone, and if her name had popped up.

Nichole barely remembered the sound of her sister's voice. It was hard to believe this was Cassie, her own flesh and blood.

"Cassie, it's Nichole."

"Nichole." Right away Cassie's voice elevated with glad excitement. "Oh Nichole, it's so good to hear from you."

"You, too, Cassie," she said, and genuinely meant it. She immediately felt bad. She should have made the effort to connect with her sister long before now. Already her mind was full of all the things she wanted to tell her, to explain.

"The last time we talked," Cassie continued, "it sounded like you'd rather I didn't bother you."

"I'm sorry . . . it was a shock hearing from you," Nichole said, making up a weak excuse and then feeling sorry she had. It shouldn't be this difficult to tell the truth.

"I know. I would have called again, but I assumed you'd rather not hear from me."

Unfortunately, Cassie was right. "It was a few months after Mom died and I wasn't myself." Again, a half-truth.

Cassie's voice dipped. "I know. I wasn't myself, either."

Nichole was afraid her voice was about to betray her. She yearned to say more but was worried the words wouldn't be able to make it past the lump in her throat.

"I know you and Karen were upset with me that I couldn't be at Mom's funeral. I would have given anything I owned to be with you, but it was impossible."

"None of that matters now," Nichole whispered. Because she was afraid to say anything more about their mother or their last conversation, she quickly changed the subject. "Karen said you were over to the house last weekend."

"A friend drove me and we collected Mom and Dad's furniture. I can't tell you how grateful I am. I had no idea you still had the piano. I was sure Mom would have sold it long ago."

"Dad wouldn't let her," Nichole told her. "He was convinced you'd come back one day."

Her words were met with a sudden, abrupt silence, and then it sounded as if Cassie had stopped breathing.

"I shouldn't have said that," Nichole whispered. She'd known her calling Cassie would be a bad idea. She was going about this all wrong, saying the wrong things, upsetting this tentative start between the sisters. "I'm sorry."

"No, no, it's all right," Cassie said. She seemed to have found her composure. "I just want you to know how grateful I am to have it."

What Nichole said was true. Their father refused to sell the piano with the hope that one day

Cassie would return home. He never seemed to give up on her, even though her leaving had devastated him. Before he died, he let both Karen and Nichole know that he'd forgiven Cassie for running away with Duke. In fact, he blamed himself that there'd been no contact through the years. Nothing anyone said could convince him otherwise. But Nichole would never tell Cassie this—she couldn't lay that on her sister.

"It was good to see Karen and Garth." Cassie, too, seemed determined to turn the conversation to more pleasant topics. "Lily and Buddy were away for the afternoon. Hopefully, they'll be there next time and Amiee will meet her cousins. How are Jake and Owen?"

"Great. I'm with a friend this weekend, so Owen is with Jake's mom."

"That's wonderful."

"Anything exciting happening with you?" Nichole asked, struggling to keep the conversation going.

"Well, I'm going to a hoedown on Saturday."

"A what?"

Cassie laughed. "I know it sounds crazy, doesn't it? It's a charity event for Habitat for Humanity. I'm working it . . . did Karen tell you that I'm getting a house through Habitat? Amiee and I are going to have our very own home for the first time in her life. Every time I think about how much my life has changed in the last few years I get goose bumps. It just doesn't seem real that I should be this fortunate."

Nichole hardly knew how to respond. "You sound happy."

"I am, oh Nichole, I am happy, and hearing from you doubles my joy. Thank you for calling. It means the world to me."

A lump in Nichole's throat grew to the size of a golf ball. "I should have reached out much sooner. I won't wait so long next time." She had a dozen questions she wanted to ask, but she feared it would destroy this fragile thread that felt so tentative. How was it that after all this time Cassie would come out of her marriage with so little? Although Cassie had never come out and said it, Nichole had the feeling Duke hadn't been the husband Cassie deserved.

"Can I . . . would it be all right if I called you next?" Cassie asked.

"Yes, of course. Please do."

"Bye, now."

"Bye." Nichole ended the call to find Laurie closely watching her.

"How'd it go?" her friend asked, carefully studying her.

Nichole covered her mouth for fear she was about to break down and cry. "Better than I expected," she whispered, and then swallowed down a sniffle. "My sister is heading to a hoedown this weekend," she said, in an effort to make light of the conversation. The last thing Nichole wanted was to sit by this beautiful pool and cry. And yet that was exactly what she was doing—tears leaked from the corners of her eyes and wove crooked paths down her cheeks. How could she have been so insensitive to her own sister?

Chapter 24

All week Cassie had worked feverishly to put Steve out of her mind, but it hadn't worked. She couldn't wait to see him, and a week had never dragged on for so long. Nothing felt the same without him at the construction site, running the project.

Saturday morning, Cassie was up early. The Hoedown was being held in an airport hangar, and a lot of work had to be done in order to get the space ready. Several other volunteers arrived to work off their hours by putting up long folding tables and chairs, placing red-and-white checkered plastic tablecloths across the tables, and then setting the tables, lining each place setting up perfectly.

To the front of the hangar was a mechanical bull quartered off with stacks of hay. In the middle of the room were tables displaying items for the silent auction. Cassie was touched by the number of companies and individuals that had donated. It made her hope that sometime soon she'd be in a position to help others in the same way she had been lent a hand up. At the other end of the hangar was a stage with room for the band, plus a faux jail for funny pictures. People could stand behind the bars and have their snapshot taken.

Steve had said on Wednesday he'd definitely see her at the Hoedown. She could only hope nothing had kept him in eastern Washington longer than he anticipated. His electrical company was one of the major sponsors, so she was pretty sure he'd make at least a token appearance.

Cassie feared that telling Steve about the letter from Duke had upset him. He'd grown quiet after asking her what she intended to do, and it wasn't long afterward that he'd made a convenient excuse to end the conversation.

By the time the work crew finished with the setup, it was mid-morning. Cassie didn't have a chance to relax, though—she was scheduled to work at Goldie Locks until three that afternoon. Amiee had gone camping with her friend Claudia's family for the weekend. It was her daughter's first camping experience and she was excited. Claudia was back to being her BFF—or was that BAE?

The apartment felt empty without her when Cassie returned from work. After quickly showering, she dressed and paid special attention to her hair and makeup. This was a big night for Habitat and for her, and she wanted to look her best.

Steve had said he wanted a dance. He'd just been making conversation, but her mind had blown it up into something it was never meant to be. One night she'd actually dreamed of them dancing together. Steve's arms had been around her, holding her against him as though he never intended to let her go. The dream had been so good that when she woke, she had wanted to hang on to it for as long as possible, lingering in bed with her eyes closed, reliving it. Several minutes passed before she forced herself out of bed.

Once she was dressed and ready, she drove to the Hoedown. By the time she arrived back at the hangar, her stomach was in knots. It wasn't nerves about her job for the night—that would be fun—it was all about seeing Steve. It felt like weeks, months, when it had been only a few days since she'd last seen him.

By six-fifteen the first guests started to arrive. Fourteen Bones, the local barbecue restaurant, had set up shop in the parking lot, with three huge portable barbecues. The scent of mesquite and smoke filled the evening air.

One of Cassie's assignments was to greet the guests and escort them to their tables. Although she kept a look out for Steve, she didn't see him anywhere.

Once everyone was seated, volunteers from

the restaurant and Habitat worked inside a large tent outside the hangar, preparing the appetizers of stuffed jalapeños, crispy fried chicken wings, and plump pink skewered shrimp. Cassie helped dish up the trays of food. Every chance she got she peeked outside, scanning the hangar, but Steve wasn't anywhere in sight.

By the time dinner was served, she'd lost hope that he'd been able to come. Something at the job site in eastern Washington must have prevented him from leaving. Her heart was heavy with disappointment.

Still, there was work to be done, and she couldn't allow herself to be too distracted. This Hoedown, she'd learned, was one of the major fund-raisers for Habitat for Humanity, and seeing that she had a vested interest in its success, she needed to give her full attention.

With or without Steve.

During the buffet dinner, Cassie was responsible for replenishing the large bowls of cole slaw for the two buffet lines. At first it hadn't sounded like much of a job, but to her surprise she was continually hurrying to and from the makeshift kitchen, carting out bowls.

Most everyone, she noticed, had come dressed in cowboy and cowgirl gear. The men wore Stetsons and boots and many of the women had donned fringed vests, red neck scarves, and fancy, colorful boots.

Cassie was too busy working to pay much attention. At one point, however, she saw a familiar face—an unwelcome one. It was that woman Britt, the one who had seen to it that Cassie had lost her job at CenturyLink Field, and who Steve was involved with. She was with an older gentleman and there was enough resemblance for Cassie to guess the man was Britt's father.

The band, which had been warming up earlier, took the stage and an announcer stepped forward. Cassie was busy carting empty serving dishes into the kitchen and didn't pay much attention until she heard Steve's name announced. She held a tray of corn bread and nearly stumbled when she saw a male figure move toward the front of the room. Steve had arrived at the Hoedown, after all.

As Steve climbed the steps leading to the platform, he glanced her way. When he saw her, he momentarily paused. Their eyes met and locked. In that brief half second, Cassie's heart leaped straight into her throat. It was then that she realized Steve had been looking for her, too.

While introductions and announcements were made, Cassie finished her duties. Megan Victory from Habitat's office thanked the volunteers for their participation. The cleanup crew would take over from this point and she was free to go or to stay, whichever she wished.

Earlier Cassie had been smart enough to bring a change of clothes. She quickly escaped into the ladies' room and slipped off her red T-shirt with **Soon to Be Home Owner** scripted across the back. She put on a buttoned blue checkered shirt that was about as western as her closet held, and a pair of blue jeans. She didn't have cowboy boots, so sneakers would have to do.

By the time she reappeared the music had started and couples had taken to the dance floor. It seemed Steve was waiting for her, because the instant she reappeared she made eye contact with him. He was on the other side of the dance floor, but right away he started walking toward her, weaving his way between couples, sidestepping around the dancers.

Cassie met him halfway.

They stood in the middle of the dance floor, doing nothing more than foolishly gazing, wide-eyed, at each other. Neither spoke as the music swirled around.

"I didn't see you," she said quietly.

"I arrived late . . . dinner was already served."

His eyes held hers. One of the dancers bumped into him and apologized.

"We should dance," he suggested, reaching for her.

Cassie stepped forward into his arms. "Sorry, I'm . . . I'm not much good at this."

He ignored her protest, pulling her close to him. He held her the same way he had in her dream.

Their feet barely moved. If this wasn't heaven, she decided, then it was pretty darn close.

Cassie closed her eyes, wanting to savor each moment, hold on to it before this happiness that bubbled up inside of her fizzed away and vanished.

"I missed you," he whispered, close to her ear.

The words washed over her. She wanted to tell him how empty her world had felt without him, but discovered she couldn't speak. It was better that way. She had too much on her plate to add romance to the mix. Still, for one night, she would indulge.

"Have you decided about Duke and Amiee?" he asked.

She lifted her head in order to look into his eyes. "Are you worried I'm going to let Duke back into my life?" she asked. "I'm not that stupid."

He grinned and seemed to relax his grip on her. "I didn't think you were."

"I'm going to wait until Amiee is thirteen, then I'll let her decide if she is interested in reconnecting with her father."

He nodded. "That seems like a good decision." Then he brought her head back down close to his shoulder and whispered as he had earlier, "I thought about phoning you every day."

"But you didn't."

"No. But I wanted to. Talking to you, being with you—it's addictive."

Wrapped in the warmth of his words, Cassie smiled. This was what she'd hoped to hear, and at the same time it was the very thing she feared. Although she was reluctant to admit it, she had strong feelings for Steve. He was constantly on her mind. And yet she couldn't allow her thoughts or her life to get tangled up in him. Not when she had so much else happening.

After all these years she had finally found a connection with her sisters. Cassie needed her sisters, they were her family, her last link with her roots. Now, at last, the first tentative steps had been taken. Little by little, Cassie was gaining the stability she'd so wanted to give her daughter. As tempting as it was, she couldn't allow her heart to get involved with Steve. Not yet. Not when she had so much else to accomplish first.

"You've been messing with my mind," Steve added.

She lifted her head long enough to look up at him. She wanted to say something but didn't know what. Tonight, all she wanted was this one night. She didn't want to mislead Steve, but she was selfish enough to indulge in this warm romance fantasy. Even Cinderella had one night with her prince.

His arms squeezed her closer as if to absorb her body into his own. "I have dreamed of this moment, of holding you like this."

Cassie thought of her own dream.

Just then someone tapped hard against her shoulder. Cassie lifted her head to find Britt standing next to her. "My turn," Britt said, smiling sweetly at Cassie and Steve.

"Britt?" Steve said with a frown. He didn't release Cassie.

"You haven't danced with me even once," she protested. "In fact, you've barely said hello. Dad wants to say hi, too."

"Then let me talk to your father." Steve reached for Cassie's hand and steered her off the dance floor and toward the back of the room to where the older man who'd accompanied Britt sat. He left Britt to trail along behind.

Joe Osborne stood as Steve approached. Smiling, he extended his hand. "Good to see you, Steve."

"You, too, Joe."

The other man looked pointedly at Cassie and then his daughter, who had joined the small group. Britt glared at Cassie.

"This is Cassie Carter," Steve said, introducing her to Joe.

"Hello, Cassie," Joe said, his smile genuine and warm, even while his daughter stared daggers at Cassie. Both men either didn't notice or chose to ignore it.

"It's a good thing you've done here," Joe told Steve.

Steve brushed off his words. "I didn't do much

of anything. It's the volunteers who put all this together." He made a gesture with his hand toward
the area around them. "Volunteers like Cassie."

"You work for Habitat?" Joe asked, turning
to her.

"I'm working on building a home for my daughter and me," Cassie explained, not wanting Britt's
father to misunderstand. "I'm one of the recipi-
ents of the generosity."

"Oh." Surprise showed in the older man's eyes.

"Yes," Britt said, "Cassie is one of the charity
cases."

Her words were met with a strained, uncomfortable silence.

"So that's how the two of you met, then," Joe
said, covering the awkward pause that followed.

"Yes," Steve answered, reassuring Cassie with a
glance. "And I'm grateful."

"I am, too." Cassie wasn't about to let this
spoiled rich girl intimidate her. Steve had his arm
wrapped around her waist, as if letting it be known
that the two of them were a couple.

"Good to see you, Joe," he said, moving to step
away. "Now I'd like to take my girl back to the
dance floor."

My girl? Oh goodness. She glanced up at him,
wishing she could slow things down a bit.

"By all means," Joe said, and sat back down and
reached for his glass.

Just before she turned away, Cassie saw Britt

slump down in the seat next to her father, fold her arms over her chest, and glare at Cassie. It was funny—it looked more like something Amiee would do than something a grown woman would do.

As they made their way back to the dance floor, Steve said, "Good girl, you held your own."

"If Britt thinks she's going to intimidate me, then she's in for a shock. I've dealt with tougher characters than her."

Steve snorted softly. "I know you have." They reached the dance floor once again and Steve brought her back into the circle of his arms.

It felt like this was home, exactly where she belonged. Cassie pressed her head against his shoulder.

They danced to every song, if shuffling their feet and holding on to each other could be referred to as dancing. It didn't matter what the beat or the rhythm, their steps remained the same. Dancing was merely an excuse to touch and be together.

"We've probably made a spectacle of ourselves," Cassie told him, as the band announced the last song of the night.

"Probably," he agreed. "Do you care?"

"Not really. You?"

He hesitated. "No doubt I'm in for a lot of ribbing from the guys."

Cassie smiled.

"You find that funny?" he asked.

Her smile grew even bigger. "A little."

He kissed her cheek sweetly.

The evening ended, and those who were left started to vacate the hangar. Fourteen Bones had already packed up the portable barbecues and left. The cleanup crew was in place. Cars began to leave, their headlights shooting beams into the night as vehicles lined up single file and drove toward the exit.

Holding her hand, Steve led her to his pickup.

"I drove my car here," she reminded him.

"I know." He continued walking her toward the back of the lot where he'd left his truck.

"Where are we going?"

He glanced at her and smiled. "Nowhere."

"Nowhere?"

"Exactly." He let down the tailgate of his truck, took hold of her about the waist, and hoisted her up.

Cassie sat on the edge, her legs dangling. Steve quickly joined her and placed his arm around her shoulders. She leaned her head against him.

"I had all week to think," he announced. "Most of my thoughts revolved around you."

She couldn't deny the same was true for her. But as good as this felt, it also really shook her. She'd fallen head over heels in love before, with disastrous results. Steve wasn't like Duke, she reminded herself, but the feeling of giving her heart to a man was also so closely associated with risk, even danger. She was keenly aware of how much she had to lose. The climb up from rock bottom had been long and hard. Now everything she'd worked for was so close, she was scared of being sidetracked by falling in love.

"This time apart was good," he told her.

"It was good for me, too," she added.

"It gave me perspective, and I needed that."

"Me, too," she added, looking up at the sky. The stars were out in a dazzling display. No evening she could remember had been more perfect.

He leaned over and raised her chin so he could kiss her. His mouth moved hungrily over hers. Only when Cassie was convinced she was about to melt and fall off the tailgate did he break off the kiss.

Steve dragged in several deep breaths before he continued. "I've made a decision."

"Oh?" Lost in the moment, Cassie could barely speak, let alone think clearly.

His gaze held hers for the longest moment. "I'm excusing myself from the construction work on your and Amiee's home."

Cassie let his words sink in and then nodded. He, too, understood their relationship was moving too quickly. It was time to take a step back and slow things down. Put some distance between them.

"I think that's a good idea."

"You do?"

"Yes . . . I think we both realize that things have gotten pretty intense, and pretty quickly. We need breathing room, and that's difficult if we see each other nearly every day at the job site."

Steve frowned and leaned back on his hands. He seemed to be weighing her words. "I never expected to feel the things I do with you. After Alicia died, I assumed I would be incapable of loving anyone else. We were close, so close . . ." His voice drifted off, as if saying the words ripped open a half-healed wound.

Cassie reached over and placed her hand on his, wrapping her fingers around his and giving him a gentle squeeze.

"I'd like to take this relationship wherever it leads us, Cassie," he said, keeping his head lowered and not looking at her. "It might be two steps forward and one step back for a while, but if you're game to give us a chance, then so am I."

She squeezed his hand again. If he understood that they were going to take things **very** slowly, she thought she could do this. "I'm game."

Chapter 25

Sunday morning Cassie woke with a happy feeling. The Hoedown had been magical, by far the most romantic night of her life. After their talk, Steve had kissed her again and then walked her to her car. For the first time since she was eighteen Cassie felt the possibility of being truly free, unencumbered by the past, her own woman capable of making good decisions. At least that was what she kept reminding herself.

The evening with Steve couldn't have been any more lovely. A dream come true. They understood each other; this was a night out of time. Like her, he accepted that they needed to take a step back and analyze where they were headed, and slow things down for the time being.

Amiee was due home from the camping trip late that afternoon. Cassie used the morning to clean the apartment, do laundry in the coin-operated machines in the back of the apartment complex, shower, and then paint her toes and fingernails. It was such a luxury; she rarely had time for herself like this.

Amiee burst into the house shortly after five, full of chatter and excitement.

"Sounds like you had a good time," Cassie said, helping her daughter lug her three absolutely essential pieces of luggage into the apartment. She'd required three bags for a single overnight stay. Three bags!

"We had the best time. Claudia's dad took us on a hike in the rain forest. Did you know Washington state has one of the largest temperate rain forests in the continental United States? It's called the Hoh Rain Forest, in Olympic National Park and Forest."

"Really?" Cassie did know, but she didn't want to squash her daughter's enthusiasm.

"There was moss and it was slippery in places and the forest was so beautiful you wouldn't have believed it. We walked and walked and it seemed like we'd gone ten miles but it was only two. I didn't know a mile could be so far. Claudia's dad had a walking stick. I always thought those were for old people, forty or fifty, but Mr. Anastasia isn't that old."

Cassie did her best to hide a smile.

"And we cooked on a camp stove. Claudia's mom

made this amazing soup that had everything you can imagine in it, and it tasted so good. Oh, and we made s'mores—you know, with graham crackers, marshmallows, and melted chocolate? They were yummy. I could have eaten ten of them, but I only ate three."

"We'll have to try making them ourselves sometime," Cassie said, loving the way her daughter's eyes sparked with joy.

"We can't, sorry. It only works with a campfire."

"Oh, then we'll just need to go camping one day."

Amiee grew serious. "Mom, this is **real** camping. This isn't car camping or eating-dinner-under-the-table camping. We hiked to our site!"

"I'll take that into consideration."

"What's for dinner?" Amiee asked, blinking at Cassie. "I'm starved."

"I have an excellent idea of how to cure that," Steve said.

He stood in the open apartment doorway, looking handsome enough for Cassie to stuff between two graham crackers, coat in chocolate, and munch on.

"Hi," she said, knowing her voice sounded breathless and happy, mainly because she was both. At the same time, her head was telling her to take it slow. Before they parted, Steve had mentioned seeing her again before he returned to eastern Washington.

"You didn't answer your phone," he said, looking at Cassie.

"Oh sorry—I was in and out of the apartment doing laundry. I must have missed your call."

His eyes were warm and gentle, his gaze lingering over Cassie before he turned his attention to Amiee. "How was the camping trip?"

Cassie held up her hand, stopping him. "Don't get her started, she'll talk your ears off."

"That good, huh?"

"The best," Amiee assured him, beaming him a wide smile.

Steve leaned against the doorjamb. "I stopped by to see if I could talk you girls into letting me buy you dinner."

"I could be persuaded," Cassie said, "and I don't think you'll have a difficult time convincing Amiee, either."

"Let's go." Her daughter was more than eager. Amiee grabbed her purse and was already halfway to the door. "KFC?" she suggested eagerly.

"Not this time, okay?"

"Okay." She didn't sound disappointed, and Cassie was pleased her daughter hadn't put up a fuss.

Steve drove them to the outskirts of Kent, to a mom-and-pop drive-in that had outside seating. He ordered cheeseburgers, along with french fries and drinks, and carried them over to the picnic table where Cassie and Amiee waited.

Steve set the sack down and then swung his leg over the bench and sat down next to Cassie so that he was directly across from Amiee. He'd grown progressively quieter as they drew close to the drive-in. After spreading out a napkin and cutting her burger in half with a plastic knife, Amiee took her first bite. "These are really, really good."

"As good as KFC?"

"No, but close."

Steve held his burger with both hands. "This is one of my favorite places to eat," he said. "I used to stop by here for lunch at least once or twice a week."

"You don't anymore?" Amiee asked between bites. She'd already managed to scarf down the first half of her burger. Camping apparently made her extra-hungry.

"I spend a lot more time dealing with the paperwork these days than actually working on the construction site. So I end up eating at my desk. That's one reason why I enjoy working with Habitat—it gets me back out," he explained.

Cassie noticed Steve hadn't done anything more than remove his sandwich from the brown paper sack. He was quiet for a second, then cleared his throat.

"There's a reason I asked you to dinner," he said, directing the comment to Amiee.

"You mean other than being hungry?"

"Yeah, it's more than that." Steve shot a speculative glance toward Cassie and grew even more serious. "I wanted to talk to you about dating your mother."

Amiee frowned and looked from Cassie to Steve and then back again. "I thought you were already dating her."

Cassie held up her hand, wanting Steve to slow down. All this talk made it sound as if it was a foregone conclusion that they were together now. They had an understanding, she thought. They'd talked about the need to take one day at a time and not rush into anything, certainly not speed up.

"I want to **officially** start dating your mother," Steve explained.

Amiee tossed a look to Cassie and then back to Steve and seemed confused. "What's the difference between official dating and unofficial dating?" she asked.

"Hold on a minute," Cassie said. Steve was getting ahead of himself. Way ahead.

But Steve cut her off. He expelled his breath as though gathering his thoughts. "Amiee, I want you to know I'm serious about your mother."

"Serious?" Amiee repeated, elevating her voice. "You mean like you want to marry her?"

Cassie sucked in her breath but before she could protest that any such idea was completely premature, Steve answered.

"It's a bit soon to decide that just yet. I'm not

taking marriage off the table—that is, if your mother is agreeable and if you'd be willing to let me be your stepdad—but that's something for us to discuss in the future."

Cassie was speechless. Of its own accord, her mouth moved up and down a couple times but no words escaped, which was probably a good thing. Had she been able to speak, she wasn't sure what she'd say without the words tumbling out of her mouth and tripping over her tongue.

Steve was taking a whole lot for granted. She had thought he understood. It was clear now that they weren't in agreement about this relationship. Despite their earlier conversation, it appeared that she'd given him the wrong impression.

Amiee's eyes grew dark as she set her burger aside. "You must really like my mom."

Seeming more relaxed now, Steve reached for his own cheeseburger. "You could say that. She's not half bad, you know."

"She has a bit of a temper," Amiee informed him, lowering her voice, as if whispering would prevent Cassie from hearing her.

"Steve," Cassie protested, finding her voice. "You and I need to have a **serious** discussion."

Steve and her daughter ignored her. "I've seen this temper of hers a time or two myself. Any other bad habits you want to warn me about?"

"Hey, you two," Cassie said, indignant now. "Stop it! Steve, we need to talk." She made sure each word was spoken distinctly, so there was no room for misunderstanding. Seeing that she'd already made that mistake once, she wanted her meaning perfectly clear now.

Steve paused and turned toward Cassie.

"In a minute, Mom," Amiee insisted. "This is important."

"What I have to say is important, too," she said, but both Steve and Amiee continued to ignore her.

To his credit, Steve smiled apologetically before turning his attention back to Amiee. "Do you have any other important questions for me?" Steve asked. "Anything you want to know before your mother and I start **officially** dating?"

Amiee reached for her soda, took a sip, and then folded her forearms on top of the table. "Do you believe in God?"

Steve nodded. "Yup."

She took that into consideration and then asked. "Do you go to church?"

Steve hesitated. "I haven't in a while."

"Why not?" Amiee wasn't letting up.

"Enough, you two," Cassie cried, growing more frustrated by the minute.

Steve gave her a gentle shake of his head, letting her know he fully intended to answer Amiee's questions.

"I've been sort of mad at God."

"How come?" Amiee pressed, unwilling to drop the matter.

Steve expelled a long breath. "Because my wife died. I prayed that God would heal Alicia. It didn't happen and so I figured if He wasn't going to listen to me, then I'd ignore Him, too."

Amiee tapped her fingers on the top of the picnic table as she mulled over his answer. "I guess I can understand how you felt."

"I appreciate it," Steve told her. "Anything else you need to know?"

Amiee nodded aggressively. "Yes, there's more. This is my mother you're talking about, and if we're going to let you into our lives there's several important factors for us to take into consideration."

Cassie interrupted. "This has gone on long enough. It's far too early for you two to be talking like this. Steve, I appreciate you considering Amiee's feelings, but I believe this is a discussion you and I need to have **first.** I am nowhere near ready for this to move so fast. I thought you understood that."

Amiee's gaze was focused on Steve and his on her. Both reacted as if she hadn't spoken, as if they hadn't heard a single word she'd said.

Cassie couldn't take this any longer. She scooted off the bench and, with her arms folded, paced the area.

"Anything else?" Steve asked, gesturing toward Amiee. It seemed he was more than ready to take on whatever it was she wanted to toss his way.

"If you and Mom get serious, you know, really

serious, and you decide to marry, will you want children?"

"Yes," Steve said. He glanced toward Cassie and held her eyes for a moment.

"As far as I'm concerned, this is a moot point," Cassie said.

"Good," Amiee pronounced, with a sharp nod of her head.

"You approve?" Steve asked.

"Well, duh. Ask Mom. I've wanted brothers and sisters forever. It takes the pressure off me."

"Right," Steve said, agreeing with her.

"One more thing, and this is important."

"Ask away."

Amiee leaned forward and with all the wisdom of her twelve years said, "My mother is a wonderful person and she's been through a lot. Don't hurt her."

"It would never be my intention to hurt either one of you," Steve vowed. "And I promise to think about everything you said. Now, is that it? Any other questions or suggestions?"

Amiee let out a lengthy sigh. "That's about it, but I reserve the right to ask questions later if I think of something else." Satisfied, Amiee resumed, munching on a french fry.

Steve reached for his burger.

The only one not eating was Cassie, and that was because her head was buzzing. Neither Steve nor Amiee seemed to think her feelings on the matter were of any significance. That rankled and now she was angry and growing more so by the minute.

As if she had a sudden thought, Amiee leaned forward and looked at Steve. "When I'm sixteen, you'd let me drive, right?"

"Amiee!"

"If your mother approves."

"What about a car? Would you be willing to buy me my own car?"

Cassie couldn't believe this. "Amiee, Steve, stop right this minute," she snapped, nearly shouting in order to gain their attention.

"Okay, okay," Amiee muttered. "I probably shouldn't have asked that, but you can't blame me for trying."

"Oh yes, I can," Cassie declared. She turned and glared at Steve. "And Steve Brody, this is serious, I don't appreciate you making assumptions you have no right to make."

"Was I getting ahead of myself?" he asked, and to his credit, he looked at bit chagrined.

"You and I need to talk ... privately, and the sooner, the better."

"Okay. Whatever you say."

Her daughter turned to look in Steve's direction. "When would you like to start?"

Steve blinked. "Start?"

"Dating Mom?"

"Soon," Steve assured her, dragging his troubled

gaze away from Cassie. "That is, if your mother agrees."

Amiee sighed expressively. "Of course she agrees. She'd be a dope not to. She's really busy these days with Habitat and work, though. She's at the salon early and at the house site late."

"And I need to return to eastern Washington for the time being. Which, given the look on your mother's face right now, might be a good thing."

"For how long?" Amiee demanded.

"I don't know. Hopefully for only a few more days. But before I leave," Steve said, "I think your mother and I need a few minutes alone."

Amiee's eyes brightened. "Are you going to kiss her?"

Steve grinned before answering in a whisper, "If she'll let me."

Chapter 26

Steve drove Cassie and Amiee back to the apartment. Cassie clenched and unclenched her hands several times while she debated what to say to Steve. Earlier she'd felt ready to explode, but her anger had dissipated as they headed back to the apartment. Nevertheless, she felt it was important that she set him straight. Sitting in the truck, Amiee was already talking wedding dresses and asking if she'd serve as the maid of honor when Cassie married Steve.

Just as they neared the apartment Steve got a phone call. Cassie could hear only one side of the conversation, but it was enough to glean that he was needed back at Grand Coulee Dam as soon as possible.

Steve walked them back to the apartment, where Amiee settled in with some homework. Cassie followed him back outside and stood by his truck. He climbed in the cab and rolled down the driver's-side window. With a heavy heart, Cassie leaned against the door.

"We still need to talk," she said.

"I don't understand why you're so upset." His look was sheepish. "Okay, so Amiee got a bit carried away, but I found it amusing and rather sweet. You have to admit the kid's got a lot of enthusiasm."

"It isn't right to lead her on, Steve."

"I wasn't. I'm serious about us, Cassie. I know you want to go slow with this and I understand. I feel the same way, but it's important that we're on the same page, don't you think?"

"Yes, that's what I've been trying to say all afternoon."

"I want us to get to know each other, and the only way that can happen is if we're committed to this relationship. I'm not going to date anyone else, and I hope you won't, either."

Truth be told, there wasn't anyone she would rather date.

"Can we agree to that then?"

She nodded.

"I want to be sure you understand," Steve said. "I excused myself from your project not because I wanted to see less of you. I want to spend more time with you. I felt working on your house and us dating might be considered a conflict of interest."

"Okay." That made sense.

"We're square, then?"

"We're square."

"I'd like to talk this out a bit more, but unfortunately I've got to get on the road." The hesitation in his voice was evident.

Cassie felt it herself. She'd been angry, and with barely an effort he'd managed to turn it around with a few words. He was a good negotiator, a good businessman. It unsettled her.

"We will talk soon," Steve said. "I'll call when I can, okay?"

She nodded.

"Kiss me before I go."

Cassie leaned in to give him a quick kiss, but he placed his hand on the back of her head and made sure she understood he was going to miss her. Standing on her tiptoes, Cassie leaned into his kiss, opening up, weaving her fingers through his hair.

He released her slowly. "A guy could get used to a send-off like that," he whispered.

Cassie was breathless and leaned her forehead to his.

"I can't remember a time I've wanted to travel out of town less."

"It's only for a few days. We'll talk again when you get back, okay?"

"What about Saturday night?" he asked.

"Yes," she whispered, "that will work."

He grinned and gently placed his lips over hers.

The kiss made her knees weak. It frightened her how quickly he could melt away her resolve. Many more of these exchanges and she'd agree to just about anything.

"Dinner, then—just you and me—on Saturday," he said.

"Someplace quiet where we can talk."

"Sure." He held her gaze a moment longer and then whispered. "Until Saturday."

"Saturday." Cassie repeated and stepped back from the pick-up. She remained standing on the curb until Steve's truck was well out of sight.

Amiee was waiting for Cassie when she returned to the apartment.

"I was thinking," her daughter said thoughtfully, "about you and Steve marrying and then sometime later you giving me a sister."

"Amiee, please. Steve and I aren't getting married."

A horrified look came over her daughter. "You're not?"

"Well, who knows—maybe someday, but not anytime soon. You're getting way ahead of yourself."

"But Mom, Steve said—"

"I know what he said and he shouldn't have." She walked into the kitchen and reached for a hand towel to dry off the last drops of water from the dishes she'd washed earlier. It was completely unnecessary, but it occupied her hands and it helped her avoid eye contact with her daughter.

"Why not? You really like him; I can tell. You were kissing just now. I saw you."

Naturally, Amiee would have been watching them. It wasn't like Cassie could deny that she was strongly attracted to Steve. "You're right, I . . . do like him . . . a lot."

Amiee slapped her hands against the sides of her thighs. "Then what's the big deal? You heard Steve. He's serious. He wants to **officially** start dating you. That's like one step away from marriage."

How kind of her daughter to enlighten Cassie on the ins and outs of romantic relationships. "No matter what it means," Cassie clarified, "any talk of marriage is premature. Do you understand that just because a man wants something in a relationship, that's not all she wrote? You will have to know this when you are old enough to date—you need to make sure **your** voice is heard in any relationship you're in."

Amiee slumped down on the sofa. "But I've wanted a sister since forever."

"I know you have."

"When can I meet my aunts and cousins?" Amiee asked her.

"I actually talked to my sister on Friday," Cassie said, happy to steer the conversation away from Steve.

"You did?" Amiee immediately sat upright. "Aunt Karen or Aunt Nichole?"

"Your aunt Nichole. She called me. We're going to get together, with Karen, too."

Right away Amiee brightened, her eyes flashing with excitement. "Can I come?"

"Of course. My sisters are excited to meet you and I want you to meet them."

"Can I tell them about you and Steve, or do you want to do that yourself?"

Cassie resisted the urge to groan. "I prefer to tell them myself."

"Are they coming here? When?"

"I don't know yet. Karen said she's hoping it will be in a couple weeks." She was wading from one crocodile-infested conversation to another. While Cassie sincerely hoped she would be able to truly reconcile with Karen and Nichole, she had no guarantee it would happen.

"Don't you have homework?" she asked.

"No. I finished my science worksheet and that was it. You made me finish all my other homework before I left for the camping trip. Don't you re-member? You checked my pre-algebra worksheet."

"I did?"

"Mom, what's with you lately? You looked at Steve like you were upset and all he wanted to do was be good to you. Didn't you notice?"

"Notice what?"

"The way he looked at you. It's like it's a hundred degrees outside and you're holding out an ice-cream cone just for him."

"Please, just stop." Setting the pan and the cloth aside, Cassie turned her back to her daughter and pressed her hands against the edge of the kitchen counter while she gathered her thoughts. Duke had rushed her, too. She'd wanted to wait before they married, give her family a few weeks to adjust to the fact that she loved Duke and then tell them about the pregnancy. Duke refused to listen. He made it sound like marrying her was the honorable thing to do and her wanting to wait was a slap in his face. When they finally did come before a justice of the peace he'd made it seem like it was the two of them against the world. He'd convinced her that he was her family now and she didn't need her parents or her sisters. For the first couple months she'd believed him. By the time she saw her mistake, it was too late.

"Mom?" Amiee's voice seemed to be coming from a long distance away.

Cassie had to pull herself back into the present, and it seemed to be a long, treacherous journey through the years. "Yes?" she asked.

"Tell me what you and Nichole talked about."

"Oh, we had a nice chat." Cassie had been thrilled to hear from Nichole. She suspected Karen put her up to it—not that it mattered. The conversation had gone well after a strained start. Cassie understood her sisters' hesitation to let her back into the circle—she didn't blame them.

Amiee interrupted her musings with a loud yawn. "You're tired," Cassie said. She checked her watch and was surprised to find it was after eight.

Amiee yawned a second time. "Camping was a lot of fun, but sleeping on the ground wasn't all that comfortable."

"I thought Claudia said there were air mattresses."

"There were, but it wasn't like sleeping in a real bed." She stifled yet another yawn. "I'm going to bed."

After the busy day she'd had, Cassie was more than ready to turn in herself, but she had a few more things to do around the house first.

It was around nine-thirty when the phone rang. She was just getting ready to crawl into bed with her book. It was her friend Rosie from Goldie Locks. "I called to see if Steve made it to the Hoedown."

"He was there." Although she tried, Cassie hadn't been able to hide from her friends how badly she'd missed Steve while he was away.

"So? Did you have a good time?" Rosie asked.

She remembered the way he'd looked at her from the other side of the dance floor. He'd started walking toward her and it was as if an invisible thread had pulled them together. "We had a fabulous time," she admitted, and then added, "The best ever." No matter what happened between her and Steve in the future, she would always have the romantic memory of that night.

"Tell her about you and Steve," Amiee insisted, shouting from her bedroom, not asleep yet herself.

Cassie walked to the doorway of her room and glared at her daughter.

"What did Amiee say?" Rosie asked.

Cassie sighed and shot her daughter a warning look. "Nothing much. Steve was by earlier and very kindly asked me out to dinner next week."

"You're going on a date?" Rosie sounded as excited as Amiee had.

"He wants to start officially dating Mom," Amiee shouted.

"**Officially** dating Steve?" Rosie asked. "What does that mean?"

"According to my daughter, it's the step right before getting engaged, which is ridiculous."

Rosie laughed with what sounded like glee. "So when's your first date?"

"Next Saturday."

"Wonderful." Rosie reeked excitement. "I'll set up an appointment for you with Shirley late Saturday afternoon."

"Shirley hasn't got time—"

"Shush, if you're **officially** dating Steve, it's our duty to make sure he wants a second date, got it?"

"Uh . . ." Cassie wasn't sure that involving her friends in this dinner date was such a good idea.

"You'll need an appointment with Alice, too. She'll do your nails."

"I just painted them this morning," Cassie protested.

Rosie sighed expressively. "Apparently, you weren't listening. Hair and nails we can do at the shop. What we need to think about next is your outfit. What you wear is ultra-important."

"She hasn't got anything decent to wear," Amiee said loudly.

The kid had radar a bat would envy.

"Let me check with Elaina," Rosie continued. "You're about the same size, aren't you? She has that pink dress . . ."

"Not the dress she wore for her wedding," Cassie protested.

"Yes, that dress. It isn't like she's planning on getting married again, so it's just hanging in her closet. Someone else might as well make good use of it. It was a lucky dress for her. Come to think of it, though, that dress is a little demure. Scratch Elaina's pink wedding dress."

"Thank goodness."

"We'll go shopping," Rosie insisted.

"I can't afford—"

"Stop. There are places where we can find the right dress at a bargain price. What do you have in the way of jewelry?"

"Ah . . ."

"Don't worry about it. Maureen has lots of beautiful pieces. She'll donate to the cause."

The same feeling she'd experienced earlier when Steve had initiated his little chat with Amiee returned. "Look, Rosie . . . I know you mean well, and I appreciate what you're trying to do, but—"

"Don't say another word," Rosie barked. "Put Amiee on the phone."

"Amiee? Why do you want to talk to my daughter?"

Rosie exhaled loudly. "Just do as I ask."

"When did you get so bossy?"

"Me, bossy? You haven't seen anything yet. Now let me talk to Amiee."

Dazed, Cassie stretched out her arm to hand the phone to her daughter. Amiee leaped up as if Cassie was extending her the Holy Grail. She grabbed it and took it over to the sofa, where she knelt on the cushion.

"What's the plan?" Amiee asked, smiling as her eyes followed Cassie, who'd taken to pacing in the small apartment.

Cassie's hearing wasn't nearly as good as her daughter's. She was able to make out only a few words here and there of the conversation. What she did hear gave her just enough to get the gist of what they were discussing, and it didn't sound good.

Amiee approved because she mumbled words like: **Great. Perfect. That'll work.**

At one point Amiee laughed out loud.

"What?" Cassie demanded. She had no inkling of what the two were plotting.

Amiee waved her off like she was swatting a pesky mosquito.

The two continued deep in conversation when Amiee abruptly pulled the phone away from her ear. She glanced at the face of the cell phone, pushed a button, and then continued her conversation with Rosie. It must have been fifteen minutes later when Amiee ended the call and handed Cassie back her phone.

"You don't have a thing to worry about," her daughter assured her. "Rosie and I've got it all figured out."

"That's nice to know." Cassie was being sarcastic, but Amiee took her seriously.

"Rosie said you're gonna knock Steve's socks off."

"Really? Do I have a say in any of this?"

Amiee considered the question, tapping her index finger against her cheek as she mulled it over. "Not really."

Cassie was afraid of that.

"Oh, and Mom."

"Yes?"

"A call came in while I was talking to Rosie. It was Steve. You might want to call him back."

Chapter 27

Karen Goodwin sat at her desk at Spokane Title, going over the closing documents for a retired couple who were due in that afternoon. When the phone at her desk rang, she automatically reached for it and was surprised to hear Nichole's voice on the other end of the line.

"Why didn't you call my cell?"

"Oh sorry," Nichole said. "You have so many numbers I sometimes forget which is which."

"Did you talk to Cassie?" Karen asked.

"I did."

"How'd it go?"

"It went great. You were so right . . . I should have called her long ago . . . I don't know why I didn't." She hesitated and then added in a hushed voice, "That's not exactly true. I do know why I delayed."

"It's awkward for us all—"

Nichole cut her off and blurted out, "Back when everything happened with Duke? I read Cassie's journal . . . I knew she was pregnant and she knew what I'd done. She was afraid I'd tell Mom and Dad, and that's why she left."

"Nichole, what? That isn't why."

"Yes, it is," she insisted.

"Did Cassie tell you that?"

She paused for a moment before she answered. "No . . . we didn't talk about anything from back then."

It sounded as if her sister was close to tears. Karen carried her own guilt—they all did, but it was time to put the past behind them and become a family again.

"I have a business meeting in a few minutes. Listen, we'll talk more about this later, but before we hang up, tell me how your weekend went," Karen said. She wanted to end their conversation on a positive note.

"The spa was fabulous," Nichole admitted. "And really, how could it not be? I was pampered and catered to for three entire days, and also managed to drop a couple pounds."

"That's great." Karen couldn't help being envious. It'd been three years since their last family vacation.

"I came home refreshed and deeply in love with my husband. Unfortunately, Owen didn't do well without me. By the time I got back to Portland Sunday afternoon, Jake and his mother were worn to a frazzle."

"It's nice to be needed, isn't it?" It was easy to remember what it'd been like when her own two children were toddlers. There didn't seem to be enough hours in the day. It was a blessing they'd had Garth's parents and her own close at hand, and as first-time grandparents, both sets had been eager to help.

"Needed and wanted," Nichole said, lowering her voice. "You'd think I'd been away for a month the way Jake reacted."

Nichole was still enough of a newlywed to appreciate romance. Karen did, too, but after several years of marriage, her love life with Garth had become predictable and low-key, though very good.

"I'm buying Jake that fancy BMW he wants so badly," Nichole announced. "He'd never ask for it, but I saw the brochure and it's his birthday next month, so as a surprise, I called the dealership and bought it for him."

Karen knew what that meant. Her sister had now spent the majority of their parents' inheritance on a fancy car for her husband. Of course, that was her choice—Karen wouldn't fault her for loving her husband and wanting to give him a special birthday gift.

"You aren't going to talk me out of it, are you?" Nichole asked.

"Not at all. It's none of my business what you do with the money we got from Mom and Dad."

"I know . . . it's just that Jake has been so wonderful lately. He's always so thoughtful and kind, especially since I've had Owen."

"Nichole, you don't need to justify it to me."

"I know, it's just that—"

"Stop," Karen said, cutting her off. She didn't know why her sister felt like she needed permission. Everyone seemed to want approval in one form or another. They said good-bye and hung up.

Ten minutes before the Anson couple were due to arrive to sign the closing papers, her desk phone rang again. Karen reached for it.

"Karen Goodwin. How may I help you?"

"This is the nurse at Thomas Jefferson Elementary," the voice on the other end of the line said.

"Is everything all right?"

"It's Buddy. He's come down with the flu and is sick and vomiting. Can you come for him?"

"Oh boy. Okay—I'm just about to go into a meeting." The timing was the worst. "I'll call my husband to see if he can pick up Buddy."

Poor Buddy. More than anything, her young son hated throwing up. He must really be sick. Karen tried Garth's cell, but it went straight to voice mail. Garth sometimes turned it off, especially when he was working hard on a project, so she tried the direct line to his office.

"Mark Holmes's office."

"Hi, Michelle," Karen said, sitting up straight. "Mark Holmes's office?" she repeated. Garth hadn't said anything about his number changing.

"Mrs. Goodwin?" Michelle asked. "Karen?"

"Yes. I need to talk to Garth." Looking out the glass door of her office, Karen saw that the Ansons had arrived and were seated in the waiting area. "It's kind of an emergency. Buddy needs to be picked up at the school."

Her words were met with silence.

"Michelle, did you hear me?"

"Yes. Karen, listen . . . um . . . Garth hasn't worked here since the first week of April. I guess maybe you forgot and dialed this number from habit?"

Karen laughed softly. Surely there was some mistake. "Very funny, but this isn't a joke. I want to talk to Garth."

"This isn't a joke," Michelle insisted. "I'd never joke about something like this. Garth was laid off weeks ago . . . Are you saying he didn't tell you?"

Karen was stunned.

"Karen? Mrs. Goodwin?"

Karen ended the call. Clearly something was drastically wrong. True, she'd noticed Garth hadn't been himself for the last few weeks, but she had no clue he'd lost his job. Now that she thought about it, he had seemed depressed lately. When she'd asked him about it, he'd claimed it wasn't anything serious. He might have mentioned problems at work, but certainly not that he'd been laid off.

If Garth was going without a paycheck she would know, and they'd be bouncing checks left and right. In fact, Garth had been paid regularly according to the bank statements, right down to the penny. This was crazy. Nuts. Of course Garth had a job.

Not knowing what else to do, Karen phoned his cell a second time. As before, the call went directly to voice mail. "Garth, if you're there, then please answer. This is important. Buddy is sick and needs someone to collect him at the school. I have a signing and the people are here. Send me a text in the next five minutes if you get this message—otherwise, I'll need to leave the office."

Shuddering a sigh, her head swimming and her heart pounding, Karen stood to greet Mr. and Mrs. Anson. By the time she returned to her desk she heard her cell ping. The message was from Garth and read: **On my way to get Buddy.**

Garth didn't know that she'd called his office. Nor was he aware that she was on to his secret.

But he'd learn soon enough. Oh yes, he'd find out the minute she was home to confront him face-to-face.

Karen wasn't sure how she'd managed to get through the signing, not to mention the rest of the day. She called and talked briefly with her son but not to Garth. She needed the afternoon to think, and even then, she wasn't sure what she would say to her husband. It was beyond the scope of her imagination that Garth would keep the fact that he'd lost his job a secret from her . . . from everyone.

As had become Garth's habit, he was cooking dinner by the time Karen arrived at the house. It all made sense now that he'd been getting home from the office before her every night. He'd told her he was working fewer hours . . . yet another lie.

"Hi, honey," he said, greeting her with a big smile.

She set her keys and purse aside. "How's Buddy?"

"Better. He slept most of the afternoon."

"Where is he now?"

Garth continued slicing tomatoes for the salad and didn't look up. "In his room playing games on his iPad."

"And Lily?"

Garth added the sliced tomatoes to the lettuce and reached for a handful of radishes, slicing those. "She's with Elise Jefferies. They're working together on some end-of-the-school-year project. How was your day?"

"Upsetting."

"Oh? Didn't the closing go well?" he asked, looking up for the first time since he'd greeted her.

"It went fine."

"Oh good. Something else happen?"

A long time ago Karen had read parenting advice that suggested not setting her children up for a lie when she already knew the truth. She figured the same would hold true with her husband.

"Why didn't you tell me you'd gotten laid off?"

Garth's head came up fast. He set the knife down on the cutting board and wiped his hand on a kitchen towel he had tucked into his waistband. "Who told you?"

"Does it matter?"

"I guess not." Using both hands, he leaned against the counter as if he feared his legs might not support him.

"Michelle said your last day was weeks ago."

Garth nodded. "It's true. At first it felt like a bad joke, but unfortunately the joke was on me."

In the hours since she'd learned her husband's secret, she'd had time to think. "The day you got laid off was the day you forgot to pick up Buddy from baseball practice, wasn't it?"

Garth swallowed hard and nodded. "I was in shock, worried and ashamed. I didn't know how I was going to tell you . . . didn't know what I was going to do."

"Did you honestly believe I'd blame you?"

"I didn't know what to think," her husband snapped. "We'd gone through this once before and I wasn't sure our marriage would survive. I couldn't face that again and I wasn't sure you could, either. I assumed I'd be able to find another job quickly—I have good references and plenty of experience, and I figured I'd tell you when I'd found something new and save you the worry. There was all this business with your sisters. And it hadn't been that long since we'd buried your mother. I didn't want to burden you with more bad news."

"Those are not good excuses. I'm your wife! Don't you think I have a right to know?"

"Okay, of course. I should have told you," he said defensively. "But it isn't easy to admit to your wife and family that you're a loser."

"Because you lost your job? Don't be ridiculous, Garth."

Straightening, he placed both his hands on top of his head. "Cut me some slack, Karen. A man has his pride."

Did he really think she would think less of him? People got laid off all the time. Pulling out a kitchen chair, Karen slumped into it. "It hurts, Garth, that you wouldn't trust me enough to tell me what you've been going through." A number of things played back in her mind. His insistence that he take over the bill paying, the bounced check, and the "misunderstanding" when they went to the storage unit and found it locked up for nonpayment.

"I didn't want you to know . . . I hoped to have another job in a few days, a couple weeks at the most."

"You've been looking?"

"What do you think I've been doing every day?" he demanded. "I've sent out my résumé, pounded the pavement, looked online. It just seems like no one is hiring." This last part was practically shouted in his frustration. "I know, because I have done everything within my power to find work." His voice wobbled with emotion and his hands shook.

Silence vibrated through the kitchen.

"You got a severance package?" That was the only way she could explain the money that had continued to be deposited into their joint checking account for the last two months.

Garth hung his head.

"Garth?"

"No. There was no severance package."

Karen frowned. "But what about the pay that kept showing up in our checking account?"

Turning abruptly, Garth left the kitchen, walking out the sliding glass doors to the backyard. Karen reluctantly followed only to find her husband on his knees, doubled over. His hands were folded protectively on his head.

Racing to him, she knelt at his side. "Garth, Garth, what is it?"

Her husband rocked back and forth as if in agony.

"Tell me," she pleaded. "Just tell me."

To her shock and horror, her husband started to cry, great sobs that shook his entire upper body.

Wrapping her arms around him, Karen felt tears gather in her own eyes, feeling his pain, his loss, if not knowing the cause.

"I thought the only way out was to kill myself," Garth whispered.

"No," Karen nearly screamed. "No. Garth, nothing is worth losing you. You're my husband . . . what would the kids and I do without you?"

"I used your parents' money," he said, burying his face in his hands.

Shock nearly sent her reeling. Her inheritance . . . For a minute she said nothing, absorbing this news. Finally, she whispered, "It doesn't matter . . . it doesn't matter."

"I tried to make up what I'd lost . . ."

A chill went down Karen's back. She didn't know how she knew but she did. "You played the stock market?"

He nodded. "It's gone, Karen, it's gone."

"All of it?"

"There's a couple thousand left . . . that's it. I'm so sorry . . . so, so sorry."

Karen held on to her husband as they both wept.

Chapter 28

Steve phoned Cassie on Monday, but their conversation was short and rather awkward. She didn't hear from him on Tuesday, although she wished she had. They were both treading carefully, as if approaching a bed of hot coals in their bare feet.

Wednesday night he called again, looking to confirm their dinner date on Saturday. They both knew that was just an excuse. Cassie didn't mind; she'd missed him and was eager to talk, going out of her way to keep the conversation light and friendly. She could almost hear him relax, and because he did, she did, too.

As it happened, she had a good reason to be more lighthearted—she'd gotten good news. "You'll never believe what happened today," she told him, eager to share. "I heard from my sister."

"Which one?"

"Oh sorry, it was Karen. She called to set up a time to come to see me and Amiee in Kent. And it gets even better. Nichole is coming, too, from Portland."

Steve laughed. "Slow down, will you? You're talking so fast I can barely make out the words."

"You have no idea what this means to me," she burst out. It felt as if everything was coming together for her at last. This was exactly what she'd hoped and prayed would happen! The deepest desire of her heart was to reconcile with her two sisters.

"Tell me," he said.

Cassie sucked in a deep calming breath and tried to say each word slowly and distinctly. "Karen and Nichole are coming to Seattle a week from Sunday. It's hard to believe, but I was a teenager the last time I was with both my sisters."

"I'm happy for you, Cassie."

It would be difficult for anyone to fully appreciate the significance of this meeting. When she first moved to Seattle, and Karen and Nichole had rejected her efforts to reconnect, it had devastated her. It was as if she'd made this long journey home, facing huge obstacles, only to have the door politely closed in her face. For weeks afterward she'd been deeply depressed. Amiee's constant questions regarding family hadn't helped. It had taken her a long while to regroup. Finally, she had, and a short while later was when she applied for a home with Habitat for Humanity.

"That's really great about your sisters," said Steve. "And I'm anxious to get back to Seattle so we can clear the air. I feel bad about the way we left things. We didn't really have time to sort it out before I needed to get on the road. I'm making progress here, slowly. I'll be back by Saturday no matter what. Seeing you, talking this out so we're both comfortable with where this relationship is going, is a priority."

The frustration in his voice was palpable. Before she could respond, Amiee walked into the room. Her daughter waved her arms above her head in order to get Cassie's attention. "Mom, can I talk to Steve?"

"Amiee," Cassie whispered under her breath. "Not now . . ."

"Mom," her daughter insisted, "this is important."

"I . . . I don't think that's a good idea."

Amiee's eyes rounded. "Mom, please."

Cassie handed her daughter the phone and Amiee immediately disappeared inside her bedroom. Although she closed the door, the walls were thin and Cassie was able to hear every word.

"Rosie and I have everything planned for Saturday night," Amiee was telling him. "Goldie Locks is fixing Mom's hair and she's even getting a pedicure. That means we're looking for a pair of open-toed shoes. Mom has small feet and no one at the salon wears a size six and a half."

Cassie rolled her eyes. She could only imagine what Steve must be thinking.

"Oh, and one of the girls at Goldie Locks, I think her name is Bridget, is taking a special makeup class and she volunteered to do Mom's makeup. Mom is going to wow you, so I want you to be prepared to have your mind blown."

Cassie had to put an end to this. She opened Amiee's bedroom door and stuck her head inside. "My turn," she insisted.

Amiee sat on her bed cross-legged. She lifted the phone away from her ear and covered it with her hand. "Give me a minute, Mom. I'm just to the best part."

"Amiee!" Cassie protested.

"Rosie found her a dress," Amiee continued, speaking quickly, as if she knew Cassie was about to rip the phone from her hands. "It was one her cousin had—"

"Amiee, give me the phone right this minute."

Her daughter sighed and said, "Mom insists I return the phone."

A short silence followed and then Amiee added excitedly, "That would be perfect. Okay!"

Amiee climbed off her bed and thrust out her arm, handing Cassie the cell.

Cassie took in a deep breath and told Steve, "I wish she hadn't done that."

"You mean telling all your secrets?"

"That's just it, I have no secrets. You, Amiee, the gals at Goldie Locks are building this date up to be some huge thing I never intended it to be . . . Amiee convinced Rosie you and I are headed to the altar . . ."

"Aren't we?" he asked, and seemed to be getting a lot of pleasure from teasing her. But then maybe he wasn't teasing, which sent her mind spinning.

Cassie was befuddled. "All I know is that between my daughter and my friends they've concocted this crazy agenda to turn me into some kind of bombshell." Cassie wanted no part of it, but nothing she said would dissuade her daughter and the girls from Goldie Locks.

"A lot of women would welcome all that," Steve said.

"I don't want any of this," she insisted.

"Then put a stop to it."

If only it was that easy. "I can't."

"Sure you can."

He made it sound easy and it wasn't. In all the months she'd been working at the salon, she'd never seen her friends get more animated or excited about anything. It was as if she was providing them with the golden opportunity to prove their worth as her friends, and Cassie didn't want to take that away from them. Nevertheless, it was important that she make it clear that all this preparation was not her idea.

Cassie tried to explain why. "I like you, Steve . . . I can't deny that I'm strongly attracted to you, but all this talk about us officially dating and you asking Amiee's permission has made me really uncomfortable."

"I believe I got the message already," he said.

She hadn't meant to get into this on the phone, but she couldn't stop now. "You should never have talked to Amiee the way you did without consulting me first. We were enjoying our time together and then all of a sudden you and my daughter are talking about the two of us as if it's understood that you and I were involved in a serious relationship."

"That wasn't the way I intended the conversation would go," he admitted, "and you're right it was premature to be discussing my intentions with your daughter. But remember, after the Hoedown I'd thought we were on the same page."

"I know and I'm terribly sorry. We can resolve this, Steve. I do care about you."

"I know."

Something else was troubling her. "The thing is, I can't have you using Amiee . . ."

"Using Amiee?" he shot back. "I wouldn't ever . . ."

It had been a mistake to bring this up now. "Not intentionally you wouldn't," she agreed. "Let's not get into this now."

Silence followed. "You sure you want to wait to finish this conversation?" he asked.

"Yes. Let me clear my head first."

He hesitated for an uncomfortable moment and then asked, "The night of the Hoedown was a fluke, wasn't it?"

"No," she cried. "It wasn't. That was the most romantic night of my life. It would be so easy to fall in love with you based entirely on the way I felt with your arms around me on the dance floor. I'll never forget that closeness, the connection. It seemed like . . . I don't even know that I can find a way to tell you everything I felt that night."

"Cherished," he suggested.

"Yes." That was the perfect word to describe it.

"Seriously, Cassie, I don't see a problem," he said, sounding all the more confused. "If you feel the same way about me as I do you, then why all this angst? You want to go slow, that's fine by me. I have my own issues to deal with, but we both know where we're headed, right?" He didn't wait for her to answer. "There's no need to rush into anything. I'm with you," he said.

Cassie let his words soak in before she responded. While he claimed to be on the same page, she still wasn't convinced that he was.

"The problem, in a nutshell," she said, gripping hold of the phone so tightly that her fingers ached, "is that I'm not emotionally ready for this. You have to understand I'm carrying a full set of baggage. It's only been in the last three or four months that I've been able to get my life together. I'm not looking for a hero to ride in on a white steed and rescue me—not when, for the first time in my life, I've succeeded in getting things on track."

"Okay, point taken."

"Although you claim to understand my concern and you're content to take matters one day at a time, I feel . . . like . . . like you're pressuring me."

"That was never my intention," he returned.

"I know. I think you're a good man, Steve."

"You think . . ."

"Yes, you have to admit that my judgment about men to this point hasn't exactly been stellar . . ."

"So now you're comparing me with Duke?" He sounded angry.

She returned fire just as quickly. "Unfortunately, Duke's the only comparison I have. He was loving and romantic, too . . . in the beginning."

"I don't believe this," he muttered, sounding disgusted.

"It was a bad idea to discuss all this now. It'll be much better when we can talk face-to-face. We'll clear the air Saturday night," she promised.

Steve ended the conversation shortly afterward and that was probably for the best. It didn't come as any surprise that he didn't call her again that week.

Saturday morning, Cassie woke with a mixed bag of feelings. She was dreading the date and at the same time was eager to see Steve again. She really wanted to be with him, but she felt anxious about making a mistake.

That morning she was able to work three hours of equity time at the construction site before she arrived at Goldie Locks for her beauty treatments. Rosie had an entire crew assembled. Cassie reluctantly submitted to their fussing.

At one point she had three people working on her at the same time. They circled her, one with a comb and a hairspray can, another with fingernail polish; the third was busy painting her toenails. It was utterly ridiculous. Forcing down the urge to demand that her friends stop, Cassie smiled and did what she could to look excited and happy.

"Steve is smoking hot," Rosie said. She mimed jerking her hand up, making a hissing sound as if she'd bounced cold water against a red-hot griddle. "You're going to have a good time tonight."

Cassie forced a smile.

"My guess is that man's got a fat diamond ring burning a hole in his pocket."

"No, no, I'm sure that's not the case," Cassie insisted, fighting a rising sense of panic.

Teresa agreed with her cousin. "If not tonight, then soon. He's not the kind of man to dally with a woman's feelings. He's solid, you know."

"You hold on to that man," Bridget advised.

"You know what they say about a man with a truck like his. Big truck, big—"

"Bridget!" Teresa broke in. "We get the point."

"Yes, but does Cassie?" Bridget asked, speculative, cocking one finely shaped eyebrow.

Cassie didn't answer one way or the other. Her mind continued to whirl at a frantic pace. By submitting to all this fuss and bother, she was suddenly wary. By allowing her friends to make such a big deal out of this date she might be undermining her credibility on everything she'd claimed earlier. Her head started to pound, and the urge to leap out of the chair and escape was nearly overwhelming.

"She gets it," Rosie insisted.

Bridget stared at Cassie with such intensity that Cassie became unnerved. Her friend frowned and lifted Cassie's bangs from her forehead. "What?" Cassie demanded.

"Your eyebrows," Bridget muttered disparagingly.

"What about them?" Cassie was in no mood for a tweezers attack.

"When was the last time you had them shaped?"

Cassie frowned. "I have no idea." Right away she recognized that was the wrong answer.

Bridget took immediate control. "It's time, girl-friend. In fact, it is long past due."

Before Cassie could protest, the back of her chair was lowered and strips of hot wax were pressed against her eyebrows. She yelped when Bridget ripped off the tape. Then, with tweezers in hand, plucking away, Bridget chastised her for letting herself go so long.

By the time her friends were finished with her, Cassie had been prodded, pinched, plucked, and polished. She was exhausted and frankly not in the best of moods. At this point all she could think about was the burning need to escape.

"You're beautiful," Teresa said, stepping back to judge their work. She had her index finger tucked under Cassie's chin as she examined her face and her hair.

"If he proposes tonight, we want full credit," Rosie said, beaming with pride. "Steve's going to take one look at you and swoon. You'll have him eating out of your hand in no time. Don't you take second best, either, understand?"

Cassie blinked with eyelashes thick enough to swat flies. "Second best?"

"Don't you dare move in with him without something sparkling on your finger. Call me old-fashioned if you want, but we didn't go through all this trouble for nothing." Rosie stood with her hands folded as if she were about to take out her rosary and pray.

"You don't need to worry," Cassie assured her.

Rosie looked more than pleased. "That's what I thought. Now go out there and bring that man to his bended knee."

"He's going to be salivating for sure," Teresa commented.

This was ridiculous, Cassie thought, yet again.

Once back at her apartment, Cassie set her purse aside and sank into the nearest chair. Her friends meant well. This was her own fault for not having the heart to disappoint them. It was a good thing Amiee was out, because Cassie felt close to losing control. She had the urge to cry, but knew what tears would do to her mascara. If that wasn't bad enough, the headache that had been threatening now arrived with reinforcements. Her temples throbbed.

The doorbell rang and Cassie stared at it for a full thirty seconds before she found the courage to answer it.

Steve stood on the other side of the screen, dressed in a suit, looking more handsome than she could ever remember seeing him. His hair was combed back and he was clean-shaven, exposing a dimple in his chin—one she'd never noticed before. His eyes widened with appreciation when he saw her. He held a clear plastic flower box in his hand. Inside was a pink rosebud corsage with a silver bow. He cleared his throat and released a low whistle. "Wow."

"Don't," she demanded.

"Don't?"

"I don't want to hear it."

"That was a compliment," he said, and then added, "Are you going to let me in or not?"

Cassie felt tears gather at the corner of her eyes. "I can't."

"Let me in?" he asked, clearly confused.

"Do this," she said, as if the answer should have been obvious.

"Do what?"

Cassie didn't understand why he was being so dense. "I can't go to dinner with you. This is wrong. This isn't me and you might think . . . I'm sorry, Steve."

He ran a hand distractedly through his neatly combed hair, ruffling it in a way that made him all the more striking and attractive. Another woman would have tossed open the door, grabbed him by his tie, and jerked him inside so fast it would have half strangled him.

He frowned. "I thought you wanted to talk?"

"I did . . . I do, but not now."

His look darkened. "Are you saying you don't want to go to dinner with me?"

She nodded, nearly choking on the knot in her throat. "Another time, please."

"Tomorrow?"

Even that sounded far too soon. She shook her head.

"Are you feeling all right?" he asked. "This isn't like you, Cassie."

She was all too aware of how weak and out of control she sounded. She couldn't imagine what he must be thinking. "Please, just go."

He backed away a couple of steps. "If that's what you want."

"I'm sorry."

"Quit saying that."

"Sorry." She wrapped her fingers around the side of the door and slowly closed it.

"Call me when you're ready to talk, okay?"

She nodded and shut the door. As it clicked into place, she had the strongest notion that she was closing the door on far more than one night.

Chapter 29

Cassie wasn't sure what to tell her friends after the fact, especially since they'd all put such effort into the beautification project.

When she arrived at the salon Monday morning, she expected to be bombarded with questions. Teresa, Rosie, and Bridget were sure to want a minute-by-minute description of her romantic date with Steve.

Sure enough, as soon as she arrived, her friends fell in behind Cassie like she was the Pied Piper.

"Well," Bridget demanded. "Don't keep us in suspense. How did your hot date go?"

"Was I right?" Rosie asked. "Did he have a diamond ring in his pocket?"

Cassie never was sure where Rosie got that idea, unless it came from Amiee.

"Um . . ." She did her best to avoid eye contact, then squared her shoulders, ready to face their disappointment.

Teresa threw out her arms, warning off the others. "Give the girl some breathing room, you two. Okay, Cassie, what happened?"

"We didn't go."

All three of her friends gasped.

"He canceled?" Rosie asked, after a moment of shocked silence.

"No, I did."

"You did?" all three cried in unison.

"It's a long story, and if you don't mind, I'd rather not discuss it."

Bridget wasn't going to let this matter drop easily. "What did he do?"

"Bridget," Teresa whispered, steering the hairstylist away from Cassie. "Leave it be. Cassie will tell us when she's good and ready."

Cassie thanked her friend with a look and a gentle sigh. The problem was explaining to her coworkers what she had yet to fully understand herself. She wasn't shy, nor was she inclined to emotionally crumble at the least provocation. Since leaving Duke she had overcome every obstacle, tackling it all head-on. In a matter of a few years she'd forged a new life for herself and her daughter. She'd learned a trade, helped build houses, reached out to family, and she'd done all this without thinking twice. But when it came to falling in love she was a quivering mess, second-guessing herself, second-guessing Steve. Uncertain. Afraid. Lost.

Cassie made it through the rest of the workday, doing her best to keep her spirits up and her customers happy.

She wasn't needed at the construction site because at this stage a skilled craftsman was installing the electrical system. So for a change, she could go straight home from work.

"Mom." Amiee glanced up when Cassie walked in the door. Her daughter sat in front of the television with her legs braced against the edge of the cushion, knees tucked under her chin, eating a bowl of breakfast cereal. "You're home early."

Cassie set aside her things and walked over to her daughter, hugging her close from behind.

"Mom?" Amiee set aside the bowl, unwound her legs, and stood. It was the same owl look her coworkers had given her.

Cassie hadn't told Amiee anything more than what she'd told the girls at Goldie Locks.

"Are you ready to tell me why you didn't go to dinner with Steve?"

"Not yet."

For once in her life Amiee looked like she was at a loss for words. "Did you have a bad day . . . like yesterday?"

"Something like that."

"Steve called. He said he tried to reach you but you didn't pick up."

"I was at work. It isn't like I can chat when I'm doing someone's color treatment." To be fair, Steve had tried to contact her when she normally took her lunch break, but Cassie hadn't been ready to talk to him, and frankly she would rather not have that conversation in front of her coworkers.

"Are you going to call him back?"

"Of course."

Amiee's gaze followed her as Cassie wandered into the kitchen.

"When? You should do it soon. He sounded anxious to talk to you."

"I'll connect with him soon. Let it be, okay?" She needed to clear her head before they spoke.

Amiee set her cereal bowl aside. "Are you mad at him? Did he do something bad that you don't want to tell me?"

"Steve didn't do anything wrong," Cassie assured her daughter.

Amiee's gaze narrowed. "You're just saying that, aren't you? He did but you don't want to tell me." Her daughter walked a full circle around their sofa.

"Would you please listen to me?" Cassie pleaded. "Steve didn't do anything wrong. I was the one who canceled our date."

From the way Amiee continued to pace the area it was clear she didn't believe her.

Cassie was about to sit her daughter down and explain what had happened as best she could when someone pounded against their front door. She guessed it was Steve, and she was right.

She answered the door, and for a long moment all they did was stare at each other. "Why didn't you answer my calls?" he asked. "I left you three messages."

"Is that Steve?" Amiee demanded.

Steve came into the apartment. "It's me," he said, but he kept his gaze focused on Cassie.

Before Cassie was aware of what Amiee intended, her daughter walked up and kicked Steve in the shins. Hard.

"Ouch." Steve bent over to rub the injured part of his leg.

"Amiee," Cassie cried, aghast at her daughter's behavior.

"What was that for?" Her daughter had his full attention now.

"For hurting my mother." Amiee crossed her arms and gave him the evil eye. "I said you could date my mother as long as you didn't hurt her. My mom can talk to you if she wants, but I never want to see you again. Got it?"

"What did you tell her?" Steve demanded.

"The truth—that I broke the date, not you— but she refuses to believe me. She's convinced you've done something awful. I'm so sorry, Steve."

His eyes widened with frustration. "Would you stop apologizing? What's gotten into you?"

"Mom," Amiee cried, "you aren't actually going to talk to him, are you?"

"Amiee, please," Cassie pleaded. "Give me a few minutes to sort this out with Steve privately, okay?"

Amiee nodded and retreated to her bedroom, slamming the door.

"That girl's got a powerful kick," Steve said, rubbing his shin.

"Three years of playing soccer will do that," Cassie said. "I should have taken your call, but I was busy at work, and . . ." She left the rest unsaid, certain he would be able to fill in the blanks.

He rubbed his hand through his hair the way she loved. "I've been stewing ever since Saturday night. I don't understand what's happening with us, Cassie."

He had every right to be frustrated with her. The only way she could explain, could talk to him, was to share her fears. She led him to the sofa and they sat side by side, so close their knees touched. Cassie pressed her hand over her heart.

"The bottom line is that I don't think I'm ready for a serious relationship."

"Okay," he said, dragging out the word. "But I'm not sure what that means. I need a little direction here. Are you saying you don't want to see me at all?"

"No," she rushed to tell him. "I do want to see you. I want us to be friends."

"Friends?" he repeated.

"You agreed we could take this one day at a time," she reminded him.

"Friends," he repeated. "Cassie, you sound like you aren't really sure what you want."

She capped her knees with her hands and stared down at them. "Falling in love is a scary prospect for me. My sole experience with being in love left me battered and scared, and while I would like to claim I'm a new woman, I seem unable to let go of the fear or the past." Shifting on the sofa, Cassie crossed her arms in a defensive, protective way over her heart. She felt she had to explain further. "The thing is, when it comes to falling in love, I haven't exactly shown the best judgment."

"You were a teenager, for the love of heaven. You were young and naïve when you met and married Duke."

"Even so, I've come a long way, but I have an even greater distance to go. This isn't the right time for me to give my heart away. And really, what do I know about love and relationships? It would be the easiest thing in the world to fall for you. I'm more than halfway there already, and it scares me to death.

"I know you might not understand any of what I'm saying, that's the risk, but I'm hoping you do and are willing to give me the room I need to grow, make my own decisions, and rebuild my life. Then and only then will I be ready for love."

Steve exhaled slowly and rubbed his hand along the back of his neck. "So where does that leave us?"

They sat facing each other as he awaited her answer, but Cassie didn't know what to tell him. She didn't doubt for an instant that Amiee had her ear pressed to her bedroom door and was listening to their exchange. That made what she had to say all the more important.

"I don't know, Steve. I thought I did, but I don't."

"Would you like some time to think all this over? I'm content to wait until you've got this figured out. I never meant to pressure you, although it appears that's exactly what I did. In which case, I suppose I'm the one who owes you an apology."

Cassie didn't know how to answer him.

"Cassie?"

Slowly she nodded. "I think that might be the best for now."

The room went shockingly silent.

"Okay, that's the way we'll play it," he said, his voice gaining strength. "I'll step aside while you figure out what it is you want. I'll wait for you to contact me. Is that fair?"

"More than fair."

Amiee's bedroom door opened. It seemed that Steve was about to say something more, but he swallowed whatever it was.

"Do you need me, Mom?"

"No, honey. I'll manage this. Thank you."

Her daughter looked doubtful, but then did as Cassie requested and returned to her bedroom. This time she didn't close the door completely.

Steve stood and looked down at his shoes. "So this is it, then."

"For the time being, until I get everything sorted out in my head." She was certain pride demanded that he not give her any indication of what he was feeling. She wondered if he'd move on while she had him on hold. But she knew it was what she had to do, even if that's the risk she was taking.

"Okay, I've got it. I'll give you all the breathing room you need." He headed for the front door.

"We can still be friends, right?" she asked, hurrying after him.

"Sure," he said, shrugging off the question. He walked out the door, and he didn't look back even once.

Cassie had assumed she'd feel relief after she'd talked to Steve. But the only feeling she had was a deep sense of loss.

Chapter 30

"Your sisters are coming **here**?" Amiee was beside herself. "To our house? This Sunday? This isn't a joke, is it? Because it would be the worst joke ever."

"Yes, they're coming this Sunday," Cassie repeated. If her daughter was thrilled, it paled in comparison to the exhilaration Cassie felt after hearing from Karen. This was exactly what she needed after the difficult decision she'd made with Steve.

"Karen is driving from Spokane and Nichole is coming from Portland."

"It will be the first time you've all been together since before I was even born," Amiee cried, leaping up and down like a five-year-old. She clapped her hands several times, seeming much younger than she was.

Cassie laughed.

"What are we going to do . . . I mean, other than visit and talk?" Amiee asked, all of a sudden looking worried. "Should we cook, or should we all go out to dinner?" Her daughter continued to chatter, speaking so fast her words nearly ran together. "Can we afford to take them out to dinner? And is Nichole bringing her baby, because I'd be happy to play with him while you visit, though I'd like to listen in with the adults. That would be all right, wouldn't it, because if it isn't I wouldn't be mad or anything, just disappointed." She stopped and gasped for breath.

Cassie had to smile again, her own excitement spilling over. Her daughter's face was bright with joy. "Which question do you want me to answer first?" she asked.

"I don't know. I'm just so happy for you, Mom." Her daughter impulsively reached out and hugged Cassie.

Cassie had just walked into the apartment. Her purse strap was crisscrossed over her torso, and she had on the sweatshirt she'd worn at the construction site. After several hours working, she was badly in need of a shower and a place to put up her feet.

"Here, sit down," Amiee insisted, as if reading her mind. "And start at the beginning and tell me absolutely everything." She scooted her textbook aside and cleared a space for Cassie on the sofa. Then, sitting on the edge of the coffee table, Amiee waited impatiently for Cassie to start.

"I got the call just before noon that they're definitely coming," Cassie explained. "I was with a client and almost didn't answer, but I'd just finished putting the perm solution on Mrs. Ruotolo's hair and had about twenty minutes to wait so I took the call."

"Was it Karen or Nichole?" Amiee leaned in.

"Karen. She wanted to make sure we were available on Sunday and I—"

"What did you tell her?" Amiee interrupted.

"That we had no other plans and that we'd set aside the entire day for them."

"When did you find out that Nichole was coming, too?" Amiee pressed her hands between her knees as if to keep them from flying about with gestures of joy.

"Karen mentioned that Nichole and she had timed it so they would arrive together. Nichole is taking the train from Portland and Karen is picking her and Owen up at the depot in downtown Seattle, and then the three of them will come to the apartment."

Right away Amiee looked around and sighed. "We should clean, don't you think?"

"Probably a good idea." Their apartment wasn't dirty, really. A load of clothes that needed to be folded sat in a wicker basket on the chair at the kitchen table. Amiee's schoolbooks were tossed about the coffee table and sofa, but that was really all. The real issue was the old, outdated furniture and mismatched pieces that Cassie had managed to scrounge up at Goodwill. When she'd arrived in Seattle, Cassie and Amiee had possessed next to nothing. They considered themselves fortunate to have what they did.

"Maybe we should meet them somewhere else," Amiee said, thinking the same thing Cassie was.

"It'll be fine," Cassie assured her. "Once they see our apartment they'll understand why we're so grateful to have my parents' things."

"I'll say." Amiee released the words on the tail end of a sigh. "I can hardly wait until we move into our new house. It's going to be so great."

"It will be." In her mind, Cassie already had the furniture neatly arranged in every room. She had the perfect place in the living room for the piano, and her father's old desk would go in the largest of the three bedrooms. The kitchen table was the very one where the family had eaten dinner nearly every night.

"I'll teach you to play if you like," Cassie said absently.

"Play what?" Amiee asked.

Caught in her musings, Cassie smiled and rested her head against the back of the sofa. "The piano. I'm a bit rusty. It's been several years since I last played, but it's something one never really forgets.

I haven't told you that my old piano was one of the things Steve and I collected."

"Really?" Amiee said. "I can learn to play the piano?"

"If you want. But like I said, it's been a few years." Nearly thirteen years . . . that was hard to believe. In her entire marriage, Cassie had played the piano only once. It'd been in a tavern—Duke had been drinking and making a lot of noise with his friends. Because she was sober and feeling out of place, she'd been drawn to the piano. She sat down at the keyboard, loving the feel of the cool keys beneath her fingers, and experienced a pang of homesickness so strong she'd stifled the urge to cry. Before she could stop herself, she'd started playing. Without realizing it, she soon had the attention of the entire tavern.

Once Duke realized she was the one at the piano, he'd dragged her outside and said she was showing off. He vowed if he ever caught her at the piano again he'd break all her fingers. She didn't doubt him, either. From that moment on, whenever she saw a piano Cassie forced herself to look the other way.

Any time he felt she did something he didn't know how to do himself, then she needed to be put in her place.

"Mom?" Amiee said, and placed her hand on Cassie's knee. "Are you feeling sick? You went quiet all of a sudden."

"Sorry, honey. I was just thinking."

"Did it have something to do with Dad?"

Her daughter seemed to be able to see straight through her. "Yeah. How'd you know?"

Amiee tilted her head to one side. "You get this sad look when you think about him. I know you got a letter from him. Did that scare you?"

"No. We are completely safe, honey. You don't need to worry." Amiee reached for her hand, folding her own fingers over Cassie's.

"Does he know where we're living?"

That had always been a primary concern, wherever they lived. "Nope."

"Good," Amiee said, nodding once.

Cassie had held on to that letter for a while now without mentioning Duke's request to her daughter. "It pains me to tell you this, Amiee, but your father is in prison."

Amiee shrugged as if that meant nothing to her. "It's where he belongs."

Cassie couldn't disagree on that point.

"What did he want?" Amiee asked. "Money?" She laughed then and added, "As if we had any."

"Among other things, he wanted money, but mostly . . ." She hesitated, unsure whether now was the time to tell her. She'd intended to wait awhile. But maybe it was time. "He wanted to stay in touch with you. He wanted to write to you. I wasn't sure I should even let you know, but you've grown up a great deal in the last five years and I decided that if you wanted to be in touch with your father, I wouldn't stand in the way. The decision is yours."

This was a big risk. Every little girl wants her father, and Cassie had protected Amiee by not telling her everything, so she didn't really know the worst of it. But her daughter was no dummy; she knew how Cassie felt about him, and she trusted her mother.

"Can I think about this and tell you what I decide later?" Amiee asked.

"Of course. There's no rush; you do what feels right to you." Cassie understood that she could be prying the lid open to Pandora's box, but that was a risk she was willing to take.

They talked the rest of the night away, mainly about Cassie's two sisters and their impending visit. It was bound to be an eventful weekend. Amiee asked to be in charge of cooking on Sunday and decided she would serve a light lunch. Salads, maybe. While her daughter mulled over the menu choices and pored through cookbooks, Cassie took a long, hot shower and got ready for bed.

Tired as she was, Cassie couldn't sleep. Different subjects popped up and down in her brain, demanding attention. She so badly wanted to reconnect with Karen and Nichole. There was a lot that needed to be settled among them. Unspoken hurts. Lost years. Disappointments and enough pain to pass around for second helpings.

It wasn't only Karen and Nichole that were on her mind, either. As always, Steve lingered in her thoughts. Their last meeting played over in her mind again and again. True to his word, he'd stayed away all week. Cassie hadn't heard from him since their talk on Monday—not that she expected she would. If nothing else, Steve had his pride.

Everything she had told him was true: She wasn't ready for a serious relationship. And yet her world felt empty without him.

Chapter 31

Cassie was nervous waiting for her sisters to arrive. They were due at the apartment around two on Sunday. The minute Cassie and Amiee had gotten home from church, they cleaned and scrubbed every inch of the shabby place. It helped work off some of the anxiety and kept Cassie's mind occupied.

When they'd finished cleaning, Cassie stepped back and viewed the living area with fresh eyes. "This would make even my mother proud," she proclaimed. Sandra Judson had been a meticulous housekeeper. If cleanliness was next to godliness, then her mother was strumming a harp at that very moment.

"Grandma said there was a place for everything and everything should be in its place, right?" Amiee said, quoting the grandmother she had never met. Little wonder, seeing that Cassie had mouthed those very words often enough herself.

They sat now, impatiently awaiting Karen and Nichole's arrival. Cassie rubbed her palms together and glanced at her watch for the second time in as many minutes. "They should be here soon," she told Amiee.

"Mom?" Amiee said, lowering her voice and darting a look toward Cassie. "I've sort of missed seeing Steve."

Her daughter wasn't the only one. "Yeah, me, too."

"It's been over a week now. He hasn't called or anything, has he?"

"No, but I was the one who said I'd contact him when I was ready."

Amiee sighed, her shoulders moving expressively. "I'm sorry I kicked him."

Cassie tried to hide a smile.

"But he deserved it," her daughter added. "I was thinking that maybe I should text him and tell him I'm sorry. Do you think I should?"

Cassie was touched. She wrapped her arm around her daughter's shoulders and kissed her cheek. "Nice thought, but I think it's best to leave matters as they are for now."

"But don't you miss him?"

Oh yes, she missed him, more than Cassie thought possible. It might be better to tell a lie, but her daughter knew her too well. There was no point in trying. "I do. Big-time."

The sound of a car door closing came from a distance. Right away Amiee was on her feet, racing toward the front door. "They're here!" she cried, throwing open the screen and hurrying outside even before Cassie was off the couch.

"Are you my aunt Karen?" Amiee asked. "And my aunt Nichole? I know all about you. Aunt Karen stole my mother's curling iron and hid it so Mom had to go to school with her hair looking freaky, and Aunt Nichole, you used to wear pigtails. My mom put my hair in pigtails, too, and said I looked just like you!"

Cassie stood in the doorway and smiled even while tears gathered in her eyes. Her heart swelled with emotion and love, watching her daughter greet her two aunts.

"Hello, Amiee," Karen said, hugging her niece.

"Can I babysit Owen?" Amiee asked Nichole. "Mom said it was up to you, but I'm good with babies. I'm signed up for a class at the Y and will get a certificate and everything. I like babies. I want my mom to have a baby, but she put everything on hold with Steve, so it's probably a lost cause."

Cassie reached out and hugged Nichole, who held a sleeping Owen in her arms. Tears streamed down her cheeks and she found it difficult to speak. "You're all grown up," she said, laughing to hide her emotion. Releasing her younger sister, she wiped the moisture from her face with the flat of her hand. "And look at my handsome nephew!"

Karen was crying, too. "I knew this would happen," she whispered, and covered her words with a weak laugh.

"Please come inside," Cassie said. After hugging Karen, she ushered them into the apartment.

"Mom wanted to bake a cake from a recipe your mother used to make, but we don't have an oven so we bought a cake. I thought about making salads but Mom said a cake was better because this is a celebration. I bet the cake isn't nearly as good as the one your mom made, but it is what it is. My mom says that all the time. Did your mom say that, too, because my mom says a lot of things that your mom did."

"I'm sure a store-bought cake will be fine," Karen assured Amiee.

"You can put Owen down on my bed to sleep. I'll put pillows around him so he won't fall off. If you want I can sit and watch him until he wakes up," Amiee offered, eager to please.

"Okay, but let's leave the bedroom door open so we'll be able to hear him."

"You won't have a problem. The walls in this place carry sound real well," Amiee assured her. "But I'll keep the door open, too."

While Cassie cut the cake and poured the coffee,

Amiee gave her two aunts the grand tour, which took all of ten seconds.

"That's your bedroom?" Nichole asked Amiee, looking shocked at the closet-size space.

"Small, isn't it?" Amiee said, "but Mom is building us a real house with Habitat for Humanity. She works every spare minute she can on putting in her hours. We're hoping to have the house completely done before Christmas. It seems like years from now, because we're both so, so ready. The fastest anyone has managed to get in their hours was six months. Mom checked. Mom thinks she can do it in eight months. Pretty cool, huh? I'll have a much bigger bedroom then."

Amiee went with Nichole to put Owen down on her bed.

"Come sit down," Cassie invited, offering her sister the sofa and taking one of the mismatched kitchen chairs for herself.

Karen joined her first and hugged Cassie. Her sister clung to her for an extra-long moment. She hugged her back just as tightly. "Before anything else—I want to tell you how sorry I am, Cassie. We didn't talk about this when you came to get the furniture, but we should have. More than anything I regret our last fight and the awful things I said to you. I called you some dreadful names and then you ran off with Duke. When we discovered you were gone I was sure it was because of the

things I said. Mom and Dad were beside themselves with worry and I blamed you. I shouldn't
have, but I did. Afterward I held on to that anger
because it was easier to hold you responsible than
to accept that I played a part in you leaving with
Duke."

Cassie had never thought she'd hear these words
from Karen. Leaning forward, Cassie placed her
hand on her sister's forearm. "There's enough
blame to go around. I was foolish and rebellious.
I'm sorry, too, Karen, so, so sorry. We were both
in the wrong. I've regretted my own words and
wanted so badly to tell you I wanted to take back
every ugly thing I hurled at you."

Karen's hands trembled slightly. "When we
didn't hear from you, no one knew what to think.
And later, when you did reach out needing help,
I was so awful to you . . . so righteous and angry."

"It's okay," Cassie whispered. "Really. It hurt
at first—I won't lie about that—but Amiee and
I found what we needed. None of that matters
now."

The two sisters clung to each other and openly
wept. After a few moments, they broke apart and,
embarrassed at all the emotion, they laughed. All
that mattered was the fact that they were together
and were able to talk heart-to-heart.

Nichole stepped out of the bedroom and announced, "Owen's sleeping and Amiee is watching
him so he doesn't roll off the bed."

Cassie wiped the moisture off her face. Karen reached for her purse and dug out the tissues, took one, and handed another to Cassie.

"I apologized to Cassie for our big fight . . . and everything else," Karen explained to Nichole, rubbing the tissue across the top of her cheekbones.

Nichole sat down next to Karen and looked at Cassie, and in short order tears formed in her eyes. "Karen isn't the only one who's sorry." She sucked in a deep breath. "I owe you an apology, too. Right before you ran away, I . . . I read your journal."

Cassie had figured that out almost right away. Clearly someone had, and it made sense that it would be Nichole. "I know."

"I found it in your half of the closet and then realized that you knew that I'd read it."

"You knew I was pregnant with Amiee."

Keeping her eyes lowered, Nichole nodded. "But I wouldn't have told Mom and Dad. I wouldn't, and then you ran away and I was sure it was because you didn't trust me not to tell. I wouldn't have—I swear it, Cassie. Before I could reassure you . . . you were gone. And you left your journal behind as if to say it didn't matter if I knew your secrets or not, because I never would have access to you again."

"You blamed yourself for me going with Duke? Both of you?" Cassie had a hard time assimilating this. All these years her sisters had assumed part of the responsibility for her decision to marry Duke.

Each one had been convinced that their action had led to the rift between them. "No," she whispered.

"No?" Nichole repeated.

"No, before any of this happened Duke convinced me that leaving was the only option available to us. I had two hundred dollars in my savings account and that was all we would need to get to Florida, where we could both get jobs."

Karen and Nichole looked at each other and then at Cassie, and smiled through their tears.

"I have missed you both so much."

"And we've missed you," Karen said, speaking for them both. "It was never the same after you left."

"For me, either, and all the while I wondered how I was ever going to make it back home. Remember our hide-and-seek games every summer in the park?"

"Last one home, but you're home now, Cassie."

Amiee stood in the doorway to her bedroom. "Is everyone done crying yet?"

Cassie beamed a smile at her two sisters and it felt as if the doors of her heart had been tossed open. "I believe so."

"Tell me a story from when you were kids my age," Amiee pleaded.

"Let me see," Karen lounged back in the sofa. She glanced toward Nichole and Cassie. "Remember Grandma Coulson and the fun things she used to cook for us?" Karen asked.

"Yum—those pizzas she used to make us with English muffins," Nichole said.

"She made us green eggs and ham once, too, remember?" Karen said.

"And she served us sauerkraut for dessert and it was good," Nichole added.

"Are you nuts?" Cassie said. "That was gross!" All three laughed at the memory.

"Oh, Karen, Nichole," Cassie said, tearing up again. "I have so missed you."

Owen stirred and Amiee immediately went back inside her bedroom.

"You never called," Nichole said, but her voice wasn't accusing or critical.

"I couldn't," Cassie admitted, lowering her gaze and clenching her fingers together. "Duke wouldn't allow it."

"What do you mean he wouldn't allow it? How could he stop you? You had your own cell, didn't you?"

"No. He made sure there was no way I could communicate with any of my family. Once he caught me; I'd borrowed a neighbor's phone and . . . and let's just say I paid the price for defying him." She told them how he'd dislocated her shoulder and given her two black eyes. He refused to take her to the hospital and had a friend reset her shoulder. The pain was so severe Cassie had briefly passed out. She never tried to use a friend's phone again.

Both were silent, aghast.

"I don't understand," Nichole continued. "If Duke was so cruel, why didn't you leave him?"

This was a question Cassie had asked herself a million times. She gave Nichole the same answer she gave everyone. Getting away from Duke wasn't as simple as it sounded. "The thing is, walking away from an abusive situation is hard. Harder than anyone realizes."

"I don't mean to criticize you," Nichole said. "I'm just trying to understand."

"Dad missed you something terrible," Karen said, taking hold of Cassie's hand.

"And I missed him and Mom and both of you so much. I don't think you'll ever know how I longed for my family." Tears filled Cassie's eyes again and she valiantly tried to blink them away. It was the memory of her parents and sisters that helped her through those lonely years; the belief that one day they would all be reunited.

Amiee returned to the doorway. "Mom talked about you all the time. I know just about everything there is to know about both of you. Aunt Karen, when can I meet my cousins? I'm the oldest, you know, and I want to meet Lily. Does she wear makeup yet? Mom won't let me until I'm thirteen. She said that was because that was how long her mother made her wait."

"Lily will love meeting you."

"Can I see her sometime this summer?"

"You bet."

"We'll arrange a time later," Cassie promised.

"Did you know Mom is no longer dating Steve?" Amiee said.

Karen's eyes connected with Cassie's. "I thought I heard something about that earlier. Are you okay?" The question was directed at Cassie.

"We miss him," Amiee answered for her. "Mom doesn't talk about it much, but I know she does."

Owen stirred awake and right away Nichole was on her feet. "He's going to need a diaper change."

"Can I help?" Amiee asked, hurrying back into her bedroom.

Karen took hold of Cassie's hand. "I'm sorry about Steve."

Cassie nodded. "Me, too, but I'm not ready for a serious relationship."

"I can understand your hesitation. Relationships are hard. Marriage, too." Karen lowered her head.

Cassie hesitated before gently squeezing her sister's hand. "Is everything all right between you and Garth?"

Karen nodded. "For the most part. Garth lost his job about three months ago . . . he was afraid to tell me and so he took money from our retirement account. It's like we have to start all over again. My husband has hit bottom and frankly so have I. We're in a tight place financially, but . . . but that doesn't concern me nearly as much as seeing Garth in this kind of emotional anguish. I've never seen him like this."

Cassie wrapped her arms around her sister. "I know what it is to hit bottom and to have to start over with nothing. The thing is that there's only one direction left to go and that's up."

"He's out every day job-hunting and comes home discouraged and deeply depressed. There's nothing available in his field, and I mean nothing."

"Is there anything else he'd like to do?" Cassie asked.

"I . . . I don't know. I've never thought to ask him."

"I had no job skills when I left Duke, but I'd always enjoyed working with hair. I decided to learn to be a stylist."

"Garth enjoys golf, or at least he used to, but now it's too expensive." She hesitated. "He does a lot of crossword puzzles and works sudoku. From what I can figure that's how he spends most of his days. To be fair, he does almost all of the household chores now and the cooking, but I can't see him opening up a housecleaning service."

"Talk to him. You might be surprised."

"I will. We both need to look at options. At this point he's butting his head against a wall. I feel like such an idiot. I should have known something was wrong, but like a fool I ignored what my instincts were telling me."

"It will get better, Karen, trust me. I've been at this same point myself. God will make a way where there is no way. He did in my life, and He will with you, too."

Her sister smiled and her eyes revealed the light of hope.

Nichole returned with baby Owen on her hip. The baby leaned his head against his mother's shoulder.

"He wouldn't come to me," Amiee said in a dejected tone. "I held out my arms and he turned his head away and refused to look at me."

"He will once he gets to know you better," Nichole promised her.

Amiee, however, wasn't about to let it go at that. "I'm your cousin, Owen, and one day maybe your mother will let me babysit you."

Nichole laughed. "I think that could be arranged."

They sat down and ate their cake and talked nonstop for nearly two hours. By the time her sisters left, Cassie was exhilarated and overwhelmed, giddy with happiness. Their visit had gone even better than she'd hoped.

"I like my aunts," Amiee said, as they stood on the sidewalk and watched Karen and Nichole drive away. "They're exactly as I pictured them."

"They really haven't changed that much."

"You have," Amiee insisted.

Karen had brought along the family photo albums their mother had kept, and they'd laughed their way through most of the pictures.

"Do you have pictures of me as a baby?" Amiee asked.

"Very few." It did no good to remind her daughter there hadn't been money for frivolities such as cameras and film when Duke needed beer and drugs. She didn't mention that whatever photos she'd managed to get had been left behind.

"It's good to have family, isn't it?" Amiee asked, wrapping her arm around Cassie's waist.

"Yes, it is," she agreed, and kissed the top of her daughter's head. Steve came to mind then, and she wondered where his family was and if he was close to his parents. They hadn't talked about so many things. The thing was, even so, he was never far from her thoughts.

Chapter 32

After waiting impatiently for two months to hear from Cassie, Steve had given up hope of hearing from her. The next move had to be from her. He'd never meant to pressure her and now it seemed there was no going back and correcting his mistake. For the first couple weeks, he'd been calm and cool about it, but when she didn't reach out the way he'd hoped he grew irritable. For the last six weeks he'd been angry at the world. It'd gotten to the point that even his best friend had taken to avoiding him.

"I don't know what your problem is," Stan snapped at him late one Friday afternoon, "but whatever it is, fix it." And with that Stan stalked away.

It didn't help matters that Britt had become a constant thorn in his side. He couldn't make her understand that no matter how fond he was of her son, he wasn't interested in dating her.

Steve had lost count of the number of times he had to stop himself from contacting Cassie. He would have in less time it took to breathe if she hadn't made it abundantly clear that she had to be the one to seek him out. The next move had to come from her and thus far it didn't look like she was inclined to make one.

He made a point of checking on her through Stan and Megan at the Habitat office. Her house was coming along ahead of schedule. From what Stan said, Cassie was working every spare minute on the project. Her furniture was stored in his warehouse and would remain there until she was ready to collect it. He'd sent word via Stan that he'd hold on to it until needed. He hoped for a personal reply. None came.

As the weeks progressed, his mood darkened. He was back to visiting Alicia more often now, talking out his troubles while standing over her grave site. Now sitting in his pickup at the cemetery, Steve mulled over his conversation with Stan. If he had a clue on how to fix this thing with Cassie, he would have done it two months ago. As it was, they were at a complete standstill.

Climbing out of his truck, Steve walked over to his wife's grave site. It eased his mind to talk to Alicia, which was sort of absurd, seeing that she couldn't respond. Still, it'd become a habit.

In the months following her death, he'd been to the cemetery nearly every day. He'd stop by three or four times a week on his way to or from work and then on weekends. As time progressed he'd come less frequently. Alicia would have understood, and he was fairly certain she'd approve of the way he spent his time these days, working with Habitat.

He felt responsible for looking after the grave site, bringing her flowers. Alicia's family all lived on the East Coast and he was the only one to keep her grave tended.

When he arrived at the grave site, to his surprise, he saw that someone had left a bouquet of flowers. They looked like they were a couple of days old. Steve couldn't imagine who would have brought them. He would probably never know. He removed the older bouquet and replaced it with the fresh one.

"It's been awhile," he whispered, straightening, and then felt he should make an effort to explain. "I meant to come sooner."

He bent over and brushed away grass clippings. He'd had Alicia's picture placed on her gravestone as a reminder that she'd been beautiful and far too young to have lost her life. Seeing her photo smiling back at him made talking to her feel less strange.

"Stan said I needed to fix what was wrong. I wish I could, but I can't do anything about Cassie," he said. "It was her choice. I was in the wrong and apologized, but that wasn't enough." What frustrated him most was that at one point she'd actually compared him to her ex-husband, as if Steve was some kind of lowlife. It tightened his jaw every time he thought about what she'd said. "If she can't tell the difference between a man like me and a man like Duke, I'm better off without her," he said, talking out loud again.

His shoulders sagged. He'd been telling himself that repeatedly, not that he was anywhere close to believing it.

Steve knew he'd been walking around like an injured bear for nearly two months. He had to fix this. Looking down at his wife's grave marker, he released a sigh.

He waited for a moment while he mulled over his dilemma.

"Do I love her?" he asked himself.

"I think so," he said, answering his own question. "My gut's been in a perpetual knot ever since we split."

He walked a complete circle around the grave site.

He stopped and abruptly rammed his fingers through his hair.

Finally, he headed back to his truck. He'd brought the old wilting floral bouquet and tossed it into the flatbed to discard at home. As he did, a card fell out. Steve reached down and took hold of it—it was printed with the name of the grocery store where the flowers had been bought.

A store in Kent.

The store that was only a couple blocks from Cassie and Amiee's apartment. The same store where she routinely shopped.

Steve mulled it over and then shook his head. It wasn't possible that Cassie had brought the flowers. For one thing, she would have no way of knowing where Alicia was buried unless . . .

He grabbed his cell and hit the button that would connect him to Stan. His friend answered on the second ring.

"Steve?"

"Question," he said.

"You gonna bite my head off if you don't like the answer?" his buddy asked.

"No."

"Good thing, because otherwise I wouldn't be inclined to answer."

Despite himself, Steve smiled. "Did Cassie happen to ask you where Alicia was buried?"

Stan hesitated. "Why do you want to know?"

"Because I found flowers at Alicia's grave site and I wasn't the one who put them there."

"Was Cassie's name on a card or something?"

Stan was avoiding the question, which was an answer in and of itself. "Nothing with her name on it. It was the name of the grocery store near her apartment. Seems to me they could only have come from her."

"A lot of people shop at that same grocery store, you know."

"I'm sure they do," Steve concurred. As far as he was concerned he had his answer. "Thanks for your help."

For the first time in two months, the knot in Steve's stomach loosened. He started up his truck and headed out of the cemetery. He'd come, feeling low and blue, seeking Alicia's advice and expecting nothing. And yet his wife had given him the very answer he needed.

He heard himself whistling when his cell chirped. Glancing at his phone, caller ID told him it was Britt. He let the call go to voice mail as he headed to the construction site, knowing Cassie was probably there working off the last of her equity hours.

Arriving at the site, Steve was surprised by how far along the house was. The frame and roof were all up. Stan was busy supervising but stepped toward the curb when he saw Steve drive up.

"You looking for Cassie?" Stan asked.

"How'd you guess?" Steve propped his elbow in the open window.

"She isn't here."

Steve frowned. "You're not hiding her from me, are you?"

His friend grinned. "No. I'd know better than to do anything that stupid."

"Then where is she?"

"Do I look like her keeper?" Stan demanded.

Thwarted, Steve realized now probably wasn't the best time to seek Cassie out anyway. He'd give it time, he decided, wait a day or two even, mull over how best to approach her. This was a delicate matter and he shouldn't act on impulse.

Instead of searching out Cassie, Steve drove to his office, where his desk was stacked high with paperwork that needed to be processed. His cell rang again and once more it was Britt.

"Hello?" he snapped, in no mood to deal with her.

"Steve, it's Britt."

"Yes, I know."

"You haven't returned my calls," she said with a small pout. "Jeremy wanted to ask you to come to the house this weekend."

"I'm busy this weekend. Can you put him on the line and I'll talk to him?"

Britt hesitated. "I'm beginning to think you're not interested in seeing me or Jeremy."

She sounded hurt now and Steve felt wretched. "Listen, Britt. I'm already involved with someone." His heart was involved, if nothing else. Despite the fact that Cassie appeared to want nothing more to do with him, he'd fallen for her hard. She wasn't going to be easy to forget.

"You don't mean that girl from the Hoedown, do you? You can't mean her! Steve, really, she's one of those poor women who are charity cases. You can't be serious."

"I'm very serious, Britt. You're beautiful and Jeremy is a great kid. I'll be happy to remain pals with your son, but as for you and me, it's not going to work."

"Okay," she said defiantly. "Well, that's just fine." She hung up before he had a chance to say anything more, which, frankly, was probably for the best.

Steve felt bad about Britt, but not for long. He got busy with paperwork and the next time he looked up it was dark. He glanced at his wrist and was shocked to see that it was after nine o'clock. His stomach growled. He hadn't eaten since midmorning and he was ravenous.

He locked up the office and headed out. For reasons he couldn't explain, he ended up parked outside of Cassie's apartment. Her beater car was on the other side of the street, so in every likelihood she was home. And the lights were on inside, so he knew she was awake.

The evening was warm and her front door was open, allowing the air to cool the apartment. Driven by something beyond his pride and his stubbornness, he climbed out of his truck. He'd sworn he wasn't going to contact her. Sworn she had to reach out to him. Even while he reminded himself of that, Steve checked traffic and then ran across the street.

When he got to the sidewalk outside her apartment, he glanced up and saw Cassie framed in the doorway. Like a hook that was sunk deep into his heart he felt drawn to her. Step-by-step he came toward her until the only thing that separated them was the screen door. Not more than five feet from her, he stopped, his breathing shallow and labored as if he'd just finished a 10K run.

For a long moment all they did was stare at each other. He swore she'd never looked more beautiful.

He stepped nearer, so only inches separated them now. Mere inches and one thin screen.

Steve's throat was tight. Earlier he'd asked himself the question if he loved Cassie, and looking at her now, there wasn't a single doubt left in his mind. He was head over heels in love, crazy about her.

This was different, totally different, from what it'd been like with Alicia. They'd been college students, high on life, ruled by hormones. They'd been in love, deeply in love, and they'd married and had wonderful plans for a home, a family, a future. Cancer had robbed them of the opportunity.

What he felt for Cassie was more mature, deep, profound. Hardly aware of what he was doing, he raised his hand and pressed it against the screen, seeking a link with her. After only a slight hesitation, Cassie's hand met his on the other side.

While it was their palms that touched, he felt as if the gesture had linked their hearts.

"Hi," he whispered.

"Hi," she whispered back.

"I've missed you."

She smiled and then bit into her lower lip as if she was trying hard not to cry. "I've missed you, too." She lowered her hand and unlatched the screen and held it open for him.

The very instant he could, Steve reached for her and brought her into his arms. He sucked in a deep breath and closed his eyes. He took in the scent of her, cherished the joy of holding her.

Cassie buried her face in his neck and clung to him. He longed to kiss her, to show her the only way he could think how miserable he'd been without her. He'd been angry, depressed, lost, and it took until this very moment to realize how convinced he was that this was home. He belonged with Cassie and she belonged with him.

They'd both made the long, arduous journey toward each other. Nothing would be right without Cassie in his life. She offered him everything that he thought he'd lost with Alicia. A home, a daughter, a sense of belonging, but he wouldn't pressure her. He'd learned his lesson. He'd be patient, bide his time until she was ready.

"I'm sorry I rushed you," he whispered, needing to say it. "Will you give me another chance if I promise to take this one day at a time?"

She raised her head and placed her fingers over his lips, shushing him.

He wrapped his arms around her waist and lifted her off the ground, and with her arms linked around his neck she tossed back her head and started to laugh.

Steve twirled her around and around, laughing with her, loving her so much that it felt as if his heart was about to burst wide open.

"Mom?" Amiee asked, and then immediately followed it with, "Steve?"

The girl stood in the doorway to her bedroom. She looked from her mother to Steve.

Steve set Cassie's feet back down on the ground.

Amiee looked from one to the other. Steve kept his arm around Cassie's waist, unwilling to let her go for even a moment.

"Are you back?" Amiee asked him.

Steve looked to Cassie and saw the joy in her face and nodded. "I'm back."

"Amiee, honey. I thought you were reading," Cassie said.

"I was, but then I fell asleep. And then I woke up."

"So did I," Steve said.

Cassie looked at him and her smile widened. "So did I," she whispered.

Steve got back in the truck and went to get a bucket of KFC, then brought it to the apartment. The three of them sat around the table and dug in to the feast. More than once Steve leaned over and took Cassie's hand, unable to restrain himself.

Amiee ate mashed potatoes but refused to let anyone eat the chicken legs so she could have them all the following day.

Soon after they finished clearing off the table, Amiee returned to her room and Cassie and Steve cuddled on the sofa.

"You took flowers to Alicia's grave site," he said.

Cassie twisted her head back to look up at him. "How'd you know?"

"Why would you do that?"

She pressed her head against his shoulder. "I was miserable, and don't laugh, please, but I wanted her advice. I know it sounds ridiculous . . . she wasn't going to answer. I . . . I don't know. It made me feel better, I guess."

"I went to her for advice today myself," he said, his lips grazing Cassie's cheek. "And she answered me."

"She did?"

Steve kissed her again, longer this time, letting Cassie know how much he'd missed her and how empty his life had felt without her. "She led me back to you," he said, as he lifted his head. "She led me straight back to you."

Chapter 33

Nichole felt jubilant. In the four months since her visit with her two sisters, the three of them had made a point of routinely getting together. Reuniting with Cassie had changed everything. She had never expected to feel this close to Cassie again. It was as if reconciling with her had completed the circle. The three sisters were in almost constant communication. They texted back and forth all day long, as if to make up for lost time.

Although her sister didn't speak of it often, Nichole learned more of the horrors of Cassie's marriage to Duke. She'd met Steve Brody and liked him a great deal. The two were definitely an item, but they were taking it slow. If she married again, Cassie wanted to be sure.

Nichole was astonished when she saw the home Cassie was building. Cassie routinely texted her photos of the progress. It was nearly completed now, and Karen and her family, along with Nichole, Jake, and Owen, all planned to attend the dedication ceremony the following month. Cassie didn't know they were coming—it would be a surprise.

Until Cassie's return, Nichole hadn't fully appreciated the importance of family connections. Oh, she'd kept in touch with Karen, but after their father's death so closely followed by their mother's, the two had drifted apart. They each had busy lives and living in different states didn't help. Without realizing it, Nichole had allowed the ties that had bound her to her oldest sibling to grow slack. That was no longer the case.

It felt wonderful to be part of a family again. Her family. While life had been treating her and Jake well, Karen and Garth had undergone their share of problems. But they seemed to be straightening it out. Three months ago Garth had taken the real estate exam and begun selling commercial property. Within a few weeks he'd had his first major sale. Karen was excited for him. He was a natural: personable, detailed-oriented, and knowledgeable. With Karen working at a title company, the two made a great team.

When she thought about how important family was, she included Jake's side of the family. She'd been growing closer to the Pattersons as well, especially her mother-in-law, Leanne. They often visited Jake's parents, and while father and son golfed together, Nichole and her mother-in-law shopped or took Owen on an outing, exploring the zoo or a park. It was nice to have such a great relationship with her in-laws, since they were the only grandparents Owen would know.

Her son was getting into everything these days, growing like a dandelion in lush green grass. He was a constant source of joy. Nichole was eager to get pregnant with a second child. She smiled as she set breakfast dishes in the dishwasher. Owen sat on the floor, playing with his xylophone, looking up at her gleefully as he made a racket.

He'd outgrown his morning naps shortly after his first birthday but could be counted on to take a two-hour nap every afternoon. Nichole used the time to work in the garden, which she loved.

The small vegetable garden she'd planted in their backyard had yielded lettuce and cucumbers and a small pumpkin that was the perfect size for her son. They'd be carving it soon.

If Nichole had any concern, it was the long hours her husband put into his job. Jake came home at the end of the day, emotionally drained and physically exhausted. Lately she noticed that he seemed a little depressed. She'd hoped driving his new BMW would lift his spirits, and it had in the beginning, but lately she'd sensed a growing discontent in him. Just recently she'd suggested that he consider changing jobs, seeing how demanding this one seemed to be. He wouldn't have a problem finding other employment, especially with his successful background with the wine company.

By noon, the autumn day had cooled considerably. The weather was forecasting snow flurries in the foothills. Karen had sent her an email that morning that said Spokane had already had their first snowfall of the year. Cassie had emailed that rain was in the forecast in Seattle. Autumn was upon them.

The doorbell chimed and Nichole grabbed a kitchen towel to wipe her hands before answering. She wasn't expecting anyone, especially mid-morning.

She opened the door to find her mother-in-law standing on the other side.

"Leanne, this is a surprise," Nichole said, holding open the door for her.

Owen toddled toward her with outstretched arms.

"How's my boy?" Leanne asked, leaning down and scooping up Owen. She spread eager kisses across his face and Owen squealed with delight.

"I hope you don't mind me stopping by unannounced."

"Of course not," Nichole said, leading her mother-in-law toward the kitchen. "How about a cup of coffee? It's chilly out today. I collected the mail earlier and was sorry I hadn't put on a sweater."

Leanne pulled out a chair and bounced Owen on her knee until he grew bored and wanted down. Eager to display his great musical ability, he returned to his xylophone and happily beat away. He really was a cheerful little boy.

Leanne was a wonderful grandmother, and in a recent conversation Nichole had shared her desire to have another baby. Her mother-in-law had been thrilled. She didn't ask outright if Nichole was pregnant; she wouldn't, that wasn't her way. She looked a bit pensive, doubtful. Nichole thought to clear the air.

"I was hoping I'd get pregnant this month," Nichole said, as she delivered two mugs of coffee to the table. "Unfortunately, my period started yesterday."

"Some things are meant to be," Leanne said, but didn't quite meet Nichole's eyes.

"I was really hoping this time."

"I always wanted more than one child," Leanne said, as she reached for her iced tea. "But it didn't happen for me." She hesitated and looked out the sliding glass door toward the patio, and when she spoke she lowered her voice. "It wasn't until Jake was in junior high that I learned that Sean had had a vasectomy without my knowledge."

"Oh." Shocked, Nichole hardly knew what to say. "I'm sorry, I didn't know."

Again her mother-in-law looked into the distance. "I'm sure you can figure out why Sean would do such a thing and not tell me."

"Well . . . I . . ." Again Nichole was at a loss for words, although there'd been plenty of rumors floating around regarding her father-in-law's extramarital affairs.

"You can't imagine how upset I was when I learned what he'd done. I hungered for another baby and desperately yearned for a daughter, but it never happened, and when I discovered why, it was too late."

"You've been like a mother to me," Nichole said, and gently patted Leanne's hand.

"Oh dear," she whispered. "I told myself I wasn't going to do this." She reached for her purse, opened it, and searched for a tissue.

"Leanne, what is it?" Nichole asked. She'd never seen her mother-in-law this upset.

Leanne dabbed at her eyes, sipped her coffee, and took a couple minutes to compose herself. "I believe we were married about three years before I learned that Sean was having an affair. Hindsight being what it is, I should have divorced him then. I didn't because Jake was a toddler, around the same age as Owen, and deeply attached to his dad, much the same way Owen is to Jake."

"Did you . . . never mind."

"Did I what?"

"Sorry, this isn't any of my business." At times

like this, Nichole wished she thought before she spoke.

"Did I confront Sean?" Leanne asked. "Is that what you want to know?"

Nichole nodded.

"No, fool that I was, I turned my head and looked the other way and pretended it didn't matter. Sean was a good provider. There'd never been a divorce in my family and I was too embarrassed to tell my parents what I'd learned. All those excuses sound so weak now." She dabbed at her eyes again and then blew her nose.

"I'm so sorry," Nichole whispered, wishing she had some words of consolation, of comfort.

"Sean got the vasectomy so he wouldn't be in danger of getting any of his girlfriends pregnant. When I learned what he'd done, I was outraged. I felt cheated and cheapened. I threatened a divorce and Sean begged me to stay. He never admitted to sleeping with other women, but he was well aware that I knew. He promised to remain faithful, and for a period of about six months I think he was, but it didn't take long for him to return to his old ways. It's part of his nature, the need for conquest.

"Funny, isn't it?" Leanne asked, although she didn't really seem to want Nichole to answer.

"Funny?" she repeated.

"Even now I'm making excuses for Sean." Leanne looked down at the wadded tissue in her hand.

Nichole knew why Leanne had stopped by un-expectedly. After thirty years of marriage, she'd had enough. She was going to ask Sean for a divorce and she wanted her and Jake to know. "Leanne," she said softly. "I hope you realize that whatever you decide in your marriage, Jake and I will sup-port you."

Her mother-in-law turned to look at her for the first time since they'd started this conversation. "Whatever I decide?" she asked. "What do you mean?"

"I thought . . . I'm sorry if I misunderstood. I thought you were here to tell me you're about to ask Sean for a divorce."

Leanne gave a short, humorless laugh. "By all that is right, I should. I should have done it years ago when I was young. I might have had a chance of finding happiness with a man who understood the meaning of fidelity and commitment. A man who is honorable."

"Leanne," Nichole protested. "You're not old. You're a beautiful woman." She wasn't just say-ing that, either. "You're one of the warmest, most generous-hearted women I've ever known. I bless the day I married into this family. I wasn't joking when I said that you're like a mother to me."

Fresh tears moistened Leanne's eyes and rained down her cheeks.

Without either of them noticing, Owen had toddled away and returned with a box of tissues, looking up at her with big beautiful eyes, so like his father's.

The action was just the comic relief needed to break the tension. Both women laughed. Leanne reached for her grandson and lifted him onto her lap to kiss him again. Owen struggled, twisting away, and Leanne set him back down on the floor. He disappeared and returned with a wooden puzzle and sat down at Nichole's feet, pulling out all the pieces and then promptly replacing them again, smiling up at her, awaiting her praise.

"Good job, Owen," she said.

"You're a good mother," Leanne whispered, smiling down on her grandson.

"Thank you." Nichole realized she had her own mother to thank. Sandra Judson had set an amazing example as a homemaker and a wife.

"You're like the daughter I never had, which is why I felt I had to come to you," Leanne said. The words trembled as they came from her lips. She grabbed hold of Nichole's hand, her fingers gripping hers to the point it was almost painful.

"I realize now what a terrible mistake I made," she said, her voice gaining strength. "If I'd left Sean when I was young, perhaps it would be different for Jake, perhaps he would . . ." She hesitated and seemed unable to go on. "I'm doing this for Owen and for you, so that you don't repeat the mistakes I made."

A chill ran down Nichole's spine, one so cold

and terrifying that she found it difficult to speak. Leanne couldn't possibly be implying what Nichole thought she was. "Leanne, what are you saying?" she asked slowly, enunciating each word carefully so there would be no misunderstanding.

"Jake came to the house to talk to his father last night. He didn't know I was close enough to overhear their conversation. I didn't intentionally eavesdrop, but I got the gist of what he was saying. I felt you had to know."

"Know what?" Nichole was almost afraid to ask, but it was as if she'd stumbled on a horrible car accident and couldn't keep from gawking. She needed the truth.

"This is going to deeply hurt you, Nichole. I would give anything to spare you this pain, but there's nothing I can say or do that is going to help."

"I prefer to know," she insisted. She squared her shoulders like a defiant soldier standing before a firing squad.

"Jake has gotten another woman pregnant."

Nichole gasped and jerked violently. She couldn't help it, the shock of it, the pain of it, nearly knocked her off her chair.

Leanne gripped her hands with both of her own. "Jake came to ask for his father's advice and help."

Tugging one hand free, Nichole covered her mouth, fearing she was about to scream. The only thing that prevented her from crying out was the thought of frightening Owen.

"I would do anything to spare you this," Leanne said, tears running down her cheeks. "The only reason I'm telling you is for Owen's sake. I had no idea Jake was aware of his father's infidelity . . . like father, like son. This has to end, and I'm determined to make sure it ends with Jake. He's my son and I would gladly give my life for him, but I will not allow him to destroy you the way Sean has destroyed me. I absolutely refuse to let him teach his son to disrespect and dishonor his wife the way Sean has me."

Nichole gripped hold of her mother-in-law's arm. She closed her eyes as the pain made its way through her heart. Her first reaction was intense anger, and then a nearly overwhelming desire to lash back and hurt Jake in return.

All the nights he claimed to be working late. The gifts he brought her. It all made sense now. It wasn't love. It was guilt, and perhaps fear.

He would pay. Nichole was determined she'd get him where it hurt him most. Right away her head was filled with thoughts of retaliation, vengeance.

"Nichole," Leanne whispered. "I am so sorry."

"You did the right thing." Her voice barely sounded like her own. Nichole's mind was in turmoil.

"I know what you're thinking," Leanne continued, "if not now, later. You'll be tempted to rationalize what Jake has done, blame yourself as if there was something lacking in you. That's what I did. I was convinced if I was prettier, thinner, a better lover Sean wouldn't need other women. I was a fool. Don't believe any of it. The lack isn't in you, it's in Sean and in Jake. Do you understand me? Don't fall into that trap."

"I won't," Nichole whispered.

"There's comfort in looking the other way and pretending, but I'm here to tell you the price is far too high. It will rob you of your self-worth, of your dignity, of your soul."

Nichole could see the truth of those words in her mother-in-law's eyes. Her hands trembled as she tried to assimilate this news.

"I . . . I don't know what to do," she whispered.

"For now, do nothing. Think this through carefully before you act, and be smart. Make an appointment with an attorney and find out your rights. I heard Jake mention that he had a business trip coming up."

"He leaves in the morning."

"How long will he be away?"

"Four days—no, five." Nichole could barely think straight. What Leanne said hit home. She needed to be smart about this and carefully think this through. She would obviously talk to him and hear what he had to say, but she would go in knowing what her options were. "Thank you," she whispered, struggling to keep her voice from wobbling. "I know this couldn't have been easy for you."

Leanne reached over and hugged her. "You're smart and you have your whole life ahead of you. You'll do what's best for you and Owen, I know you will."

Nichole sincerely hoped her mother-in-law was right.

Chapter 34

Karen and Cassie sat with Nichole in her living room. Hearing the pain in her sister's voice was all it took for Cassie to drop everything and, with Amiee in tow, head to Portland. Thankfully, Steve had insisted she drive his car . . . the one Alicia had once owned. Karen, too, had left Spokane and rushed to her sister's side.

"I'm so grateful you were both able to come," Nichole murmured, for what seemed like the hundredth time.

Nichole had contacted Cassie the morning after the visit from her mother-in-law. She was so upset she had hardly been able to speak coherently. Jake had an out-of-town business trip, which gave Nichole five days to form a plan.

"I can't think straight," she whispered.

"You don't need to make a decision this weekend," Karen advised her.

"Jake knows something is up. I did what I could to act normally, but I could barely stand to look at him."

"If he knows you know, then all the better," Karen said. "That makes it easier."

"None of this is easy."

"It can't be," Cassie agreed.

"How could I have been so blind?" Nichole demanded. "The evidence was right there in front of me and . . . and I didn't see it. All those late nights, the excuses, the Saturdays he played two rounds of golf and didn't seem the least bit tired. He was with . . . her."

"You trusted him," Karen said, patting Nichole's shoulder.

"I definitely want a separation," Nichole whispered. "He's going to have to leave until I sort out what's best for me and Owen."

"Don't you move," Karen advised. "Not yet, at any rate."

"That's what Leanne said."

Nichole had mentioned her friend Audrey earlier. Nichole and Audrey had been college roommates. Audrey had continued on to law school and was currently working for one of the premiere Portland law firms. She'd immediately advised Nichole on how best to protect herself financially.

"I just never thought something like this would happen to me and Jake. I could see that it about killed Leanne to tell me what she'd learned. She said she did it for Owen, so that he won't grow up believing that it's acceptable to cheat on one's wife the way his grandfather and father did."

"She has a good point," Karen said.

Cassie leaned over and reached for Nichole's hand, which was cold. Her sister trembled slightly. "Would you rather not know?" she asked gently.

"Yes," she cried, and then quickly changed her mind. "No. The thing is I don't know what to do. Leanne has lived with a cheating husband all these years, but she also told me that the price she paid for looking the other way was far too high."

Cassie understood her sister's waffling all too well. For years she convinced herself life with Duke wasn't always miserable. There'd been good times, too. When it was good it was very good, and when it was bad, well, it was beyond miserable. She clung to the good times, convinced herself the bad days weren't really that bad. As the years progressed, there were far fewer good times and far more bad days and nights. But if it hadn't been for that night and Duke's search for a knife, Cassie still had to wonder how long it would have taken for her to gather the courage to leave.

It wasn't easy to pick up the pieces of one's life and quite literally start over. She knew exactly how difficult it could be.

Amiee and Lily kept young Owen entertained while the three sisters sat together.

"Whatever you decide, we're here for you," Cassie assured Nichole.

"One hundred percent," Karen added.

"What if . . . what if we decide to stay married and go to couples counseling? Would you . . . do you think that would help? I have to believe that Jake loves me and Owen and that he would want to do whatever he could to save the marriage."

"That's something you and Jake need to decide."

"You'd support me in that?"

"Of course." Both Karen and Cassie nodded.

"Leanne . . ."

"You aren't your mother-in-law; you and Jake need to make your own decisions."

"Jake has a weakness. We all have flaws, right?"

"Of course we do," Karen reiterated.

"Some are worse than others. Having him move out will shake him up enough to know I'm serious. Dead serious. I can't and I won't live with a cheating husband."

"As long as you make that clear and stick to your resolve, then you might have a chance of salvaging your marriage," Karen said.

Tears swam in Nichole's eyes. "I love you both. I couldn't be more grateful to call you both sisters."

Nichole hugged Cassie and Karen joined in. They clung to one another for several seconds, and then one of them started to laugh. Soon they were all laughing for no reason other than the fact that if they didn't laugh they were sure to cry.

A short thirty minutes later, Karen and Lily left in order to drive back to Spokane.

"We need to head out, too," Cassie said. Amiee continued to play with Owen. She was especially good with him, and the youngster had quickly taken to her.

"Before you leave, there's something I need to give you," Nichole said, as she stood and disappeared down the long, narrow hallway that led to her bedroom.

Cassie exchanged looks with her daughter. She couldn't imagine what it could be.

Nichole returned and set a wooden box on the coffee table in front of Cassie. The box was old and looked vaguely familiar. As soon as Cassie reached for the box, she remembered where and when she'd last seen this box, now weathered with age. Reverently, she picked it up and held it in her hand. The lump in her throat made it hard to breathe.

"Do you know what it is?" Nichole asked.

Cassie nodded and struggled not to openly weep. After she composed herself enough to speak, she said, "It's the cameo."

"Dad always intended that you have it."

Cassie opened the box, but tears blurred her eyes and made it nearly impossible to view the cameo. The very one their grandfather had purchased as a wedding gift for the woman he loved. Their grandmother had worn it on her wedding day. And Cassie's mother had worn it the day she married the man who was their father.

"But . . ."

Nichole closed Cassie's hand over the box. "Dad wanted you to wear it at your wedding."

"But . . ."

"If you're half as smart as I think you are, then one day in the future you'll marry Steve. And this time, Cassie, I want to be invited to the wedding."

Cassie choked down a sob and nodded. "You will be, both you and Karen."

"Mom," Amiee said, sitting down on the sofa next to Cassie. "What is it?"

"A family heirloom."

"What's that?"

"It's a piece of my parents' love being passed down to me."

Amiee looked down at the cameo. "Will I get to wear it on my wedding day when Macklemore decides he wants to marry me?"

Cassie smiled. "Sure."

Cassie hugged her sister again.

Nichole whispered, "Having you as my sister means the world to me. You have every reason to resent Karen and me for the way we treated you, and instead you patiently loved us. Your forgiving attitude is helping me decide how best to deal with the situation with Jake. I don't know what the future holds, but I do know that I have two incredible sisters who will support and love me no matter what I decide."

"And so do I," Cassie whispered.

She'd been the last one home, but she was here, having come full circle.

Epilogue

The day had finally arrived. After months of work—five hundred sweat-equity hours—Cassie's house was finished. She had the required funds for one year's home-insurance premium gaining interest in the bank. The keys to the house were about to be handed to her and Amiee.

Unlike the Youngs, Cassie didn't plan a big party to go along with the ceremony. Steve would be with her—Stan and Megan, along with Maureen and her children, too. All had been instrumental in bringing this project to fruition. She couldn't have done it without their encouragement and support. Steve and Stan had delivered the furniture from Steve's warehouse. The very first item to be placed inside the house had been her piano. Cassie had run her hand over the keyboard, grimaced; when she could afford it she'd make an appointment to have it tuned. The boxes of her parents' other items had been left at the warehouse for Cassie to sort through later, but the rooms were all furnished.

The pastor from the church she and Amiee attended had promised to do a short dedication prayer. Every time Cassie caught a glimpse of the house, she experienced an overwhelming sense of pride and accomplishment. She recalled the first day she'd walked on the vacant lot. It'd seemed an impossible dream back then, and yet here it was, finished and furnished. Amiee had a real bedroom with closets and a study desk, the very one Cassie had used at her daughter's age.

Steve suggested he collect Cassie and Amiee and drive them to the house. It was a nice gesture and she appreciated it. After she officially accepted the keys, they'd return and load up the last of their things from the apartment. Not much remained— all the big items had already been transferred to the house, thanks to Steve, Stan, and George Young.

Amiee chatted excitedly through the entire ride. "Our own house, and Steve, in case you didn't know, there's a KFC just one-point-three miles away. I clocked it in the car. That's walking distance, but I don't think either you or Mom would want me walking on a street with all that traffic. I'll accept a ride if you insist."

Steve shared a smile with Cassie. "I think a KFC dinner once a week should be a bare minimum, seeing how close it is and all."

"I wish you'd hurry up and marry this man," Amiee murmured under her breath.

"All in good time," Cassie promised.

Steve reached over and squeezed her hand. They had given a great deal of thought to their ongoing relationship and decided to hold off discussing getting engaged for six months. But a wedding was definitely a possibility.

"Aunt Karen and Aunt Nichole are coming this weekend," Amiee told him. "They wanted to be here for the ceremony, but there was a scheduling conflict."

"I'm sorry to hear that."

"You'll like them," Amiee said. "Aunt Karen's a lot like Mom and, well, so is Aunt Nichole." She lowered her voice. "Her and her husband have separated."

"So I heard."

They rounded the corner to their new home and Cassie sat up straighter. "What are all those cars doing parked outside the house?" she asked.

"Someone must be having a party," Steve said, completely deadpan.

"Steve?" Something was up, and Cassie didn't doubt for a moment that he was behind it. "What's going on?"

"Just a few friends."

Amiee's arm shot out. "Is that Aunt Karen's car?"

Cassie looked closer and her heart started to race.

She recognized several cars. Teresa's and Rosie's, Shelly and George Young's, and several others.

Cassie pressed her fingertips over her lips. "Look at all these people," she whispered. A bright red ribbon was stretched across the front door, with a huge bow centered there. The garage door was open and long tables had been set up with folding chairs. There appeared to be a mountain of food and serving dishes.

"Who brought all the food?" Cassie asked, turning to look at Steve.

He grinned and looked proud of himself. "Everyone contributed. This is a celebration, and we couldn't very well let the day pass without—"

"Celebrating," Amiee supplied.

"Exactly."

Cassie had trouble believing this many people would take time from their busy schedules to share this moment with her.

"This was your doing, wasn't it, Steve?"

"I helped. We all pitched in. We love you, Cassie. Each one of us in our own way. You've touched our hearts, given of yourself, and become an important part of our lives. A very important part of mine." He raised her hand to his mouth and kissed her fingers. "I love you, Cassie. There isn't anything I wouldn't do for you."

"If no one thought of it, you could buy me a bucket of KFC," Amiee told him, completely serious.

"I believe, my dear Amiee, that you'll find several buckets waiting for you this very day. I'm not much of a cook, and when Shelly suggested a potluck, I knew exactly what you'd enjoy most."

Steve parked the car and Cassie wiped the tears out of her eyes. Amiee opened the passenger door and climbed down, racing toward her friends and the food. Cassie followed, and as soon as her friends saw her, they applauded.

The prayer and ribbon-cutting ceremony took only a few minutes, and then Cassie was handed the keys to the home she had spent so many hours building. And there on the south side of the house was space for a garden. Cassie looked again.

"Steve, is that a gazebo at the side of the house?"

He grinned. "Could be!"

"But it wasn't there two days ago. How did . . . When . . . Who?" Silly question. Cassie knew it had to have been Steve.

He grinned again. "I had help. Are you surprised? I remembered you telling me your parents had one."

Later, as the keys were placed in her hand, Cassie closed her fist around the cold metal and smiled. Her family and friends gathered around her as she lifted her eyes toward heaven and thanked God for this moment. It was then that she realized that she was truly and finally home.

ABOUT THE AUTHOR

DEBBIE MACOMBER, the author of **Last One Home, Mr. Miracle, Love Letters, Blossom Street Brides, Starry Night, Rose Harbor in Bloom, Starting Now, Angels at the Table,** and **The Inn at Rose Harbor,** is a leading voice in women's fiction. Nine of her novels have hit #1 on the **New York Times** bestseller list, with three debuting at #1 on the **New York Times, USA Today,** and **Publishers Weekly** lists. In 2009 and 2010, **Mrs. Miracle** and **Call Me Mrs. Miracle** were the Hallmark Channel's top-watched movies for the year. In 2013, the Hallmark Channel produced the original series **Debbie Macomber's Cedar Cove,** as well as the original movie **Mr. Miracle,** based on Debbie's holiday novel by the same name. Debbie Macomber has more than 170 million copies of her books in print worldwide.

www.debbiemacomber.com

LIKE WHAT YOU'VE READ?

If you enjoyed this large print edition of
LAST ONE HOME,
here are a few of Debbie Macomber's latest bestsellers
also available in large print.

Mr. Miracle
(paperback)
978-0-8041-9456-3
($18.00/$21.00C)

Blossom Street Brides
(paperback)
978-0-8041-2120-0
($26.00/$30.00C)

Love Letters
(paperback)
978-0-8041-9450-1
($26.00/$29.00C)

Starry Night
(paperback)
978-0-8041-2103-3
($20.00/$23.00C))

Large print books are available wherever books
are sold and at many local libraries.

All prices are subject to change. Check with your
local retailer for current pricing and availability.
For more information on these and other large print titles,
visit www.randomhouse.com/largeprint.